All My Loved Ones

a novel

All My Loved Ones

a novel

KRISTEN MCKENDRY

SWEETWATER BOOKS
An imprint of Cedar Fort, Inc.
Springville, Utah

ISBN 13: 978-1-4621-4026-8

Published by Sweetwater Books, an imprint of Cedar Fort, Inc.
2373 W. 700 S., Springville, UT 84663
Distributed by Cedar Fort, Inc., www.cedarfort.com

Library of Congress Control Number: 2021936731

Cover design by Shawnda T. Craig

Edited and typeset by Valene Wood

Printed in the United States of America

10 9 8 7 6 5 4 3 2 1

Printed on acid-free paper

To Eric Johnson,
the only man outside of my family to have read
all of my books and lived to tell about it

Other Books by Kristen McKendry

Promise of Spring
The Ties that Bind
Garden Plot
Beyond the White River
The Worth of a Soul (with Ayse Hitchins)
Desperate Measures
Heart's Journey
The Governess
The Song of Copper Creek

For Children

The Holy Ghost Can Help

Acknowledgments

Thank you to Rowyn for the crabby berries. Thank you to Gianni for the sleeper agent idea. Thank you to Sharon for the Rembrandt metaphor. Thank you to Gryffin for the dehydrated towel. Sorry to Anne-Marie for giving her the stomach flu—it's not personal. Thank you to Stacy Backus Martineau for the ice cream argument. And to Kevin, who asked if he was going to be in my next book: Hi, Kevin.

Chapter One

I didn't see him arrive. I was busy struggling with a long, fat roll of fiberglass insulation the size of a water heater tank, trying to haul it from truck to house without letting it touch the damp ground. When at last I got it stowed safely in the front hallway, I turned to find him standing in front of the porch as if he'd sprung from the earth.

He looked as if he'd been under ground, at any rate. His bare feet, planted solidly apart, were coated in a dusting of pale dirt that extended up to the fringes of his ragged cut-offs and probably beyond. His t-shirt was a light brown, though it had probably started out white. His longish hair was sandy blond and unruly, his brown eyes the color of Milk Duds set in a deeply tanned face. The tan was echoed on his thin, bare arms. His fists were planted on his hips, and he was watching me with completely uninhibited interest and perhaps a touch of resentment. He looked to be about nine.

When I turned and saw him, he flinched slightly but didn't look away. What could this child of nature want with me? I wiped my grimy hands on my own none-too-clean jeans and went to the top of the porch steps to stand looking down at him.

"What are you doing?" he demanded.

"I'm putting insulation in the attic," I replied.

"Why?"

"Because the squirrels got in through a hole in the roof and destroyed the insulation," I said. "I've hauled it all out and am starting clean."

"No, I mean, why are you doing it at all?" he said, frowning.

"You mean, why am I fixing up the house?"

"Yes. Are you?"

"Yes. There's a great deal to be done."

"But why are you *here*?" he insisted.

Earlier, I had found evidence that someone had broken into the house through a loose basement window and had camped out there—for some duration, judging from the number of pop cans I'd cleared away. There had also been a small nylon backpack containing a flashlight, a bag of potato chips, and a fairly expensive pocketknife. The mystery, I thought, was now solved. It also explained his proprietary air.

"Ah. I think I have something of yours," I said. I fetched the nylon bag from the front closet where I'd stowed it and held it out to him.

He stepped forward and accepted it gracefully, with no sign of embarrassment at being caught out. Shrugging one strap over his shoulder, he scowled up at me.

"Are you going to live here now?" the boy asked.

"Yes, this is my house," I said. It still felt strange to say it, the idea as confounding to me now as it had been when the lawyer at Grenville and Green had first spoken to me two months ago.

"Why do you want to live here?" His tone clearly expressed his opinion of this news. It equally clearly said what he thought of my newly acquired home. Even this urchin could see the house was a potential money pit.

"Because someone left it to me." *And don't ask me who,* I thought, *because I don't know.* It was a ludicrous position to be in, but it was the truth. The lawyer had informed me that the bequest came from someone who had specified in their will that they were to remain anonymous. I had spent many sleepless nights pondering who could have left the house to me, had pestered the lawyer beyond what was polite, and had finally given up. I would accept the gift and appreciate it—the timing had been perfect—and simply welcome it as one of the serendipitous things that seemed to happen with regular frequency in my life. So frequently, in fact, that I sometimes joked I had a guardian angel. And perhaps I did. Though I doubted angels generally owned ramshackle Edwardian houses.

"No, but I mean, why do you want to live *here*? It's falling apart," the boy observed now, in case I hadn't realized it.

"I like to fix up old houses," I said. "It's what I do for a living."

He shot a skeptical look at my truck. Battered, the color of a beet, it obviously wasn't one of those fancy pick-ups city boys with spotless cowboy boots drive to look manly. This was a working vehicle, sadly used, thoroughly worn out. The fading painted letters on the door read "K.W. Custom Renovations" and gave my old phone number, now as defunct as the life I'd left behind in Toronto. I would have to get it repainted now that I had a new local number.

"You mean you fix them up and sell them?"

"No, I fix up other people's houses for them. They hire me. This is actually the first time I've fixed up one for myself."

He thrust his chin at me. "You're a girl," he declared.

"Sure enough," I said, smiling. "You are observant."

"Girls aren't builders."

"This one is. Carpenter and tiler, plumber and painter. The only thing I don't do is electrical. I hire a man to do that," I added to placate him.

He opened his mouth and then closed it again, shooting another look at the truck. I took his moment of inattention to move closer, coming down the stone steps to stand beside him in the trampled mud.

"Do you like coming here?" I asked gently.

He glanced back at me and hitched the backpack further up his shoulder. Finally, he conceded, "Sometimes."

"I'll keep some pop in the fridge if you want to come visit once in a while," I offered.

"It's not the same," he muttered, and dug one bare toe into the earth to create a little mound. We both stood looking down at it for a moment.

"Sorry," I said. "I didn't know."

He shrugged in a what-can-you-do sort of way.

"How—how long have you been coming here?" I asked, an idea catching in my brain.

"A couple of years, maybe."

I blinked. "Has the house been empty that long?"

"Yeah."

"Do you know who used to own it? Who used to live here?"

He shrugged. "I've never heard."

Rats. I had been hoping he could help me solve the mystery of who my benefactor was. But even if he couldn't, perhaps one of the other neighbors could. I hadn't met any of them yet, but the idea was encouraging. But I wondered why, if, according to the child, the house had been empty for at least a couple of years, I had only inherited it two months ago.

"Do you live near here?" I asked next.

He neatly evaded the question. "Are you going to fix up houses for people here in Smoke River?" he asked.

"Probably, if there are any to fix up," I said. "Truth to tell, I'm not sure what I'm going to do out here. I'm starting fresh."

"What does that mean?"

"It means I'm giving up my old life and starting a new one."

He thought about this a moment, and I could tell from his half smile that the idea appealed to him.

"I'm about to lift something heavy from the back of the truck," I said. "It's a bag of drywall compound. Will you help me carry it into the house without it getting muddy?"

He brightened. "I will for a dollar," he said.

I couldn't help laughing at his impish expression. I could see we were going to be friends.

In the end, he helped me completely unload the truck, manfully struggling to do his share even though my materials were too heavy for him. At last, we got the sacks of compound, buckets, tools, and boxes of screws stowed in the front sitting room—the room I intended to turn into a workshop. A stubborn stack of drywall had already been delivered and waited in the center of the room like a challenge. I had set up a workbench against one wall, and my table saw was by the big front window where most people would have placed a table of bric-a-brac. Plush carpet, coffee tables, and lace curtains might be more traditional, but who was to see? I would fit the house to suit me. After all, there was no one to come around and see how far I had degenerated.

When the truck was empty and the front hallway was patterned with muddy footprints, I gave him five dollars and seated him at my kitchen table with a glass of milk and a Snickers bar (I hadn't focused much on grocery shopping yet). He ate the bar slowly, unwrapping it with care as if lost in thought. I puttered at the sink, washing up from my meager breakfast of toast and peanut butter (I hadn't bothered with cooking very much lately, either). I set the dried plate in the cupboard and turned to find him looking at me, elbows on table and chin in hand.

"What's your name?" he asked.

I gave a mock bow. "Kerris Adelaide Wells. You can call me Kerris," I said. The name felt odd on my tongue after six years of being Kerris Adamson—another thing to get used to, among many.

"K.W. Renovations," he observed.

"Precisely. It's clever of you to figure it out." At least I didn't have to change the name of my business, since I had started it up before my marriage and had never altered the "K.W." One less hassle to deal with after the divorce.

He took another bite of the bar. I waited, but when he said nothing further, I prompted, "What about you?"

He blinked at me.

"Do you have a name?" I asked.

He seemed to consider a moment, then nodded seriously. "Yes, I do," he said. He crumpled the wrapper and tossed it into the plastic wastebasket by the sink, then rose and reshouldered his backpack. "Thanks for the candy bar," he said. At the door he paused and looked back at me. "I like A&W root beer best," he said.

I smiled. "I know."

The house fit me. I'd known it would, instantly, the moment I'd turned the key in the front door and stepped inside. In spite of the yellow-flowered '70s wallpaper, the threadbare carpet, the hundred-year-old plumbing, it had felt familiar. Even *smelled* familiar. There had been an instant warmth and welcoming, as if the house recognized me, accepted me. *Wanted* me. That was a feeling I hadn't had for quite a while.

I suppose some people would think it weird that I can sense how a house feels. It's something I've been able to do since I was a small child. They have personalities, and I can sense them when I'm renovating. I can tell what the house wants me to do with it. Houses are meant to shelter people, and when a house is left empty for too long, it grows sad. I could feel this place cheer up the minute I set down my keys on the scarred kitchen counter, as if it could tell I intended to stay.

I had made up my mind to stay regardless, no matter what I found when I came to inspect the house. There was nothing left for me back in Toronto, and mine was the type of work I could take anywhere. As I'd walked quietly through the rooms, baffled and curious, assessing the work to be done, I'd felt I'd made a lucky escape. I couldn't have stood another month in the bleak apartment I'd hurriedly moved into following the breakup of my marriage, but it had been all I could afford at the time. Marcus's lawyer had argued—successfully—that even though Marcus was the higher wage earner, I had supported him most of our six-year marriage while he was in law school, and therefore I had to keep doing it. It seemed ridiculous, now that he was a practicing lawyer, that I should have to keep on paying. But the court had sided with him. In the end, I'd handed over everything to Marcus just to get it all to go away, including our Forest Hill condo where he and his new wife were now comfortably ensconced.

I'd managed, though, to hang onto my truck and tools. They were my livelihood, after all. I'd backed down on virtually everything else, but not that. And my first walk through the gift house told me I'd be needing those tools and all my skill.

It wasn't in as bad a condition as some I'd renovated, but there was water and squirrel damage in the attic, every wall and floor needed recovering, the wavy-glassed windows were as old as the house, there was the strong smell of mouse in the closets, and when I'd tentatively turned on the bathroom faucet, the gurgle of rusty water told me there was work to be done there too. If I didn't die of lead poisoning first.

But in spite of all that, there was a warmth and charm to the place that reached out to me. The front door opened directly into a wide hallway with living room on the left and dining room on the right. Further along there was a bathroom and pantry on the left and the kitchen on the right, with stairs going up to a landing and then turning to run up to the second floor. The stairs to the basement ran beneath them. The simple layout was not overly inspiring, but the sunlight slanting through the wavy windows turned the scarred wood floors to amber, and when I pried open the kitchen window, I could smell fresh-cut grass and early lilacs.

As I'd explored, I had searched for clues as to who had lived in the house before me, but there was little to go on. Nothing personal had been left behind. What furniture was left was inexpensive and generic beneath the dust cloths. There were no books or knickknacks, no photos or artwork of any kind. The flowery wallpaper and pink carpet in the bedrooms convinced me it was a woman's house, though. Beyond the flowers and color, there was just a feminine sort of feel to the place. The lines were graceful, the old windows tall and light filled. The kitchen, which had been redone sometime in the 80s, was laid out in a practical formation, and the sink had been cleverly brought forward to allow a person sitting on a stool to tuck their knees under it. This spoke of long hours at the sink, making me think a down-to-earth and efficient woman had designed it. I suspected she and I would have gotten along.

The plumbing would have to be entirely redone, of course, and likely all the insulation too. The stairs creaked alarmingly, and the attic was water-damaged, but the basement was mercifully dry. It was also empty other than a set of wooden shelves loaded with what looked like cans of powdered milk and oatmeal, now dusty and liberally sprinkled with mouse droppings. Beneath the neglect and musty-mouse smell, though, it was a solid, beautiful house. It might be empty and lonely now, but it had known love and contentment at some point. Vestiges of it still remained.

As I'd returned upstairs to the empty, airy kitchen, I'd felt a lightening of my soul for the first time in many months. Here was a project to distract me. Here was a home that welcomed me. As I'd picked up my keys, I'd run my hand along the Formica kitchen counter in satisfaction and whispered, "I'll be good to you."

It was as if I could hear the house whisper back, "I'll be good to you too."

After that initial inspection, I had returned to Toronto and unhesitatingly condensed my life into whatever would fit in my truck. Now here I was in Smoke River, two hours further north than I'd ever been before in a town I'd never heard of before the lawyer had said its name. I'd been living in the house for just over a week now. It was the first time I'd ever had a home of my own, just me alone. I'd always lived with my family or with Marcus. I had installed what little furniture I had, bought a new bed to remind myself that this was a fresh start, and opted to leave all the downstairs windows uncovered to let the light in. Every morning I woke with a little brighter feeling, a freedom that grew with each day as the depression of the past weeks sloughed away. It almost felt as if whoever had left me the house knew I'd needed this new beginning.

Chapter Two

In the past week I had started exploring my new town, just in short forays. I had never lived anywhere but the big city, and it was almost unsettling to discover I could drive around most of Smoke River's streets in fifteen minutes.

Smoke River was one of those self-conscious little towns with a huge sense of civic responsibility. Not content to hum along inconspicuously like most little country towns, it threw itself into being "up and coming." It branded itself as a "Great Place to Live," and declared so on the sign posted as you came into town. Baskets of spring flowers hung from every streetlamp on Main Street. An old-fashioned white bandstand stood in the park where, I had no doubt, Canada Day parades would end with dancing to live bands and fireworks. The bowling league threw charity bake sales, and the civic center, not to be outdone, held annual raffles to raise money for Deserving Projects.

There was a community newspaper, apparently delivered the first of every month, full of local tidbits and offerings that gave me a snapshot of life here: The Women's Circle met every Wednesday to knit chemo caps for cancer patients. The mayor congratulated everyone that there had been an 87-percent turnout on election day and the crime rate was next to nil. There was a sale on lamb chops at Hardy's Handymart. A new antique store had opened next to the curling club.

And the single big chain grocery store advertised everything from tofu to rabbit pellets.

So far, I had stopped to visit only three businesses in town: the library, the gas station, and one really useful store: Eamonn's Hardware. That was the first shop I hunted out, and I was pleased with its selection and prices. I would be able to find just about everything I needed without having to make the drive to the Home Depot in Port Daley half an hour away.

It was to Eamonn's I headed that afternoon, after my encounter with the nameless urchin, hoping to find a new handle for the back door and just the right shade of yellow paint for my kitchen. On my previous trips to the store, a teenage boy with a ring through his left eyebrow had served me. Today it was a tall, solidly built man in his mid-thirties, wearing a stretched black muscle shirt smudged with cement dust.

I explained to him what I wanted. He combed his dark hair back with his thick fingers and headed down an aisle.

"Spring Marigold or Banana Sherbet?" he asked over his shoulder.

"Pardon?"

"Those are the two yellows I have." He continued at a brisk pace and I hurried to follow. He stopped before a bank of stacked paint cans. "Actually, I have three, but you won't want the third one."

"No? You don't have swatches to choose from?" I asked, amused.

"We don't mix paint here. But there are a few favorites everyone seems to go for, and those are what I stock."

"Spring Marigold and Banana Sherbet."

"Those are the choices." He pointed to a slab of wood on which swabs of paint had been brushed, to demonstrate the various hues. There were about ten, ranging from cherry red to yellow, blue, green, and mud brown.

"What's that third yellow called?"

"Morning Sun, but personally I think it should be called Tipsy Man's Bile," he replied. "You don't want that one. They painted the public washrooms at the civic center with that."

"Right. Okay. Which one is Marigold and which is Banana?" I asked, looking at the other two yellow options.

"That one." He pointed to the top yellow swipe.

I was no further enlightened than before, but I shrugged and nodded. "Fine, I'll take two gallons of that one."

"Spring Marigold," he said approvingly and reached down two cans from the display.

"Is someone really paid to sit and think up these names?" I mused. "How do I get that job? I could do something like that." I could easily think of several names for some of the colors on display: Runny Meatloaf, for example.

"I know, eh?" he said.

"I need a new handle and lock for my front and back doors, too."

"Last aisle," he said, heading that way. Apparently, I was going to get personal assistance the whole shopping trip.

"I think bronze would look better than brass," I told the man. "And a lever, not a round knob or one of those kind you press with your thumb. Those look like handles off a beer stein."

He gave a deep laugh, his tanned face creasing into pleasant lines, and pulled the perfect handle from the shelf.

"That's it," I said, nodding. I followed him to the counter to ring up my purchases.

"You know," he said, eyeing me thoughtfully as he punched numbers into the old-fashioned cash register, "nobody in Smoke River bothers locking their doors."

"I do," I said. I didn't add that I had almost every penny to my name wrapped up in my power tools in the front room.

"You must not be from here," the man observed.

I pushed my weary credit card across the counter, almost expecting to hear it sigh. "No, I just moved here from Toronto."

"Ah," he said, as if that explained everything, which I suppose it did. As I signed the receipt, he leaned on the counter with his arms folded. "What do you do?"

"Home renovations," I said, and felt the usual smugness when his jaw went slack in surprise. It was the reaction I got most often.

"You don't say," he said. "For a living?"

"Yes." I smiled.

"Design stuff only? Or do you do the actual renos?"

"Actual renos. Dirty hands and all," I told him. "I'm also a licensed plumber. So I guess you'll get used to seeing me in your store a lot."

"Always a pleasure. Anything you need we don't have, we can order it for you."

"Thanks."

"Where do you live in Smoke River?"

"Rannick Road."

He unfolded his arms and straightened. "You're not the one who bought the empty white house on Rannick, are you?"

"Actually, I inherited it," I said.

"That old place? I'm glad to see someone's going to live in it," he said. "It's starting to fall apart. It's been empty too long."

"It's not so bad," I defended it loyally, though he was basically right.

"I couldn't believe it when I heard someone was actually living there. You're very brave, taking it on. I bet it will need a complete overhaul. It's still got the original glass."

"I know."

"The house will be happier now, having someone in it."

I stared stupidly at him and felt a grin start to creep across my face. This solid, jolly-looking man was a kindred soul who had tapped into the same truth I had—that houses *liked* to be lived in. When I restored them to beauty, I could feel their gratitude.

"What are your plans for the place?" he asked now, leaning on the counter and settling in for a chat. There were no other customers in the store.

"Well, it's still solid and has good foundations. The furnace was replaced about ten years ago, so that's one less thing I have to do. Some leaks in the roof. General repairs and updating. I might knock out one wall to expand the kitchen into the dining room. I think the house is Edwardian, maybe even built as long ago as the 1890s, but some cretin put vinyl siding on it, probably after the War."

"That will have to go," he agreed.

"Someday. I'm focusing on the more urgent stuff first." I didn't add that my finances couldn't handle too much right now.

"I always wondered why someone didn't buy it and fix it up," the man said. "It's a nice location, with all that land, and being right across the street from the woods. I wondered if maybe no one did because the place was haunted or something."

He lifted one eyebrow, waiting to see my reaction. I folded my arms and returned his stare levelly. After a moment, he conceded defeat and broke into a grin.

"All right, it isn't haunted. But why else would it stand empty?"

"I don't know, unless the owner was in a nursing home or something and couldn't live there. Or maybe it was tied up in probate for a long time. I only inherited it two months ago. Those are the only reasons I can think of for it to have been unlived in all this time. You don't know who the last owner was, do you? Who lived there last?"

"Wait, you don't know who left it to you?"

"No. It came out of the blue."

"Well, there's luck. I'm afraid I wouldn't know who owned it. I just moved back here last year after a few years in Orangeville. But my mother might know. She's lived here most of her life, though now she's in the new subdivision the other side of town. In one of those tidy, soul-less new houses." He put my receipt in my bag and handed it to me. "I'll give Mom a ring and let you know what she says next time you're in."

"I'd appreciate that. The mystery has been driving me crazy," I said. I smiled again and picked up my paint cans. "Thanks again. I'll see you around, Mister . . .?"

"Call me Eamonn."

"And I'm Kerris."

His smile was broad, contagious. "I'll remember that."

I hadn't yet made an effort to meet the neighbors. I'd been busy, I excused myself, wrapping up my old life and moving house. Though I suspected that was only a partial excuse. The truth was, chatting with a store owner or a stray child was different from introducing myself to neighbors. They might want to get to know me, expect me to socialize, maybe want to be *friends*. Something in me shied away from the idea of any relationship where expectations would be put on me. It all sounded too exhausting. But I'd have to make an effort at some point, and it may as well be now. After all, they might know something about who had owned my house.

After making myself go, I was disappointed to find the neighbors on the west weren't home, and from the pile of yellowing newspapers on their porch, they'd been away for a while. The neighbor on the east, however, came to the door as soon as I knocked. She balanced a baby on her hip with one arm and dragged her unruly brown hair out of her face with her other hand. She looked too young to have a child.

"Hi," I said. "I'm Kerris Wells. I moved in next door a few days ago."

The young woman shifted the baby to her other hip. I couldn't tell how old he was, but he was compact and round like a bowling ball and I imagined he weighed about as much. He leaned his head on his mother's shoulder and regarded me peacefully with big brown eyes.

"Oh yeah," the young woman said. "I've seen your truck come and go. Sorry I haven't come by earlier to welcome you to the neighborhood. We just moved in ourselves about five months ago, and it's been busy. There never seems to be time."

"Oh." There went the idea that she might have known who'd lived in my house before me. "Well, I guess we can both welcome each other to the neighborhood!" I added lamely. I no longer knew what to say, since the purpose of my coming over had now been shot out of the water.

"I'm Donna Sellers," she added in a chatty voice. "And this is Blaine. He's eleven months."

"Nice to meet you."

"Do you want to come in? I can put some coffee on."

"Oh, that's okay—" I began, but she held the door open for me, and there was no option but to step inside. I was instantly assaulted by the smell of soaked diapers, cooking oil, and cat litter box. The front hallway of her narrow little house was floored with linoleum (old—likely backed with asbestos, but I didn't have the heart to tell her so), the overhead light was dim, and the orange-flowered wallpaper was right out of the '70s, like mine. But in spite of all that, I got a plucky vibe from the house. Enthusiasm and a never-say-die sort of attitude. What you saw was what you got, I felt, and the same was probably true of its owners. People were attracted to houses because something in the place spoke to something reciprocal in them.

Before Donna could close the door behind us, someone called out, and we both turned to see a woman striding up the walk carrying a foil-covered plate. She was shorter than I by a few inches, but the curly dark hair massed on top of her head with a pink scrunchie made her look taller, and her face was lean and interesting. She wore no make-up but didn't need any, her lashes long and dark around exotic blue eyes.

"I brought you some pulla," she said and lifted a corner of the foil to reveal beautiful golden pastry, something like cinnamon rolls.

"Oh wow, that's so nice of you," Donna said, but her hands were busy with Blaine, so I ended up taking the plate.

"This is my new neighbor, Kerris," Donna explained to the woman. "She was just coming over to get acquainted. Kerris, this is Jeri Shaanssen."

The woman bared her teeth in a grin and I sensed a sort of electricity radiating from her whole being. With her frizzed hair, her muscles toned and tense, she looked poised, ready to explode into motion. As if she were fizzing just under the surface.

"Nice to meet you," Jeri said.

"Do you want to come in and join us?" Donna offered, but Jeri shook her head.

"Thanks, but I'm roofing my garage this afternoon."

"By yourself?" I asked. "Because I can help if—"

She shook her head. "Oh, I do it all the time. Whenever I feel . . . um, I mean, there are about ten layers of shingles on it by now. See you, ducks!"

She chucked Blaine under the chin and strode off again, and Donna laughed and closed the door after her. She led me toward the kitchen in the back, chatting over her shoulder in a steady stream, and I had no choice but to follow.

"Jeri's really nice. She brings us stuff all the time. You can put the plate on the counter there. So! My husband is Craig. He's a software engineer and works in Orangeville, so he's always gone. I'm here on my own most days, and some weekends too, which isn't ideal, but it was cheaper to buy a house here and do the commute, you know? Real estate is so expensive closer to the city!" She paused, waiting.

"It's just me next door," I said awkwardly. "I renovate houses for a living."

"Really? That's so cool! I love watching those design shows on TV. No wonder you said you could help Jeri with her garage roof. She should have accepted the offer. One of these days she'll fall off and break her neck." She seemed unfazed by this bald prediction.

Donna ushered me into a chair at the bare Formica table and plopped Blaine into a highchair, where he strained against the plastic tray and turned an alarming shade of red. She ignored it, bustling about and setting out coffee, cups, cream and sugar, and the plate of Finnish pastry in front of me. Then she dropped into a chair opposite and began to pour out as carefully as if she were doing a scientific experiment in a lab. While her hands moved, she continued to talk, and I decided having her husband work so far from home had left her craving company. She popped a bun out from under the foil and into her son's hands, and he settled down contentedly to gum it into brown mush.

"My favorite is when they build those tiny homes, you know?" she said. "The ones the size of a cracker box? And even though the couple says they want to go minimalist and leave materialism behind and save money and everything, they still want to fit three hundred pairs of shoes and a snowmobile into the tiny house. It's crazy, right? Me, I don't think I could ever live in something that small. I mean, this place has three bedrooms and a basement and we're still crammed in like sardines. But it's all we could afford, and we wanted the three bedrooms because we want to have more kids someday. I don't think Blaine should be an only child. Hey, do you think you could do something about my front closet? The door sticks, and there's no room for Craig's coat. He wears this bulky thing the size of a bear, right?"

Twenty minutes later I managed to escape back home, my stomach full of pulla, my head ringing with her non-stop voice, and the closet door fixed. It had been just a small job, easily done, a friendly favor between neighbors. But Donna had been overwhelmingly grateful, and I wondered how long it had been since anyone had shown her a kindness before today.

She had also burst out with the idea of having me reconfigure the front closet and entry by enclosing the front porch. Husband Craig (hastily phoned at work) agreed, and I had reluctantly taken the job. I wasn't ready to take on work yet, and I wasn't sure I wanted much contact with the Sellers family—friendly as they were, I didn't think my ears were up to it—but there was something disarming about Donna's cheerful energy, and I hadn't felt I could say no. I told myself it was just a small thing and wouldn't take long. And remembered my mother saying much the same thing when I was young: "Just swallow the broccoli down. The anticipation is always worse than actually doing it." Though after sitting stubbornly for an hour and finally downing the cold broccoli, I'd still found the doing worse than the anticipating.

Chapter Three

The boy was back again two days later. I looked up from my breakfast of toast and peanut butter and found his round, dirty face staring at me through the kitchen window, a hand cupped on each side of his head to block the sunlight. It gave me a bit of a start. I set down the novel I'd been reading (I can never eat without reading, or read without eating) and went to the back door.

"Hey," I greeted him.

Unabashed at being caught spying, he came over and looked up at me from the bottom of the steps.

"Hey," he returned.

"Want to come in?"

"What you got?"

"Root beer. I bought it just for you."

He came into the kitchen and, after glancing around a second, sat at the table. "You've changed it," he remarked.

"Not as much as it's going to be changed," I told him. "I'm thinking of ripping out that wall today."

"Why?"

"Because it will make it flow into the dining room better," I said. "I'll have to try to match the wood floor in the spot where I take the wall out. Then I'll extend the counter, refinish the cupboards in pale white, replace the chipped sink, and paint the whole room a sunny marigold yellow."

"That will look okay," he said slowly.

I was pleased by this concession. "Have you had breakfast?"

"Not really."

I saw the hopeful look on his face and had a few unkind thoughts toward his parents. Then again, here was I, plying him with root beer before eight a.m. Who was I to judge? I put two slices of bread in the toaster and dug a carton of eggs from the fridge. "Scrambled or fried?"

"Boiled. Hard, not squishy."

I fished out a pot and put it on the stove. This appliance, at least, was fairly new, bought secondhand and hauled from Port Daley. The stove original to the house had been a hazard.

"You never told me your name," I prodded as I put the eggs on to cook.

"I didn't?" He looked surprised.

"No."

"I thought I did." He took a swig of his root beer.

"There, you did it again. Evading the question. Why won't you tell me your name?"

He grinned, a winsome gap-toothed smile that would have had me promising him anything.

"Of course, I will. Why wouldn't I?" he countered. "Everyone has a name."

"Oh, fine," I sighed. "I'll pick a name for you myself, then. How about Alfalfa?"

"What?"

"Or Arliss. Or Opie."

"Who?"

"John-Boy."

"Those are stupid names," he said, contentedly swinging his feet.

"You're right. I'm sure your mother gave you a much nicer name than those."

His face grew solemn. "Yes, she did."

"I'd rather call you by a nice name."

"You can call me Alfalfa if you want to. I don't mind."

"The name has been taken," I informed him. "So what is it really?"

"Who cares?"

"I do," I said.

"My friends call me Stinky."

"They do not. What did your mother name you?"

He gave a world-weary sigh. "Finn," he said at last.

"Finn? Like Huckleberry Finn? You're pulling my leg."

"Finn, like short for Finlay," he said.

"Your mother named you Finlay? And calls you Finn?"

"Well, she doesn't call me that anymore."

"What does she call you now?" I asked, amused.

"Nothing. She died."

It was spoken flatly, matter-of-factly, and it chilled me to the bone. He turned his pop can round and round between his fingers, studying it. After a moment of silence, I murmured, "I didn't know. I'm sorry."

He shrugged one shoulder.

It certainly helped explain his dirty appearance, his hanging out in my basement, his wandering ways, and the hungry look on his face. Was he also fatherless? Where was he living? Why did no one in the town care for him? I gave him the toast, thickly spread with butter and spun honey.

"Thanks," he said, and crammed half a slice into his mouth at once.

"So should I call you Stinky?" I prodded gently.

He grinned with his mouth full. "Finn's okay."

"Will you tell me how old you are?" I asked.

He considered this a moment, then nodded once. And surprised me by answering straight forwardly.

"I'm ten."

"I thought you were about that."

"How old are you?" he countered with his mouth full.

Fair enough. "Thirty."

I turned off the stove and drained the eggs under cold water. Lacking an egg cup, I put them in a bowl and handed them to him. Finn picked up a spoon, considered an egg a moment, then smashed it with a mighty whack of his spoon. Bits of shell flew across the table.

"Have any salt?" he asked.

I gave it to him, along with two more slices of toast. For a while he munched in silence. His fingers left dirty fingerprints on the surface of his boiled eggs. I went to the sink to putter, leaving him to himself for a while.

"So what grade are you in?" I asked when it looked like he was nearly finished.

"I'll be in Six after the summer."

"Do you go to school here in Smoke River or do you have to bus to Port Daley?"

"Here in Smoke River until Grade Nine, then I'll have to bus."

At least that answered the question. Someone must be looking after him to some extent. I couldn't see him getting himself off to school on his own initiative.

"Do you live far from here?" I asked as casually as I could. I thought maybe he'd wandered up from the trailer park in the river bottoms. It had looked a bit seedy when I'd driven by it.

"You ask a lot of questions," Finn observed, wiping his mouth with the back of his hand. "My turn to ask some."

"Okay. That's fair." I sat down opposite him and leaned on my elbows. "What do you want to know?"

"Are you married?"

"Not anymore. I'm divorced." I refused to flinch.

He nodded soberly, one survivor understanding another. "You got kids?"

"No."

"Do you want one?"

"Why, are you looking for a home?" I laughed, and then stopped, wondering if he was. But he shook his head.

"Nah. Just wondered."

I hesitated, then shook my head. "I don't. I was busy with my life, my job, my . . . well, everything." It sounded like a feeble excuse. The truth was that Marcus hadn't wanted any children until after he got his law practice going, and I had just gone along with it. I'd wanted kids, but I'd thought we had plenty of time for a family later.

"Have you heard any tales about this house being haunted?" I asked to distract him from the topic.

He shot me a look that clearly said he'd expected better things of me. "I gotta go now," he announced, standing.

I saw him to the door, where he paused and turned back to me. "Kerris?"

"Yes, Finn?"

"Thanks for breakfast."

He jumped down the steps in one bound and ran off.

Fortunately, there wasn't asbestos, and it only took three days to enclose the Sellers' porch and finish their entry and closet. Even though it was a basic and simple job, it brought me a sense of satisfaction, a relief to find tools in my hands again in the service of someone else, even if briefly. But after three days of listening to Donna, it also drained me. She was cheerful and friendly and loving toward her little boy, but I had grown unaccustomed to noise and chatter. It was with a bit of guilty glee that I finished up the job and retreated to my own home and the projects waiting for me there.

Eamonn hadn't been exaggerating when he'd said my house came with a lot of land. I had two acres, most of it overgrown with weeds and some of it treed with hardwood. Two rickety sheds and the remains of a chicken coop stood behind the garage. I had no intention of keeping chickens, and the sheds were far from safe, so I planned to tear these down and reuse whatever wood I could salvage. It would be hard work to re-establish a decent lawn, so I thought I'd limit the grass to the immediate area surrounding the house, rough-mow the rest, and throw some wildflower seeds around. I didn't need a manicured, meticulous, and labor-gobbling yard, and a meadow of wildflowers would attract birds and butterflies. The idea of being surrounded by a sea of flowers appealed to me.

But first I had to get rid of the rusted and abandoned junk that filled the two old sheds. That Saturday, I backed my truck as far into the backyard as the septic tank would allow and started dragging old shovels, bottomless plastic buckets, rotting rain barrels, lawnmower bits, cracked flowerpots, and some unidentifiable metal objects into it. Whoever had owned this house had clearly liked to garden. I wondered what it would have looked like before the weeds and grass had taken it over. Maybe I could find a neighbor to tell me, and I could restore it to what it had been before.

I gave up that idea as soon as I found the axe. Not a little hatchet. An *axe*, heavy as a corpse and honed to a deadly sharpness. The handle was worn from use. If this yard had required a weapon of that magnitude, I wasn't restoring it to anything remotely resembling it. Trundling along behind a lawnmower was as "gardeny" as I got.

I'm five-foot-nine and fairly strong. I like to think of myself as capable and self-sufficient and as liberated as the next woman. But there are occasional times when an able-bodied man could come in handy, and this was one of them. The junk had been lying there for years, tangled and water-soaked and inhabited by mice. I didn't relish the work.

I was bent over what looked like a rusted plow share, legs braced apart, tugging for all I was worth and wondering when my last tetanus shot had been, when Finn's voice spoke behind me.

"You're doing it all wrong."

I jerked upright and whirled to face him. He stood beside my truck, sucking on a purple Popsicle and watching with interest. The Popsicle was melting and dripping slowly down his arm to his elbow. Some of the drops had landed unheeded on his bare feet. It looked like he was wearing the same clothes he'd worn before, unwashed and rattier than ever.

"Oh, am I?" I snarled without meaning to. "And I suppose you know how to do it better, do you?"

"Yes, I do." He finished the Popsicle and tossed the stick away nonchalantly into the weeds. "Brains over brawn."

"Tell me, then, Smarty, but don't come closer without shoes on. It isn't safe."

He shot me a disdainful look. And then turned and pointed to the winch on the back of my truck.

I felt my face flush hot with embarrassment. Brains over brawn, indeed. I didn't use the winch often and had forgotten I had it. Muttering, I dug through the back of my truck, looking for a chain. I found some heavy nylon cord that would do. I knotted it around the plow share, attached it to the short chain on the winch, turned it on, and watched the truck haul the hunk of metal neatly out of the shed as easily as pulling a carrot out of a garden bed.

The plow share slid across the ground and came to a stop beside the truck. I turned off the winch and Finn and I stared down at the thing for a moment in silence.

"Yes, well," I sighed, and untied the nylon cord.

"If you rig up a ramp and a pulley, it could haul the stuff right up into the truck bed for you," Finn pointed out, licking a filthy finger.

I swallowed my injured pride and put my hand on his shoulder.

"I gotta hand it to you. You're a brainy one," I said, and added, "Thanks, Stinky."

He shrugged but he couldn't quite hide his pleased smile.

Of course, things went much easier after that. We had the truck full by lunch time. We sat on the back porch, another five-dollar bill in Finn's pocket (justly earned), and drank Tang and ate tuna sandwiches and watched a dragonfly dive-bomb the yard.

"That biggest shed would make a neat fort," Finn observed, popping a pickle into his mouth.

"It wouldn't be safe. It's falling apart," I said.

"You build houses," he reminded me. "You could make it safe."

"Are you asking me to build you a fort?"

He gave another half shrug and swung his feet. "I'm just saying," he said. "Since I can't use the basement anymore and all."

I massaged an aching muscle in my shoulder. "I'll think about it. I was going to tear it down."

"That's a waste," he said.

"All right," I said. "I'll make it a fort. But you have to help. And when it's done, no loud parties or people traipsing through my yard at all hours, okay?"

"Okay."

"No turning it into an opium den or stashing stolen goods in it."

"Deal." He grinned. "Can I bring a flashlight and spend the night in it?"

"Only if your father says it's okay," I suggested, watching him.

Finn shrugged. "He won't care."

It was said confidently, with no sign of self-pity. Well, I thought, at least it confirms there's a relative somewhere in the picture.

Chapter Four

One of the things that most appealed to me about my house was its isolation. Only a short drive from the edge of town, it nonetheless felt as if it were in the middle of nowhere. Behind the property were the remains of an old railway, the iron rails now gone but the gravel berm still there, overgrown with weeds. Trees gathered on east and west so I couldn't see the neighbors from the backyard. The road the house sat on seldom had any traffic. Directly across the street from me was an expansive park, surrounded by a rustic wood rail fence, where a forest was kept in some sort of abeyance. A deep lawn ran beneath the trees, unmown and left natural and wild. I fell into the habit of relaxing on the front porch in the evening with a glass of icy lemonade, watching the black squirrels bounding in the long grass and wild violets under the maples. It felt a very far way from Toronto. The longer I sat, the further away the city and the life I had led there seemed.

Which was, after all, the point.

On Sunday, I decided to take a well-deserved break, packed myself a picnic, put on capri pants and a t-shirt, and went across to the park to enjoy a day out. There was no formal path, but a dim trail was cut in the grass, probably by some animal, and I followed it, enjoying the swish of the grass against my calves. The sun filtered through the maple canopy to cast spotlights here and there through the shade, like an eccentric stagehand lighting my progress. I moved from pool of light to pool of light, smelling the crushed grass and the indefinable scent of an Ontario April. It was cool in the shade, though, and I wished I'd brought a sweatshirt. How did Finn walk around in bare feet?

Eventually, I heard a musical trickling and came to a small brook winding its boggy way through the grass. The water was golden and the bottom was free of stones. I circled around like a dog until I had a small area of grass tamped down in a circle in the sunlight, and then I sat cross-legged and pulled my picnic from my knapsack. It was nothing fancy, only a cheese sandwich, a bottle of juice, and some grapes, but it tasted wonderful when eaten outdoors. I let the splotchy sun sprinkle down on my shoulders and soothe away the tension in my muscles.

I leaned back on my elbows, the grass tickling my back, and squinted up at the light in the treetops.

"How am I doing?" I whispered to the sky.

I didn't subscribe to any formal religion—my parents had made that pretty inevitable—and I was uncertain about God, but once in a while I got the sense of something or someone watching over me. Not God, I imagined, but a sort of guardian angel, and now and then, in the right mood, I liked to check in with them/it/her. I thought probably *her*. It just sort of felt like a feminine presence, distant but aware of me, like a friend you never see but think of now and then. I wasn't even sure I believed in angels. Perhaps it was just a benevolent force of some kind. Whatever it was, I had come to recognize when it was at work in my life.

I think it had always been there, but the first time I really became aware of it was when I was seventeen and had been named Prom Queen (back in the day when high schools did silly things like that). My name had been announced in a school assembly along with the name of Rod Wallace, the designated Prom King. I was delighted at the idea of attending the dance on his arm. My friends had shrieked with excitement when the announcement was made. He was the most popular student in school and a truly beautiful boy, and I floated home in a daydream about what a couple we would make.

My mother had shot that dream down abruptly with five words, "We can't afford a dress."

I had known that, of course. In the six years since my father had left, my little sister and I had learned that Mom's secretarial salary didn't extend to frivolous extras like prom dresses. Or amusement parks. Or participation in class field trips. Or piano lessons. Or skating parties. Or any of the other myriad of things all our friends got to do. Our clothes were either homemade or recycled from Value Village, the secondhand shop. I owned one dress and one skirt, both of them practical gray wool and faded.

I told myself it didn't matter. I would wear the gray dress, with a pink ribbon holding up my blonde ponytail. And if it wasn't good enough, well, then Rod Wallace could go to the dance by himself. I didn't care. But when my name was published in the local paper and I saw my school photo there in print next to Rod's, I couldn't stop crying with disappointment.

I don't know who or how, the only thing I know was it wasn't my mother's doing. A week before the prom, a box arrived at the house, delivered from The Hudson Bay Company. Mom was at work and my sister Gillian opened the door to the delivery man.

"It's for you," she said, reading the label in puzzlement.

Inside the box was the most perfect, the most lovely dress, a confection in pale blue with a floaty skirt that looked like multiple scarves bound together at the snug waist. Dark blue satin roses gathered the neckline, and the sleeves were long enough to cover the scar on my upper arm from when I'd fallen off my bike as a kid.

"It's beautiful!" Gillian breathed in astonishment. "Who sent it?"

"It doesn't say."

"Did Mom order it?"

"No way."

"Did . . . Dad?" Her voice dropped in tone and she didn't meet my eyes.

According to Mom, Dad was in Sacramento, California with his new wife, his new kids, his new life. He hadn't said so much as Happy Birthday in six years. There was no way this dreamy dress had come from him. And how would he have known I needed it, anyway?

I don't know why, but I didn't show the dress to my mother. She would have done something to ruin it for me—turned the coach back into a pumpkin, unmasked the fairy godmother, locked me in a tower.

I wore the gray dress, unquestioned, out the door that evening with the new dress in a plastic bag and made Rod stop at a Tim Hortons doughnut shop on the way so I could change.

That had been the first instance that I'd really been aware of, but there had been a number of others over the years. Anonymous flowers delivered to the door the day before my graduation from university (not from my mother—she'd left me a Hallmark card on my pillow). A job offer out of the blue when I hadn't even thought to apply there. My credit card balance mysteriously paid off when I was first starting my own business and money was tight. (I knew *that* hadn't been my mother's doing, either! Not in a million years.) In little ways I'd been shown someone was watching, someone cared. Far from being a frightening thing, it was comforting. There was someone who saw I had what I needed, when my parents (or I) failed to meet the task. And now this—the gift of the house, when I'd had nowhere to go and no one to fall back on.

Come to think of it, it had been a few years since my guardian angel had done anything blatant. I'd almost started to think it had been some childhood fairy tale and wasn't going to continue on into post-marriage adulthood. Goodness knows the last year or so had been anything but a fairy tale. But I'd been wrong. They were still looking out for me. *She.*

I tidied away the remains of my lunch and rinsed my hands in the little brook. The water was icy, and I wiped my hands on the seat of my pants and shouldered my knapsack to continue my exploration.

After a while of tramping through wildflowers and getting stickers in my socks, I came upon an asphalt path. I stopped to pick the seed pods from my stockings and then walked on, making better progress on the hard surface. The path didn't seem to have any particular goal in mind, but wandered freely through the woods, and I went along with it. I'd been rambling for about five minutes when the path turned and came out suddenly from under the trees, and I found myself blinking in the strong sunlight under a bare sky. After the half gloom under the maples, I felt momentarily blinded.

I'd emerged into a clearing. No, a field. No, a *yard.* The grass became a manicured emerald sweep stretching a hundred feet ahead of me, where it ended in a cement driveway. Turning my head to the left, I followed the driveway with my eyes and then stopped, staring at the house to which it led.

It wasn't colossal, not really, when I looked closely at it. But it had the impact of a colossal house. Built of gray granite, its sharply pitched roof black, its base thickly planted with low evergreens, it looked like a mountain popping unexpectedly from the forest. A willow tree curved gracefully at one corner, trying to soften the blunt angles of the stone, and I saw a spray of some pink flower growing on each side of the massive front door. The windows were tall and wide and without curtains, so that I could see right through some of them to patches of sky showing through windows on the other side. There was a car, sleek and gray and low to the ground, parked in the driveway before the double garage.

Good grief, this wasn't a public park at all. It was the grounds of someone's house.

I sank back into the shadows of the trees and hoped no one had seen me. I was mortified at the thought of being caught trespassing with my picnic in a sack. I should have realized it wasn't a park when I'd seen no signs, no formal car park or path. City kid that I was, I'd simply assumed things were different in country towns. Feeling stupid, I fled back the way I'd come, managed to pick up the animal track through the grass, and hopped the rail fence across from my house. I didn't slow down until I was in my own kitchen, leaning against the table and laughing at myself for my ignorance. I had no idea who my unimaginably wealthy neighbor must be, but whoever it was, I hoped they didn't mind my making crop circles in their grass.

Lying in bed that night, I remembered playing a game with my sister when she was small. We would sit facing each other and chant the words as we made the actions with our hands. *Going on a lion hunt . . . Got my slingshot . . . I'm not afraid . . . through the tall grass . . . over the fence . . . across the river . . . up the mountain . . . to the dark cave.* Of course we always found a lion in the dark cave, and we would go lickety-split backwards through all the actions as fast as we could—mountain, river, fence, grass—to get back home before the lion ate us. Remembering, I began to laugh. I had indeed gone on a lion hunt of sorts today, and I'd been just as delightedly frightened as I'd been with my childish, frantic game.

As I dropped off to sleep, I realized how long it had been since I'd really laughed.

Finn appeared Monday afternoon as I was hanging out my laundry.

"I'm here to work on the fort," he announced.

I opened my mouth to tell him I had a lot of things to do that day and maybe we could start on it tomorrow. But I stopped before any words came out. He stood before me with sturdy tennis shoes on, this time. He wore a clean blue t-shirt and jeans. He had made some attempt to comb down his hair, and, in his hand, he carried a serviceable hammer. His eyes were steady on mine, a stubborn tilt to his chin as if he knew the excuses I was about to make. His expression was braced for it, as if he'd heard a lot of excuses from grown-ups in his life and expected nothing different from me. I swallowed the words down and smiled.

"Let's get at it, then," I said.

Finn's face split into a broad smile.

We cleared the shed of the rest of its contents first, hauling away old clay flowerpots, rusty rakes and trowels, and tangles of twine and bird netting. The floor was packed earth and rot was advancing up the wood walls, but Finn insisted the structure could be saved. I had my doubts.

"They shouldn't have put the wood directly against the ground," I told him, pointing. "There should have been a cement foundation. The water has gotten into the walls."

"You can fix it," he said confidently. "It's what you do."

Yes, I sighed, it was what I did. I fixed things. "But some things are too ruined to be fixed," I said. *My own life, for instance*, I mentally whispered.

He ignored this and began swatting at the fly-blown cobwebs in the corners of the ceiling.

In the end, we compromised. I tacked a vapor barrier inside the old walls, then built new walls inside them with new wood, leaving the rotting outer shell intact. Basically, I was building a fort within the shed. If the outside structure peeled completely away in the weather, there would be no harm done to the actual fort. The windows seemed to be intact, and adding the inner walls gave them deep ledges, which Finn declared could hold his flashlight and comic book collection like shelves. As night fell, I declared it too dark to continue.

"We'll tack the tar paper on the roof tomorrow."

"We're almost done," Finn protested. "Can't we finish it?"

"Not tonight," I said firmly. "I have to order in the shingles anyway, and besides, I've been working since sun-up and I'm tired."

He began to whine, then saw my face and decided against it. He followed me to the house, his hammer shoved in the back of his waistband.

"Your laundry is still out," he observed.

"It's probably not dry yet," I said. "And if it is, I'm too tired to bring it in. It'll be all right tonight."

"It's going to rain tonight," he said gloomily.

"Is not. It's been warm and sunny all day."

"That's when we get rain, when it's been hot all day." He rolled his eyes at my ignorance of evaporation and cloud formation.

I eyed him a moment, then sighed. "You bring in the laundry. I'll go rig up a light so I can nail the tar paper on."

I didn't let him climb up to help me, but I did find him useful for handing supplies up to me. I had the roof covered in no time and was just gathering up my extension cords when the first raindrops began to fall. We ran for the house as the sky opened and the torrent began.

Laughing, we landed in the kitchen and shook water droplets from our hair and clothes. We helped ourselves to hot chocolate and then sat gently steaming at the table. I nodded toward the basket of laundry Finn had hauled in. Not only had he gathered it from the line, he had neatly folded each article. Someone had taught him at some point.

"Thanks for that," I said.

He nodded seriously. "And thank you for the fort."

Manners? From Finn? I grinned and reached across the table to rough up his hair. It was drying in dust-colored spikes, and the bridge of his nose was pink from the sun. To my surprise, he didn't duck away, but let me touch him. His eyes met mine for a long moment, then slid away.

"I'd better go. School tomorrow," he said.

"Come again tomorrow after school and we'll finish it off," I said. I remembered the rain. "Do you want a ride home?"

"I don't mind rain. It'll count as my bath."

"Want a bar of soap so you can lather up on the way home?" I joked.

"Nah, it's Monday," he replied, grinning. "I only use soap for my Saturday night bath."

Chapter Five

I decided I would surprise him. While he was in school, I went and bought shingles (Eamonn hadn't been on duty, but the pierced teenager helped me select shingles in a particularly exciting shade of red). Then I spent the morning making some adjustments to the fort. I had built a raised platform floor over the packed earth, and now I rolled out some foam and some leftover carpet on it. I installed some hooks on the walls to hold his things and laid out my sleeping bag. I painted the outside of the building brown (the Runny Meatloaf, though out in the sunlight it looked better, more like Chocolate Chiffon). On the door I painted in white: Finn's Fort, in as fancy a calligraphy as I could manage. I put three cement steppingstones leading up to the door as a welcome. And I left a six-pack of root beer on the floor beside the sleeping bag.

I stepped back to admire the overall effect. The brown color and the red roof reminded me of the box of chocolate-covered cherries my grandmother had kept on her coffee table (and let her grandchildren actually *eat*, which was better than some people). After Grandma's death, the cherries had been replaced by a covered glass dish of candy-covered almonds enameled in pink and white and green pastels. Mom had never let us lift the lid. Mom had eventually sold Grandma's house and rented an apartment of her own, and the dish of almonds made the move with her. I don't remember seeing it when I cleaned everything out after she died. I wonder if she'd finally succumbed and eaten them.

I shook off my musing and turned toward the house. As I did, a soft breeze gently lifted a strand of hair from my cheek and tucked it backward, and I paused, momentarily startled. It had felt exactly the way it had felt when Grandma had tucked my hair behind my ear and caressed my cheek with her hand. I'd forgotten that gesture she'd made so often, that small, gentle thing that I'd found so comforting as a child. It was probably the memory of the cherries that had triggered the feeling. The little moment of tenderness lingered and made me smile as I went up the steps.

There was just one more thing I wanted for Finn's fort, but I'd forgotten it when I'd gone for the shingles and brown paint. I looked up the hardware store on my iPhone, and Eamonn himself answered on the third ring.

"It's Kerris Wells," I said. "Remember me?"

"The one in the haunted house?"

"That's me. Do you carry any Coleman lanterns?"

"I do. What size are you looking for?"

"Big, like the kind the Scouts take camping. The kind that can hang from a hook in the ceiling."

"Yep, I have yellow or red ones."

"Red, please. Can you hold one for me and I'll come pick it up right now?"

"Don't worry about it. My brother Ian is just heading out that way right now. I'll have him drop it off to you."

"Really? Would he mind? That would be great," I told him. "I'm short on time today."

"Sure, he'll be happy to. You can pay me the next time you're in the store."

"Terrific! Thanks so much." *Another advantage to life in a small town*, I thought.

"Oh hey, I asked my mother about your house. I'm afraid she doesn't know who lived there before you."

"Oh, thanks for asking," I said, surprised at how disappointed I was. As I said goodbye and hung up the phone, I reminded myself that I had yet to meet the neighbors on the west. The stack of newspapers,

I'd noticed, had disappeared from their porch, so they must come to town occasionally, but I'd yet to see them. I would catch them sometime and ask if they knew anything about my mysterious benefactor.

About twenty minutes later, there was a knock at the door. I was in the middle of wrestling a slab of old countertop out of the kitchen with the idea of hauling it out to my truck. I'd misjudged the length of it and had managed to wedge it into a tight spot in the hallway, where I couldn't go forward or backward. Frustrated and sweaty, I hollered for the person to come in. There was a polite hesitation, then the front door opened and a head poked through.

At first, I thought Eamonn had changed his mind and decided to come himself. Then I saw that this man, though similar of feature and with the same thick, brown hair, was taller and leaner, his tan not so deep. He instantly took in my predicament and strode forward to grasp an end of the counter with one hand. In his other hand he held the red lantern.

"Let me help you," he said. "Are you coming out or going in?"

"Coming out. But mind the dust—you'll ruin your clothes."

He glanced down at his tan slacks and striped dress shirt and just shrugged. "They'll wash." He set the lantern aside and hefted the countertop to shoulder height. With a deft turn and some juggling I'd never have been able to do alone, he soon had the heavy slab free with only a slight mark on the walls of the hallway. Between us we managed to make it to the truck and heave the thing in. He brushed his hands together and turned to me with a smile that echoed Eamonn's easy grin. I saw his eyes were sea-gray, fringed with impossibly long dark lashes.

"Ian McGrath. Eamonn sent me."

"And just in time, too," I said. "Kerris Wells." As we shook hands, I could feel the dry callouses on my own palms and was acutely aware of the dirt under my short nails.

"Thanks for the help," I said. "It was heavier than I'd bargained for. I should have cut it in half before I tried to move it."

"I'm surprised you attempted it yourself."

"I didn't have much option," I replied, leading the way back into the house. "It had to come out, and I'm the only one here to do it."

"Do you have more pieces?"

"Three more, but they're shorter. I can manage them," I said, more confidently than I felt.

Ian McGrath didn't reply, only strode down the hall into the kitchen. He paused, looking around at the destruction and mayhem.

"You've done a lot already," he observed. "Let me help you get the rest out."

"You don't have to. It was nice enough that you were willing to bring the lantern out—" I began.

To my relief, he ignored me and proceeded to haul the countertop pieces out of the kitchen. I hadn't ordered the new counters yet, but I had the strong suspicion I'd end up hiring someone to put them in for me rather than trying to do it myself. At one time I might have attempted it, but these last few months I didn't seem to have the energy or strength—or will—I'd once had. I was learning I had limitations, and I was getting better at respecting them. It wasn't an entirely bad thing.

When Ian returned from the last load to the truck, I was sitting at the table with lemonade waiting.

"Thanks," he said, dropping into the chair opposite mine. "Usually it doesn't get this hot until June."

"I owe you a major favor," I told him.

"No worries." He took a long swallow of the cold liquid and looked interestedly around the kitchen. "Are you refinishing the cupboards or putting in new ones?"

"Refinishing. And I'm going to extend the counter out into a peninsula, with stools to sit up to it." I had carefully numbered the cupboard doors before removing them so that I could get them all put back together again when I'd finished stripping and staining them. I had changed my mind about the whitewash, thinking it would look too countrified. Instead, I was going to go for a honey-colored stain to complement the Spring Marigold walls. I found the stain sample to show him what I had in mind.

"That will be very nice," he said. "And what kind of countertops? Granite?"

"My budget wouldn't stretch that far," I told him. "And even if it did, I think I'd still go for good old laminate. It can take a beating, and my counters need to be able to take a beating."

"Ah. Yes. Granite can stain. And laminate isn't that expensive to replace down the road . . . once you've beaten it." He smiled. I gripped my glass and tried not to notice the attractive little lines that his smile caused to radiate from the corners of his incredible eyes.

"Do you work with Eamonn?" I asked, thinking he sounded like he knew what he was talking about.

His grin grew broader. "Eamonn wouldn't let me within ten feet of his precious power tools. I'm hopeless with my hands. He got all the skill in the family there, I'm afraid. But I've learned a bit, listening to him rabbit on about work."

"So what do you do?"

"I teach at Port Daley Collegiate. Biology."

"Cool."

He chuckled low in his chest. "I don't know that my students would agree with you. But I also coach rugby and soccer. That's cooler."

It felt odd to have him sitting at my table, chatting. I hadn't had a man in my kitchen since I'd parted from Marcus (though Finn would protest that he counted as one, of course). It was a rather nice feeling. I was just about to search out another topic of conversation when he set his glass down, slid back his chair, and stood. I jumped to my feet too. Of course, he hadn't meant to linger. He'd only been making the delivery on his way . . . where? Home? To a wife and family? He had the comfortable, settled look of a married man, though no ring on his finger.

"Thanks for the lemonade," he said. "I'd better head out. See you around, though."

I walked him to the door and thanked him again, and watched him fold his long frame into a white Honda Accord and drive away. He turned left at the end of the street, heading out of Smoke River. He must live out in the new subdivision I'd seen south of town, where Eamonn said their mother lived. I caught myself watching the road where he'd disappeared and told myself firmly to get back to work.

Finn loved what I'd done with the fort. He showed up promptly at 3:30 and together we inspected the changes I'd made. He especially liked the lantern.

"Great! Now I can read in bed at night."

"Yep. But not tonight, if that's what you're thinking."

"Why not?"

"For one thing, you have school tomorrow. For another, the paint isn't totally dry yet and I don't want you breathing fumes all night. Wait until the weekend."

His face fell but he nodded. "Can I bring my beanbag chair?" he asked. "It's brown. It would match really well."

"Sure. That would be perfect for in here."

Mollified, he scampered to the house for his ritual root beer. I followed behind, smiling.

I thought about Finn after he'd gone home, or wherever it was he went at night, while I was straightening the house before bed. I honestly enjoyed his company. I had found myself throughout the day thinking of things he might enjoy or things I could do to please him. I looked forward to his unexpected appearances and mischievous face. I delighted in his conversation. If I thought about it, I could even admit I'd fantasized about taking him in permanently. If I found out he *needed* a home and a mother . . .

But no, I knew better than to go there. I felt overwhelmed just taking care of myself these days, much less a child. Especially a child in as much need as Finn seemed to be. I hung up the towel I was holding and left the kitchen, snapping off the light. Briskly I changed into the baggy shirt I used for a nightgown, brushed my teeth, and went to bed. But lying there staring up at the darkness of the ceiling, I no longer had the busy exhaustion of the day to distract me, and I found I couldn't turn my thoughts off.

I was thirty years old, single again, and childless. I supposed some people who'd had the less-than-stellar childhood I'd had wouldn't be in any hurry to bring children into the world. After all, I hadn't had a great example of parenting set for me growing up. Dad had been absent much of the time, being consumed—we'd thought—by his profession. (As it turned out, he'd been more consumed by his multiple affairs with various women in the congregation over which he was the minister.) When at last he vanished for good, when I was eleven and my sister Gillian was six, the hole he left in our lives proved not to be very big.

Mom had always been a hard woman, but after Dad left, sheer exhaustion compressed her lips into a disapproving line and carved permanent frown lines between her eyes. I knew taking on the responsibility of supporting us had been difficult for her, and she missed her husband's income if not him himself. She made it pretty clear she considered her daughters burdens and inconveniences, and she raised us strictly, without joy. She also did her best to sour her children against formal religion on the premise that rotten apples came from rotten trees.

I thought it would be understandable if I didn't want to raise a child after experiencing what I had. But my family life had had the opposite effect on me—I wanted to give a child a better home than I'd had. I wanted to do it *right*, to somehow make up for all the wrongs.

Mom had moved us to Toronto from Ottawa after the divorce with the idea of living with her widowed mother to split expenses. That had been a good year, I thought, folding my pillow in half and jamming it under my head. That year with Grandma had been an oasis, a calm eye in the midst of the storm. For the first time, Gillian and I had known acceptance and warmth and what it felt like to be smiled at. We'd only really gotten to know our wonderful Grandma for that one year, though, and then she had died when I was almost thirteen, and the storm had overtaken us. But I still felt a gladness of heart when I thought about her. Her death had been more painful for me than all of my father's betrayals.

And here I was, going through yet another betrayal at the hands of a man. And Gillian had grown up and gone on through a string of relationships that always ended badly. What was it about the women in my family that doomed them again and again to be hurt by the men in their lives?

I sat up with a groan and shoved my blankets off, drawing my knees to my chest and wrapping my arms around them. I put my forehead on my knees and concentrated on breathing. Behind my eyelids I could see Marcus's face, so handsome, so arrogant, with his feathered brown hair perfectly angled on his forehead. His beautiful mouth forming the impossible words I couldn't comprehend.

I'm in love with Maddie. We're having a baby.

So, as it turned out, it wasn't having kids that he objected to, it was having them with *me.*

People talk about moments of change, as if they're as benign as turning left instead of right at a stop light. But what change really is, is collapse. When your expectations splinter, all the air is squashed out of your hope, your view of yourself dissolves, and you find yourself on your back, looking up at the ceiling, gasping for breath and wondering what flattened you. The complete annihilation of life as you know it. People try to couch it in saccharine references as growth or going in new directions or refocusing. But really, it's the end of everything vital, the suspended moment when you're not sure what—if anything—happens next.

For me, this particular moment of change had been accompanied by nausea. You can't fall that swiftly without losing your stomach. For much of the three days that followed Marcus's announcement, I'd knelt by the toilet, retching up the whole story I'd built for myself about our life together, until the realization had finally sunk in that there was nothing left to bring up. The story was over. There was still anger and protest, of course, but it had been covered by a weary veneer of numbness that carried me through the next few months, and that was all right with me. It was better than the bitter taste of bile, as I picked my way through the shattered remnants toward higher (or at least safer) ground where I was less likely to slash myself.

Tiptoeing through the broken glass, I could tell even that early on that there was nothing to salvage. Collapsed houses never looked recognizable, it was all just rubble.

Sleeping now was out of the question. I ended up sitting at the kitchen table most of that night, awash with self-pity and trying to stave it off with too much coffee. To distract myself, I scribbled plans for the house and yard. I might be in the middle of nowhere, in a town the size of my old high school, and as alone as I'd ever been as a child. I might never be a mother or have a family of my own. But I was determined I would make this little house, *my* home, a place of peace and acceptance. No child, Finn and my own younger self included, would ever be made to feel unwanted *here*.

As I drew up my plans, the idea wasn't lost on me that I was rebuilding myself along with the house.

Chapter Six

Of course, my truck—the one really vital possession in my life—decided to die the next Wednesday. I had driven into Shelburne to do some shopping and was halfway back to Smoke River when a funny sluggishness came over it and it started to grind. Just as I reached Front Street, the engine died completely. I coasted to a slow stop at the side of the road. I pumped the gas and tried to start the truck again. The engine caught briefly and then sputtered and died again.

Sighing, I leaned my head back on the headrest and tried not to cry. This was definitely not in the budget. I needed this stupid old truck. I couldn't work without it. It was sure to be something expensive . . .

A tap on my window jerked me upright, and I saw Ian McGrath's friendly face peering in at me. I rolled down the crank window and swiped at my eyes, hoping he couldn't tell I'd been on the verge of tears.

"Are you okay? I saw you just sitting here . . ."

"Thanks, I'm fine," I said. And then immediately added, "No, I'm not. My truck died."

"Oh. What's wrong with it?"

"I don't know. I was driving back from Shelburne and it was just fine. Then it started acting funny, and then it stopped altogether."

"Try starting it again."

I did so, with the same result. The engine turned over briefly and then died. When I tried again, I got only a click.

Ian poked his head further into the cab and looked at the gas gauge. "Not out of gas. I'm guessing it's your alternator or your fuel injector."

"Is that expensive?"

He glanced at the rusty side of the car, looking for a make and model. "Maybe," he said. "Then again, they may not even make parts for this vehicle anymore."

"It's not that old," I protested, feeling as if he had insulted an elderly relative. "It's just had a hard life."

"What year is it?"

I thought a moment. "I think it's a 2001."

He arched one perfect eyebrow. "Yes. Well. Why don't I push you into the service station and then give you a lift home?"

"That would be super, thank you. That's the second time you've rescued me."

"I'm not keeping track."

The service station was only a block and a half away, but it took both of us plus three friendly volunteers to push the rusting carcass that far. I'd never realized how heavy my old Ford was. I made arrangements with the bemused-looking man at the station to take care of it, and then fetched my purchases from the truck bed and loaded them into Ian's Honda. It started up with a loyal purr and we were off.

It had been easy to chat with Ian when he was in my home, but crammed into his small car with him, I found myself tongue-tied. He seemed very large and close and too tall for the low ceiling. He was wearing jeans and a Toronto Raptors t-shirt and drove with his hand resting lightly on the stick shift by my thigh.

"I'm sorry to put you out of your way," I said.

"Not at all. I'm heading home out your way anyway."

I glanced at my watch.

"Don't you have to teach today?" I asked.

"Professional development day. No classes."

"Ah. And you don't have to be there professionally developing?"

He grinned, the corners of his eyes crinkling. His eyes were more blue than gray today. "I'm playing hooky, but don't tell the principal." He glanced at my expression and started to laugh. "Actually, I was excused early today because I have an appointment with the tree man."

"The who?"

"Arborist. He's coming to look at a diseased willow tree, to see if it needs removing. I suspect it does. It's too bad, because it's very old and tall and beautiful."

Old willow tree. Not the new subdivision then. The only trees there were spindly identical maples, one plopped in front of each cookie-cutter house like flags lining a runway.

"The usual fellow retired," Ian added. "I've never met this one before."

"The usual . . . you have your own arborist?" Surely this was unusual.

"Well, I have a great many trees to tend, you see. But the University of Guelph recommended this man, so I'll give him a try."

"Well, thank you for the ride," I told him as we turned onto Rannick Road. "I hope I haven't made you late."

"No, no." He parked the Honda in my driveway in the spot where I usually parked my truck. I wondered how much it was going to cost me before the truck was parked there again. But instead of just letting me out, Ian jumped from the car and took my bags from the back seat.

"I can get those," I said, but he was already halfway to the front door. I fumbled for my key and opened it.

"You lock your doors?" Ian sounded surprised. He followed me into the kitchen and set everything on the table for me.

"I'm from Toronto," I excused myself again. "And I live alone." Now why had I added *that*? "Um, thanks for the help."

"My pleasure." In spite of his appointment, he seemed in no hurry to go. "Listen, when your truck is ready, give me a call and I'll take you back to pick it up."

I was about to protest but he was already scribbling his phone number on a piece of paper he pulled from his pocket. "You can reach me at home almost any evening. You can also leave a message for me at Eamonn's store and I'll get it."

"I will," I said.

"Please do."

I found myself fishing for something to extend the conversation and keep him there a little bit longer, and then I hit on a question I'd been mulling over.

"Hey, maybe you can tell me. Why is this town called Smoke River?"

"Oh! Hasn't anyone told you? It's really cool."

"What?"

"At about six o'clock in the morning, just as the sun is starting to rise, walk down to the river. The best place is the bridge by the Legion, where the river bends and heads toward Lake Huron. But it has to be just as the sun comes up."

"Why? What happens?"

"Go. You'll see." He solemnly slid his hand, palm facing me, from left to right. "All will become clear," he intoned sagaciously.

I grinned. "Okay. I'll go."

He dropped the pose and looked down at me—he really was very tall, maybe six-three or -four—and his eyes lingered on me for a moment. "I'm glad I ran into you. Have a good day."

"You too."

It was weird, but the kitchen felt rather empty after he left.

After he left, I went over to knock on the door of the neighbors I hadn't met yet. Their curtains were drawn, though, and no car was in the driveway, and no one answered my knock. Missed them again. I returned home feeling deflated.

I prodded myself into spending time that afternoon trying to get my life into some sort of order. I couldn't go much longer without drumming up some business and refilling the depleted bank account. The Sellers' front porch was one thing, the idea of taking on a full-scale project was another thing entirely. But helping Donna Sellers had made me think perhaps I could manage some small fix-it jobs. So I composed an ad for the local paper and printed up some homemade but nice-looking flyers to pin up on the Handymart and community center bulletin boards. I wasn't ready to relaunch my website with my new contact information, because I really didn't want to take on a major home renovation, but I told myself it was okay to start with baby steps. I figured I could handle tiling a bathroom or unclogging a sink or two.

Even that much effort to reclaim some of my old life left me emotionally frazzled. I cocooned in the house and decided to pamper myself with comfort food for supper. I was in the process of grating a small mountain of cheddar for mac'n cheese when there was a knock at the door. I opened it to find two young women on the steps.

They were dressed neatly, one in navy skirt and blazer, the other in a flowered calf-length dress. They had name tags pinned to their chests, and both wore their blonde hair long on their shoulders. They gave me broad smiles. I felt my heart sink.

"Hi! We're missionaries for the Church of—" the one in the blazer began in a bright, chipper voice.

"Sorry, I'm right in the middle of making supper," I interrupted, already starting to close the door.

"Oh, that's all right. We could come back—"

"No, thanks." I shut the door firmly and went back to the kitchen. There was no way I could handle Jehovah's Witnesses or whatever they were right now.

I might have imagined it, but the kitchen seemed to give a little sigh as I went back to grating the cheese.

The next morning, muttering to myself for being a fool, I slapped my alarm off at 5:30 and groggily pulled on jeans and a sweatshirt. Without stopping to comb my hair or make myself presentable—who would be out at this stupid hour, anyway?—I let myself out of the house and headed toward the center of town and the river. The bridge, I knew, lay just beyond the big red brick Legion building, about two blocks from the hardware store, a walkable distance. The air was chilly and gray as I stumbled along, hands shoved in my pockets.

No one was out yet other than one lone figure hunched in a coat, walking a yellow dog past the post office. Here and there a golden glow showed in upstairs windows of the houses I passed, but the street was quiet and hushed. No cars, no voices. After a while, the invigorating air woke me more fully, and I began to enjoy the slap of my shoes on the empty sidewalk and the feeling of having the town to myself. The sun was just peeking over the horizon when I reached the bridge.

Leaning my elbows on the railing, I looked down at the dark water sliding past below me and waited, though I wasn't sure what I was waiting for. There was a soft rippling sound as the river hit the bend and turned in a series of small, white rapids, making a gentle sort of music that I hadn't been aware of before in the normal hustle and noise of the day.

And then I saw it. A thick white mist rose from the river like tattered gauze, spiraling and swirling along the water and reaching up in tendrils toward the first rays of the sun. It looked like a tangible, living thing I should have been able to reach out and touch. I watched as it crawled along the surface of the river, bubbling over the small rapids at the bend. Soon the whole river valley was filled with white fog.

I waited, entranced, breathing in the mist, listening to the water I could no longer see, and understood clearly what made the early settlers choose the name Smoke River.

And then the sun rose higher and the air warmed, the sky turned from shell-pink to pale blue, and the mist dissipated and dissolved away as quickly as it had arisen, leaving the surface of the water golden in the sun.

Feeling extremely satisfied with my new home and life in general, I was just turning away from the railing to head back home when movement caught my eye. I turned back in time to see a bright yellow kayak slip out from under the bridge and glide silently along the river. A woman sat in it, wearing an orange life vest, her dark hair pulled into a curly mass on the top of her head. That hair clued me in, though I couldn't see her face, and I recognized Jeri, the woman with the pulla. But she wasn't buzzing with energy this morning. In fact, she made such an impression of stillness, gliding on the surface of the river, that I felt my breathing slow in response. Effortlessly, she dipped the oar once, gently, in the golden water, and then she was gone around the river bend into the sunrise.

I gave myself a break from house renovations that day and decided to pay a little attention to the front yard. Any potential clients in a small town might drive past my place to get an impression of my work, and I wanted my home to present a shiny face. It was a simple yard, just a patch of lawn, a cement bench, and one bed of shrubs and perennials, but the bushes needed a spring trim and grass was coming up through the cracks in the driveway. The air was deliciously fresh, and there was a wonderful breeze blowing the trees across the street, making them sound like a rushing river.

I was on my knees, digging at a particularly stubborn thistle, when a car slowed and stopped in front of the house. I looked up to see Ian's Honda. He rolled down the passenger-side window and called to me, and I stood and walked over, pulling off my gardening gloves.

"Hi there," he said cheerfully. "Any news on your truck?"

"Not yet." I was hoping that was because the garage was overly busy and not because it meant there was a complex and expensive problem with the truck. "Hey, I took your advice and walked to the river this morning to watch the sunrise."

"And?"

"And it was the most beautiful thing I've ever seen."

He grinned. "I thought you'd like that."

"I certainly understand how the town got its name, now. Thank you for telling me about it, or I might have slept in the rest of my life and never known about it."

"My pleasure."

I expected him to wave and continue on his way, but instead he cut the engine and climbed out. Coming around to my side of the car, he leaned against it and pushed his hands into his pockets. I found myself briefly wondering how it would be to have a job where you could wear light-colored slacks and a pale blue shirt and have them still in a pristine state at the end of the day. I pushed my hair back with a dirty hand and tried not to compare his cool, clean look with my own disheveled and shot-at-the-knees state. I couldn't remember the last time I had dressed up for anything.

"Great weather for gardening," he said.

"Yeah. Not too hot today." There wasn't much else to say. If a feature of small-town life was chatting about the weather with the locals at every meeting, I'd have to practice.

"Oh," I said, remembering. "When I was watching the mist, there was a woman kayaking on the river. I think her name is Jeri. I met her once."

"Oh, yeah, Jeri's out on the river most mornings. You'll likely see her around town, too. She regularly pops up in unexpected places—mowing other people's lawns, waxing the bowling alley floors, dogsledding up and down Main Street."

"Dogsledding! Really?"

"She's quite harmless, really. Just a bit . . . Well, she's our local . . ."

"Eccentric?" I asked.

"Writer. She writes novels, but reluctantly. I don't think it's writer's block, exactly. She just does everything she can to avoid actually sitting down and writing."

I laughed, thinking of how adeptly I had avoided returning to work for the past weeks. "She sounds like my kind of person. Anyway, it got me thinking, and I wondered if there's a place to rent a kayak around here. I'm thinking I might like to try it. It looked . . . peaceful."

He chuckled and nodded. "There's an outfitter in town, just past the post office. They rent everything you need, and when you've paddled as far as you want to, you phone them and they come pick you up at the other end and haul you back. You should try it. It's fun."

"I will, thanks."

I expected him to get back in his car then, chit-chat expended, but instead he folded his arms and said, "You know, I like kayaking myself. I could go with you sometime, if you want."

"Oh?" I was a bit startled. Did he mean it as a *date*?

"You know, since it's your first time, it might be good to have someone along in case of trouble."

"Ah." Maybe not really a date, then. Just neighborly concern.

"Want to?"

"Um . . ." I felt the heat rising in my cheeks and silently chided myself for my brilliant conversational skills. I straightened and managed to nod. "Sure, sounds fun."

"How about Saturday?"

"This Saturday?"

He laughed. "Chickening out already?"

"Of course not. No. Um. Sure, that would work for me. Thanks. What time?"

"The earlier the better, before the sun gets too hot. You don't have any shade out on the water. You're so fair, you'll want to wear sunscreen—the light reflecting off the river can burn you."

"Got it. How about eight o'clock? If the rental place is open that early, that is."

"It is. I'll come pick you up," he offered.

"Okay, sounds like a plan."

"Can I get your phone number in case anything comes up?"

"Oh, sure." He handed me his cell phone and I entered my name and number, then handed it back to him.

"Thanks. Well, I'd better let you get back to your work. Enjoy your day." He turned to go and paused, looking at me over the car roof. "I'm glad I bumped into you again," he said.

"Me too."

He gave a brief nod goodbye and got back in his car. I stood for a moment, bemused, listening to the fading sound of his motor and gazing unseeingly at the park across the street. And then blinked. Trees.

I straightened. He'd said he owned a lot of trees. I thought of the giant willow beside the beautiful house. Could it be . . .? I didn't stop to think about it. I dropped my gardening gloves to the grass and jogged across the street. Climbing over the fence, I set out once again on the animal track through the forest. I made faster progress this time, knowing where I was going. Over the stream, along the path, through clouds of gnats and pools of shadow, to the edge of the thicket. I was just in time to see the garage door of the big stone house sliding closed behind the white Honda.

Who would have guessed it? Ian, in his humble Honda . . . he was the king of the castle. Owner of the park. Lord of the trees. Good grief.

Chapter Seven

My walk back to my house was slow this time, thoughtful. I was no longer worried about being eaten alive for trespassing on the grounds. His own arborist, indeed. Probably his own maid and cook and groundskeeper, too. I knew for a fact that biology teachers didn't make that kind of a salary. Perhaps he had inherited money? Won the lottery? I thought about Eamonn, proud of his little hardware store, seemingly not living high on the hog. And I wondered how all these pieces fit together.

When the garage called late that afternoon, I dug my trusty bicycle out of the garage—I hadn't ridden since I'd left Toronto—and went back to pick up the truck. I didn't want to call Ian for a ride. I told myself his wealth didn't matter, didn't change anything. But it did. I could have called him when I'd believed he was just a high school teacher living in a subdivision. But I couldn't call the King of the Castle for a ride. I paid the bill almost without seeing it (only registering with distracted relief that my credit card wasn't rejected), threw my bike in the back of the truck, and headed home.

When I walked into the kitchen and tossed my keys on the counter, I caught a faint whiff of something floral and paused, trying to identify it. Maybe the previous owner had left an air freshener somewhere because I kept getting these occasional whiffs of flowers, but I hadn't been able to find one anywhere in the house. I didn't mind the scent at all; it was fresh and comfortable and reminded me of childhood summer holidays and playing in the park. But I wished I could figure out where it was coming from. And what crazy kind of freshener lasted for years anyway?

Shrugging, I pushed the puzzle from my mind and made myself a cheese sandwich for supper. And then, feeling guilty for not cooking for myself better, I cut up an apple to go with it. Anything more than that felt too onerous. It was funny how I could find the energy to rip out countertops and flooring, but the idea of boiling pasta sounded like too much to manage. This past year or so had taken too much out of me, I knew, and I could either fight against it until I dropped from exhaustion, or I could give in to the need to be kind to myself.

At least for today, I would follow the latter. I needed a little restoration myself, I knew, as much as the house did. No one else was going to do it for me. I would have to do it for myself.

So I watched a movie on TV, stretched uncomfortably on the floor with a pillow since I didn't have a sofa, and ate microwave popcorn from the bag. (Mom never used to let us eat it. She called it "death in a bag.") But the movie's plot didn't interest me and I couldn't remember the title by the time it ended. The evening stretched empty ahead of me, and I've never been the type to sit in front of a TV for long. Sitting still was dangerous, because when my body stopped moving, my brain got active. I decided to tackle my mouse problem, which sounded manageable and not too demanding.

I am generally kindhearted when it comes to any kind of animal, but the mice had clearly had free run of the house for a long time, and the situation had grown intolerable. For the sake of my health, I needed to take drastic measures. I debated between various forms of murder and decided on warfarin, which came in cheesy-looking yellow squares, like fudge gone bad. I left one in each closet and then took a few down to the basement to place in strategic locations around the shelving.

While I was down there, I figured I might as well clear out the large cans of food left on the shelves. I pulled one down and squinted at it in the light of the single bare bulb overhead. Powdered milk, with an expiry date stamped on it nine years in the future. The paper label included the words "Prepared for the Bishop's Storehouse" and "Not for resale." I looked over the rest of the cans and found they all had the same type of label with the odd wording—oatmeal, macaroni, sugar, dehydrated onions, red winter wheat, and more powdered milk.

Maybe the person who'd lived here before me had been one of those preppers, putting food away for the zombie apocalypse. I considered throwing it all out, but the cans seemed in good condition, if dusty, and all of the expiry dates were well into the future. If it was edible, it would be a shame to waste it, and if it stretched my grocery budget a little, all the better. I replaced the can on the shelf and went to find a cloth to wipe them down.

There it was again, I mused. My fairy godmother, providing groceries just when my credit card couldn't take any more.

Friday after school, Finn showed up at the door with a plastic basket of strawberries clutched between his pink-stained hands.

"These are for you." He shoved them at me and went straight to the fridge for his pop. "You're getting low," he told me, waving the can.

"Yes. I'll get more on the weekend," I said. "Thanks for the berries. Where did you get them?"

"Picked them," he said proudly, dropping onto a kitchen chair. As if there were any doubt about the stains on his fingers. I decided it would be better not to inquire too closely. If I found out they were stolen, I'd have to refuse them, and I didn't want to watch the joy die from his face.

"Thank you. I'll have them with yogurt for breakfast tomorrow."

"What's all this stuff?" He jerked his chin toward the pile on the floor.

"I'm refinishing cupboards today. Want to help?"

He considered a moment, then agreed. So I draped one of my canvas aprons over his clothes (slightly worse for wear than his usual look, probably from hunting for strawberries) and showed him how to rub the paint remover onto the wood. I did the next step myself, scraping the old paint off and wiping the wood down.

Finn thought this was the best fun ever. I had to admit he carried it out efficiently, without spilling or dropping things or wiping mess all over himself. His hands grew steadily browner, but all in all he did a fine job for a ten-year-old.

"You're good with your hands," I told him. "Maybe someday you'll be a furniture maker or a carpenter."

"Nah, I'm going to be an archaeologist."

"Oh! Well, that's very good too," I said. "That will take a lot of schooling."

"Yeah. I'm going to have a hat like Indiana Jones, too."

"I see." So that was it. He'd been watching too many movies. "You know, archaeology isn't all just adventures and discovering treasure and such."

"I know. It's about patience, too. My dad told me. You know they dig things up with tiny toothbrushes?"

We discussed methodology and digs and research for a while, which led to Egypt and Mesopotamia, which led to geography in general.

Finn sat back on his heels and set his stained rag on the drop cloth I had spread under us. "They taught us a song in school last year," he announced. "We learned all fifty of the United States. I still remember it. Wanna hear it?" Without waiting for my answer, he launched into a loud tune. "Alabama! Alaska! Arizona! Arkansas! California! Colorado! Connecticu-u-t!"

The kitchen rang with his exuberance. I stood and went to my toolbox to find my screwdriver and the hinges I had removed from the cupboard doors. Finn didn't seem to notice I was gone but belted out the names with more gusto than tone.

"Delaware! Florida! Georgia! Hawaii! Idaho! Illinois! Indiana!"

My cell phone rang and I had to cover one ear with my hand in order to hear.

"Kerris? It's Miriam."

I brightened. "Hey, good to hear from you! What's up?" I had just spoken to Miriam Gold a couple of weeks earlier, when I'd called to give her my new phone number, but it was nice to hear the familiar voice of a friend.

". . . Maine, Maryland, Massachusetts, Michigan!" Finn emphasized the last syllable, and Miriam's voice ratcheted up an octave.

"Gun? What on earth? Has someone had an accident?"

"No, it's just a neighbor kid singing."

"Kid? Oh. Well, I'll make this quick, then. It sounds like you're busy, and this is long distance, anyway," Miriam said briskly. "I thought you'd want to know Maddie's had her baby. I wanted you to hear it from a friend."

I couldn't help sucking in a gulp of air, as if she'd kicked me in the chest. Then I forced myself to let the air out deliberately and say in an even tone, "I thought she wasn't due yet."

"She wasn't. But it came early. It's—*she's*—at Sick Kids Hospital. There are some complications, but I hear she's holding her own. She'll be there a while, though. Only four pounds."

"New Mexico!" Finn was happily belting onward, and I plugged my free ear with a finger.

"I—I hope she's okay," I heard myself mumble. After all, I had no ill will toward the infant. It wasn't its fault my marriage had fallen apart.

"Ohiiiiii-o!"

"Everything going okay, Kerris? It sounds crazy there. Do you need a girls' day out on the town or anything?"

I smiled at this. My idea of entertainment and relaxation was very different from my friend's. A day shopping in Toronto sounded nightmarish to me, and she would have been appalled if I'd suggested a leisurely hike along the Bruce Trail. The only thing we really had in common was the war years of high school, but somehow that had been enough to cement our friendship over the intervening years.

"No. Fine. I'm fine."

"I'm not convinced. You call me if you need anything at all, okay?"

"I will. Thank you for letting me know about . . . Well, keep me posted." I really didn't want her to. I wanted to be able to forget Marcus and his new wife and his premature baby completely, but I knew it wouldn't happen.

"I will."

Finn had plowed ahead and was winding up to his grand finale. He had jumped to his feet, arms thrown out wide and head back to address the ceiling.

"Utah! Vermont! Virginia! Washington! West Virginia! Wisconsin! Wyoooooming!" Finn fell mercifully silent at last and beamed at me.

I said my goodbyes into the phone, but Miriam had hung up already. I returned the phone to my pocket and smiled at Finn.

"Not bad for a Canadian fifth grader," I acknowledged. My ears were ringing.

"I can do all sixty-six books of the Bible, too," he offered. "Genesis, Exodus, Leviticus and Numbers—"

"That's all right," I said hastily. "Let's start staining these doors."

Later that night, my phone rang again. I was curled in the armchair, rewarding myself for a day's hard labor with a book and a bowl of chips and salsa. It was Ian. I recognized his mellow baritone right away.

"Hi! Listen, I wanted to touch base about kayaking tomorrow."

"Okay." Part of me toyed with the idea of backing out altogether, but I forced myself not to. Why did it matter so much if he was rich as a king? It wasn't as if I were a pauper or something. At least, not on global standards. I had a roof over my head and the ability to put food on my table (even if scrounged from someone else's basement). That was more than a lot of people had.

"I called to reserve the kayaks," Ian went on, "and they mentioned there's a big group of other people going out at eight. So I wondered if you wanted to go at seven-thirty instead, to beat the rush. If it's all the same to you, I'd rather have the river to ourselves."

Something warm in his tone made a little shiver run up my spine. Maybe this *was* a date. I swallowed. "Certainly! Fewer people to see me make a fool of myself," I said.

His chuckle was soft in my ear. "You'll be fine. It's a really easy river to kayak. So I'll pick you up just before seven-thirty, then."

"That will be great," I told him. Then I tried, "I'm looking forward to it," and found it was true.

"Did you hear back about your truck? Do you need a lift in to pick it up?"

"No, thanks. I mean, I already picked it up. It was the fuel injector, like you thought. They were able to unclog it—no new parts required. Thanks again for your help."

"Any time." There was a pause as we both searched for something else to say and found nothing. "Well, have a good night, then," he finally said.

"You too."

I hung up and sat looking at the phone. If only it could just be the Ian the Biology Teacher I was going kayaking with, and not the Owner of a Great Many Trees.

Since Marcus had torn apart our lives, I'd had frequent bouts of insomnia, but on the nights I could sleep, I didn't usually dream. Or if I did, I didn't remember my dreams when I awoke. I was out too deep, exhausted both physically and emotionally. But Saturday morning I awoke with the vague shreds of a dream still floating just at my fingertips, the faint memory of flowers, the smell of cocoa, a gentle hand caressing my cheek. Even as I came fully awake and sat up, the remnants faded and were gone. I was left with a calm, peaceful feeling that soothed my soul more than I'd felt in many weeks. I dressed and went down the wooden staircase (newly refinished) to the kitchen (still counter-less) and made a cup of mint tea. I carried it out to the back steps to sit and watch the rising sun turn the long grass emerald. The morning air carried the foretaste of a hot day, and I could hear someone's lawnmower already growling further down the street, putting those of us who weren't at work yet to shame. But I ignored the tug to be up and doing and just sat, enjoying the sun. There was no hurry, it was only seven. I had bags of time left. I felt as if a bubble were enclosing my little space, protecting me. *Hugging me.*

I was surprised as the words came to my mind. But the more I thought about them, the more appropriate they seemed. That's what had happened, my house had awakened me with a hug. Warm contentment spread over me, and the feeling lasted all morning.

At least, until seven-thirty. When Ian's car pulled up and I realized I really was going to go down a big river in a kayak.

Ian wore knee-length khaki cargo shorts and a green t-shirt that made his eyes look aqua-marine. He didn't look the least bit nervous. I figured kayaking was old hat to him. But I felt a little bit sick as we pulled up in front of the outfitters and went inside.

The elderly woman at the desk soon put my jitters at ease.

"It's a very slow and shallow river," she said, briskly cinching me into my life jacket like she was saddling up a horse. "Don't worry—we haven't lost a person yet."

"Is it that obvious I'm nervous?" I asked.

"Your grip on that paddle gave you away," she laughed. "First time?"

"Yes."

"Relax. Here, hold it like this." She demonstrated the grip and paddling motions for me. "And it helps if you remember to lean forward a bit, not backward. Kayaks are very stable, you'll find. Worst case scenario, you tip over."

"Exactly," I said. "That's what I'm worried about, dangling upside down and drowning if I can't right myself."

"Oh, the river's only two feet deep in most places, dear," the woman assured me. "If you can't right yourself just pushing against the bottom with your paddle, you can always just stand up and wade out. Just remember to bring the kayak with you."

I felt extremely foolish, then, for being worried at all. "I hadn't realized it was that shallow."

"Besides," the woman said, leaning in confidentially and looking over her shoulder at Ian, who was watching in amusement. She purposely whispered loud enough for him to hear. "If you fall in, you're with a very able-bodied, handsome man who can fish you out."

To my credit, I didn't blush or burst out laughing. I nodded solemnly at her. "Yes, I am."

It was Ian who blushed instead.

In the end, we spent a wonderful morning gliding along the friendly river in two yellow crafts the shape of giant bananas. It was an entirely different experience being down on the water as opposed to looking down on it from the bridge. The river was so broad and smooth that I hardly needed my paddle. The occasional ripple indicated boulders just below the surface here and there, but they were easily avoided with the lightest touch of paddle to water. In most places I could just drift along with my paddle lying across the kayak, watching black cormorants and great blue herons rise, annoyed at my passing. There were no others out on the river this early, and I was glad Ian had thought to start us ahead of the bigger group. The water made chuckling noises in the shallower spots but was completely silent where it ran deeper, and there was a delicious taste of damp earth and stone hovering in the air. It was peaceful. Glorious.

Now and then our kayaks drifted close enough together to talk, but for the most part Ian stayed out in front, to show me the best way through the boulders and lead me into the smoothest water.

"Having fun?" he asked once when we paused in a little inlet under some willow trees.

"Why have I wasted the past thirty years not doing this?" I replied, grinning.

"The first access point is about ten minutes ahead. Do you want to stop there or keep going?"

"Keep going," I said promptly.

Another half an hour, though, and my muscles began to protest at the unfamiliar exercise. Reluctantly I called to Ian that it was probably time to stop. Our cell phones were stored in a waterproof bag the size of a pillowcase so we could call the outfitters to come pick us up at the next access point.

While we waited for their truck to come get us, Ian turned the kayaks over to let out any water, but I walked along the bank of the river, reluctant to leave it. I was filled with a funny sort of glee, in love with the river like a teenager finally discovering the perfect, dreamy guy who had sat undiscovered in her math class all winter. The river was there any time I wanted to return to it, I reminded myself. I'd made a new friend, one that suited me perfectly.

And Ian was pretty great, too.

After the lazy adventure of the morning, I made myself get to work when Ian dropped me off at home. There was so much left to do on the house, but I changed into my jeans and went at it cheerfully, filled with energy from the morning's adventure.

Of course I ran out of drywall compound within the hour and had to go into town. I entered Eamonn's store half-hoping it would be the teenager with the eyebrow ring at the counter. But Eamonn stood there, and, when he saw me, his smile broadened in delight as if I were an old friend.

"Hey there! Truck okay?" he called out. There were several other customers in the store, and I felt all heads turn to fix their eyes on me. Life in a small town.

"Yes, thanks. Fuel injector," I said automatically. I turned to scan the shelves intently, as if I were looking for hidden treasure instead of spackle.

"Hear you and Ian went kayaking this morning," Eamonn added, and I saw the speculative eyes all turn on me again. I snatched up the yellow plastic tub of compound and practically jogged over to the counter.

"Yes. It was fun," I said, plunking down my purchase and fishing for my wallet. "He told you about it?"

"It was all he talked about the last two days, he was that looking forward to it," Eamonn said.

"Ah. Yes, well, it was great." I waved my credit card at him. He blissfully ignored it.

"Mind you, he hasn't dated much since Julia died, but I did think he was more keyed up about going than the occasion warranted."

I stared at him. Julia?

"Then he said it was you who was going with him, and I understood completely." He winked at me and finally took my credit card.

I licked my lips. "Oh." I wasn't sure how to respond to that.

"My Shelley was that pleased to hear about it. Thinks he's been alone too long."

"Shelley?"

"My wife. She approved of him asking you."

"She doesn't even know me."

"No need. Has a second sense about stuff like that, Shelley does. Did the same to me, you know. I was at a friend's wedding in Ottawa and up walks this red-haired girl, bold as you please, and says, 'You don't know me, but my name is Shelley Anderson, and I have the feeling you and I are meant to be together.' Just like that."

I stared at him. "Are you kidding?"

"Nope. Of course, after an introduction like that, I had to ask her out. Married two months later. Swept me off my feet, she did."

I didn't know what to reply to that. I swallowed and took my card as he handed it back to me. Eamonn leaned conspiratorially over the counter and chuckled. "A forceful personality, that's what she has. My advice to you is, put up a struggle. Don't let her push you into anything. Hold the wedding off for, oh, three months at least."

"Eamonn! Shut your yap!"

We both jerked around. Ian stood in the doorway, a ferocious scowl on his face. If he hadn't been holding a large cardboard box, he probably would have had his fists out in a pugilistic stance. Eamonn threw both hands up in surrender.

"We were only talking, Ian. Sure, just a bit of fun."

Someone in another aisle began to titter. I felt the corners of my own mouth begin to curl upward. Ian turned his scowl on me.

"Don't you encourage him. He's pure evil. And that Irish accent is fake. He's never been out of Ontario."

I couldn't help it. I burst out laughing. Behind me, Eamonn began to join in, then, seeing his brother's expression, quickly turned it to a cough. Ian strode forward, set the box on the counter, and jerked his chin toward the bag containing my spackle.

"Is that yours?"

Helpless, I could only nod.

Ian swept it up with one hand, grasped my elbow with the other, and towed me out of the store. Behind us, as the door closed, I heard the other customers erupt into laughter.

Chapter Eight

We strode down the street a ways. I didn't know where we were going, but I went along anyway, and after a while his grip began to relax, and his stride began to slow to a regular walk. I waited and finally heard what I was listening for. A sigh.

"Sorry about that," he said, letting go of my elbow and instead looping my hand through the crook of his arm. He'd changed into slacks and a blue long-sleeved t-shirt, and the fabric was soft under my fingers. "He'd be disappointed if I didn't get riled. Teasing me is his chief pleasure in life."

"So all that was just theatrics?"

"Well, not entirely," Ian admitted. "He's incorrigible. He made my childhood a nightmare. He starts having a go at me and instantly I'm eight years old again. Old patterns are hard to break." He looked down at me, and I could see the laughter hiding in his sea-colored eyes. "Don't you find the same thing with your siblings?"

"I only have one younger sister. I think usually it was me making her miserable, not the other way around."

Ian continued to walk down the sidewalk, swinging my bag of spackle at his side. I had to stretch to keep up with him. I wanted to ask about Julia but felt a sudden attack of shyness. It seemed too intrusive. Much as I liked him, I really hadn't known him long. Instead, I asked, "Is Eamonn older or younger than you?"

"Older. There are four of us—Eamonn, myself, Margaret, and Jenny."

"Where are we going?"

He paused mid-stride and looked around, a surprised look on his face.

"I don't know. I'm just walking."

"Well, my truck is parked back at the store."

He arched an eyebrow at me. "Are you in a hurry?"

"Not particularly."

He shifted the bag, turned, and gripped my hand in his. "This way. There's an ice cream shop through the park."

"I haven't had lunch yet."

"We'll do that later. First, ice cream."

This seemed perfectly sensible to me. We went down a side street, turned to the right, and cut across a playground. This early in the morning, there were only a few mothers and babysitters standing guard over a handful of toddlers as they dug in the sandbox or drifted in the safety swings. Further down the path, several older children were climbing monkey bars shaped in a geodesic dome. As we passed, Ian nodded in recognition at a young girl who hung from a bar by her knees. Her long blonde hair hung like ropes of taffy to the ground. She waved and gave an upside-down smile.

"Hi, Ian!"

"Good afternoon, Anne-Marie. Is Kat around?" Ian glanced around the park.

"She's at Peter's ball game, but Jana's watching me." She pointed to a girl in a pink blouse and white jeans, sitting on a nearby bench and reading. If she was watching the little girl, I couldn't tell.

"Good girl," Ian replied, and kept walking.

At the Baskin Robbins, I chose my favorite, Gold Medal Ribbon, though to me it seemed a rather decadent thing to be doing. Ian took his time choosing, considering every option and finally placing his order.

"One mint chocolate chip cone, please, and two butterscotch ripples." He paid before I could reach for my wallet and glanced down at me. "You'll have to help me carry them."

I took one of the cones, and he took his other two, my bag looped over his wrist. We left the shop and headed back toward the playground. I was curious, but I didn't ask any questions, figuring all would eventually become clear. When we reached the park, Ian handed one of the butterscotch cones to the girl reading on the bench. She looked up in surprise, and then her round face broke into a smile.

"Thanks, Ian!"

The girl on the monkey bars caught whiff of the handouts, swung to the ground, and ran over to us. Ian handed her the other butterscotch cone.

"You're the best," she cheered, attacking the ice cream with no qualms at all about the earliness of the hour.

I expected Ian to eat the mint chocolate chip cone, but to my surprise, he turned and handed it to a sandy-haired boy who had come up behind us. He looked about Finn's age and his t-shirt was grubby, though his hands looked clean.

"Your favorite," Ian said with a smile as the boy thanked him.

We walked on, leaving three happy children busily eating ice cream. As we turned out of the park into the street, I looked up at Ian.

"That was kind of you. But what about your cone?"

He gave a lopsided grin and shrugged. "I hadn't noticed Seth was there before. I couldn't very well treat his sisters and not him."

I could have pointed out that he hadn't treated all the other children on the playground either. I could have suggested we go back for another cone for him. Instead, I simply held out my ice cream.

Ian glanced at it, then at me, eyebrows raised. For a moment we looked at each other. I wasn't sure what he saw in my face, but after a moment he nodded in thanks and took my cone. He carefully licked one side of it a couple of times and then handed it back to me. We continued down the street, sharing the cone back and forth until we reached my truck, parked in front of Eamonn's store.

We'd nearly finished the cone by that time. Ian looked a question at me, and when I nodded, he popped the rest of the sweet into his mouth. I took my bag containing the spackle and tossed it through the open window into the cab of the truck. I was learning not to lock up in Smoke River.

"Now lunch?" I asked. "My treat?" I knew he probably had enough money to buy the diner, if he was living in that mansion across the street, but I still wanted to pay, since he'd paid for the ice cream. It was important to me that he picked up on the fact, however subtly, that I wasn't after his money.

He laughed but agreed, and we went across the street to the little diner. It was snug and filled with vinyl seating and peeling Formica tables, but the fish and chips were fantastic, and the mushy marrowfat peas cooked just right. I finished the fattening goodness and reached for a paper napkin, thinking I wouldn't need to eat again for a week.

"This has been an unexpected pleasure," Ian said, polishing off his plate with satisfaction. "If perhaps a bit backwards, having dessert first."

"Well, yes. But it was pretty amazing, wasn't it?"

"Delicious. I was sorry to end our kayaking morning together, and it was a nice surprise to continue it after all. Let's do it again sometime. In the correct order, this time."

I looked at him sitting across from me, his easy smile, the glitter in his eyes, and found myself nodding vigorously.

"Yes, please," I said.

I paid the bill, and we left the diner and walked across the street to my truck again. I fished out my keys and turned back to Ian to say goodbye. He had moved forward to stand close, looking down at me with a gentle expression on his lean face.

"Have a good rest of the day," he said.

"You, too."

"I will. Though after such a great morning, I think the afternoon won't be able to compare."

He surprised me by leaning down and giving me a quick, soft kiss on the cheek. He smelled of vinegar and salt, with an undercurrent of chocolate. I was acutely aware of Eamonn staring at us through the shop window. Ian straightened, glanced at Eamonn, and then wiggled his eyebrows at me.

"That should keep Shelley happy." He grinned and went into the store.

I drove home in something of a daze. The sweet spring morning, the confident hum of the truck engine, the taste of Gold Medal Ribbon and battered fish, the adoring look on those children's faces . . . all combined to make me feel a warm contentment. A little bubble of something was rising in my chest, and I found myself humming as I pulled into my driveway. It had been a long time since I'd felt this way, not since the divorce, not since Mom's death, not since long before that. It had been so long that I'd almost forgotten the name of it, but now I remembered. It was happiness.

When I walked into the kitchen, Finn was sitting at my table eating a sandwich.

"Well, hello," I greeted him, not a bit fazed to find him there.

He gave me a half-guilty grimace. "You left your door unlocked. I got hungry waiting for you."

I was surprised I hadn't locked up. My truck was one thing, but my house full of power tools was another. Maybe small-town life was rubbing off on me *too* much.

"I haven't had a chance to go shopping for root beer yet," I told him. "I'll go later today."

"That's okay. I just had some milk instead." He downed the rest of the sandwich and brushed his hands tidily on his jeans. "What are we doing today?"

I shook my head. "I'm surprised you want to hang out with me all the time. Wouldn't you rather play with your friends? It's a beautiful day out there, and I'm going to be stuck inside drywalling the downstairs bathroom."

"I can help you. I'm learning all kinds of skills," he replied. "Maybe I'll be a builder someday."

"I thought you were going to be an archaeologist and have an Indiana Jones hat," I said.

"I'll do that too. You can do more than one thing for a living, you know."

So we drywalled together. The space was too small for us both to fit, but he proved himself useful handing me screws and tape and scrapers through the door. After the sheetrock was up, I showed him how to tape and mud the seams and holes. He especially liked this last part, ending up with more spackle on his face and arms than on the wall. When we were done, I hauled him into the kitchen to wash him off at the sink.

"Once that's dry, we can sand it, and then we just have to prime it and give it a couple of coats of paint," I said. "But I won't get to that for a few days."

"What color are you painting it?"

I dug through the binder I kept and found the paint chip. I'd guiltily driven to Port Daley for the paint, since Eamonn's selection was so limited. "This. It's called Sea Foam."

"It looks like mint."

I found myself thinking of ice cream. "What if I use dark brown towels in that bathroom?" I suggested. "It would be like being in a bowl of mint chocolate chip ice cream."

He laughed, finding this funny. I put away the binder and began hunting through the fridge for my own lunch. As I set out more sandwich makings, I asked him over my shoulder, "Do you know a kid about your age named Seth?"

He had been drumming his heels on the chair rung, but at my question, Finn grew still.

"Seth who?" he asked carefully.

"I don't know his last name. But he has two sisters. I met them at the playground this morning."

"Why were you at the playground?"

"I was just cutting through it to get to the Baskin Robbins."

"Ah. That's why you're thinking of ice cream," he observed. "You know, if you put a bright red toaster on your counter, this kitchen could look like a banana split with a cherry on top." He nodded at my yellow walls.

We amused ourselves through Finn's second sandwich imagining the other rooms in the house and what kinds of ice cream they would be according to their colors. My tan, white, and pink bedroom was Neapolitan. The upstairs bathroom with its white and gold theme was pralines 'n cream. His brown fort was chocolate fudge. The unfinished pale living room stumped us until Finn suggested dishwater-flavored ice cream. He suggested the gray cement walls of the garage were actually lint flavored. That led to a bunch more nonsense. It wasn't until he left an hour later that I realized he hadn't answered my question about knowing Seth.

Sunday was spent in blissful quiet. I took the day off from renovations and Finn never appeared. I spent the morning reading and the afternoon baking and just gave myself a rest. It had been a pretty frantic few weeks, moving into the house, planning the renovations, and carrying out the restoration I'd done so far. Before all that had been the weeks of inevitable paperwork associated with the uncontested, expedited divorce, the tense conversations with lawyers, and the wrapping up of my Toronto-based business. And the sympathetic friends to contend with. I think that was almost as difficult as letting go of my marriage—having to explain to distraught friends and keep up a strong front and assure everyone I was fine, while inside, my heart was breaking. Miriam and others had tried to involve me in social events and whip up a celebratory feeling, but I only wanted solitude. Instead, I got phone calls from people who were more wrapped up in trying to figure out how they now fit in my reordered life (or Marcus's—or both?) than in trying to comfort me.

So it was nice to have a peaceful day to myself, to still that howling that always seemed to be in the background of my mind and let everything—all the turmoil—just rest. The house, despite its blemishes and half-finished state, seemed to settle down around me like a warm blanket, and I dozed contentedly over my book and let the house's kindness sink deep into my bones.

Chapter Nine

It didn't last long.

Monday morning I awoke to the sound of rain and remembered I hadn't covered the pile of leftover pink insulation at the side of the driveway. While I was contending with the soggy disintegrating mass, the electrician arrived to upgrade the wiring in the living room to accommodate my table saw. He examined the outlets, looked at the electrical panel, made some doubtful noises, and announced that my aluminum wiring wasn't up to code and it would all have to be switched out.

"What has to be switched out?" I asked, not wanting to hear the answer. Rainwater was running from my hair down the back of my neck and soaking my shirt.

"All of it. Every outlet. Every receptacle."

"In the whole room?"

"In the whole house," he corrected me. "I'm surprised your insurance company will even cover this house."

I shied away from the thought of a fight with the insurance company. "What's that going to cost me?"

He paced through the house, jotting notes in a notebook and shaking his head. I left him to it and went back out to deal with the insulation. Finally, he emerged from the house and stalked toward me, screwing up his face against the rain as if it were acid instead of water.

"Five thousand," he said firmly. "And I'm giving you a deal."

It took me a second to catch my breath. "I think I'll get a second opinion," I finally managed.

"Suit yourself. But I'd hurry if I were you. If it isn't upgraded soon, I'll have to make a report."

"Who to? The electrical board?"

"The fire department."

He climbed back into his truck and drove away. I stood in the streaming rain and fumed for a while. Then I finished covering the insulation with tarps and sloshed back inside. Fine, I thought peevishly. If worse came to worst, I'd move into Finn's fort.

The rain continued all day and that night. On Tuesday morning I woke up to a flashing alarm clock and knew the power must have flickered during the night. Drat. The aluminum wiring must have heard the electrician and now it was freaking out. I walked through the house, soothing it in gentle tones, knowing I was foolish but not knowing what else to do. I got some breakfast, brushed my teeth, went into the living room, and turned on the light. A roll of thunder burst overhead. There was a popping sound, and the house went dark.

It was also silent. I couldn't hear the fridge humming or the air conditioner whirring. Feeling resentful toward the electrician—though of course it wasn't his fault, it was the storm's, but I couldn't help thinking he had *jinxed* it—I went into the kitchen where the most natural light was and hunted for a flashlight. Well, so I couldn't work today. Fine. A good excuse to spend the day reading and eating potato chips. (There was some advantage to not being accountable to anyone.) When no flashlight presented itself, I threw a sweater over my head and dashed out to Finn's fort for the lantern.

I was well into my novel that afternoon when there was a knock at the door. I took my lantern with me to answer it—the entry had no windows. Ian stood on the step with rain dripping off his big-brimmed hat.

"Hi!" He sounded repulsively cheerful for someone standing in a downpour. "I came to make sure you were all right, with the power off and all."

"How did you know my power was off?" I was so surprised for a minute that I left him standing there.

"The whole neighborhood is out," he said.

"Oh, it's not just my house?" That was a relief. Maybe my wiring wasn't sulking after all. I remembered my manners. "Come in, come in! You're sopping wet."

He took off his hat and slicker and I hung them in the shower to drip dry. When I came out again, he had placed his rubber boots on the mat and was in my kitchen, looking out the windows at the water washing away the view. It felt odd, somehow, to have him there in my kitchen in his stocking feet. Odd, but comforting.

"I was starting to get cabin fever," I told him. "I'm used to being active. Do you want something to drink?"

"I'm fine, thanks."

I told him about the electrician's pronouncement and why I had thought it was just my house that was affected. "Back in Toronto, I could look out the window at the neighbors and see if their power was out too. But here I can't see any neighbors."

"Not used to being so isolated?"

"Not really." Ordinarily I would have added that I liked isolation, but today I was happy to have the company. Particularly *his* company.

"Once you settle in and get to know some more people, you won't feel so alone."

Alone. He had no idea how alone I felt. Then I remembered Julia and realized maybe he did. Whoever she had been, whether a wife or a girlfriend, he had still known loss.

"So are you playing hooky again?" I asked lightly.

"They cancelled school and sent us all home." Ian looked as happy as first grader at the unexpected reprieve. "They're saying it might be a few hours before the power is on again. A tree fell and took out a couple of power poles."

"I hope it's not much longer than that. Everything in my freezer will thaw."

"Keep the door closed. It should be okay."

"I will. So how shall we spend the day, then?" I asked.

A shadow crossed his face and he looked at me uncertainly. "Actually, I can't stay long. I have other rounds to make. I just wanted to see if you were set for candles and batteries and that kind of thing."

"Oh. Okay." I felt a warmth crawl into my cheeks.

"I'm sorry."

"No, no, I just assumed . . . It's fine." I was feeling more stupid by the minute. "Do you have a roster of people you're supposed to check on then, in emergencies?" Maybe this was a small-town tradition I didn't know about. Like the buddy system.

"No, just a couple of families I . . . keep an eye on. The Postlethwaites—they're an elderly couple on their own—and the Jamesons. They live nearby."

I went to the sink to fill the kettle for the sake of something to do. Then remembered the power was out and I couldn't heat it up. I set it on the stove anyway. "Well, that's nice of you. Sure you don't have time to have something before you go? I have juice in the fridge that I should use up."

"Well, all right, thank you."

"I guess it's nice being on your roster," I added, my back to him. "It's good to know someone's around if there *is* an emergency."

I took two glasses from the cupboard and turned to place them on the table. Ian was right behind me, and I nearly dropped the glasses. He took them from me but stood looking down at me without moving.

"It's not a roster."

"Well, your list, or whatever it is."

"Kerris, it came out wrong. It's not just about candles and batteries. I mean, knowing you, a little power outage is nothing. You could probably handle a typhoon singlehandedly. I really came because I wanted to see you again."

It was the right thing to say. I smiled up at him.

"Thanks," I said quietly.

"I'm sorry I can't stay longer. Maybe another time."

"Sure. Any time." I thought about going back to my boring book and an idea struck me. "Hey, I could come on your rounds with you and help. Start meeting people, like you said."

I didn't understand the look that crossed his face. He looked startled, even fearful, then annoyed, then reluctant. The emotions flashing across his features so quickly I couldn't be sure I'd seen them.

"I don't think so," he said, a little too quickly. Then he tried to soften it, "I mean, not this time."

"Oh. Okay." I stepped back, a bit surprised, and also a tiny bit hurt.

"I'd better be going," he added, and left the kitchen.

"What about your juice?" I asked. He retrieved his things from the shower, thrust his arms into his slicker, and stamped into his boots at the door.

"I'll take a rain check," he said. As he opened the door, lightening flashed. He looked up at the rain, rolled his eyes at me, and went out.

The power came on two hours later, but my mood had been spoiled. I threw myself into my work, skipped supper, and went to bed early, fiendishly tired.

It wasn't until Wednesday morning that the rain stopped and I was able to leave the house at last. The ground was boggy, but the flowers had enjoyed the drink and were flaming bright purples and pinks on the roadsides. The river was running high and fast, deeper now and not so friendly looking as it had been before. The May air was warming up, making steam rise from the damp road. I went for a brisk walk to clear my head and was in a much better mood as I returned home. I caught sight of Jeri picking up sticks blown down in the park and we waved to each other, too far apart to exchange verbal greetings.

Ten meters from my house, I found a teenage girl stopped at the side of the road, fiddling with her bicycle. Her face was red with frustration and at first she didn't see me coming. When I greeted her, she looked up with wide blue eyes, and I saw that it was the girl from the playground, the one who had been sitting and reading on the bench while her sister played.

"Having trouble?" I asked.

"It's my stupid handlebars. They're loose and keep coming off. I'm late for school."

"I can fix that in a couple of minutes," I told her. "Let me just grab a wrench."

I went into the house, found the tools I needed, and hurried back out. She stood where I had left her, but her expression was relieved now that help had arrived.

"I'm Kerris," I told her as I knelt on the asphalt to bring the handlebars to eye level.

"You're Ian's friend, right? I thought I recognized you from the park."

"What's your name? I've forgotten it."

She hesitated, then apparently decided I must be all right if I was Ian's friend.

"Jana Jameson."

Ah. Jameson. That was the name of one of the families Ian said he kept an eye on. I fought with the rusted bolt of the bicycle until it began to move. In less than a minute I had the handlebars on tight and the bike was ready to ride again.

"Thanks! I really appreciate it," Jana told me.

"Where do you go to school?"

"Port Daley Secondary."

My mouth dropped open. "You bike all the way to Port Daley? Every morning?"

"Only when I've missed the bus," she muttered. "It took me so long to get the kids out the door today that—" She stopped short, then added, "Mom wasn't feeling well, so I had to get everybody out the door, and now I'm late." She threw one leg over the bike. "I have to get going. Thanks again."

"Wait. It's nine o'clock already. Why don't you let me drive you into town? It will save you half an hour."

She hesitated, and I could see her mind turning. On one hand, she'd likely been told not to accept rides with strangers. On the other hand, she was terribly late. If I was a friend of Ian's, could I be trusted?

"If you like, we could call your mom first and make sure it's okay with her," I suggested.

"No, she doesn't like to be bothered when she isn't feeling well," Jana said quickly. "I think it will be okay."

We stashed her bicycle beside my garage and climbed into the truck. Jana settled back on the seat with a sigh.

"Thanks. I really didn't want to have to bike it again."

"I hope your mother's okay," I told her as I pulled into the road. "Does she need someone to check on her?"

"No, she's all right. She doesn't like company when she's feeling bad," Jana said.

I glanced at her profile as I drove, the set of her jaw, the grim expression on her face, and thought perhaps Mom was in bed with a hangover or something along those lines. Best not to pry. But maybe I would pass along the information to Ian. If he had taken it upon himself to keep an eye on the family, he may want to know. In fact, perhaps that was *why* he was keeping an eye on the family . . .

We drove for a while in silence. I fished for something to say, because Jana didn't seem eager to start the conversation.

"Your sister has beautiful hair," I told her. "I assume she was your sister. At the park?"

"Anne-Marie. Yeah, it's pretty when she keeps it brushed."

"And the boy was your brother?"

"Yeah."

"How many kids are in your family? Are you the oldest?"

Jana shot me a considering look, then decided to answer. "Next to oldest. There are six of us kids."

"Six! Wow."

"Three girls and three boys."

"That's a lot." I waited, but she offered nothing more, so I switched the topic. "What grade are you in?"

"Nine. It's almost over, next month, thank goodness. I wouldn't care about being late, but I have an exam today."

"What in?"

"Math." She made a face.

"Oh, I know," I commiserated. "I hated math all through school. I could never see what good it would ever do me. But now look, I use it every day in my work."

"I," she said firmly, "will never choose a career that requires math."

"Well, you might find you need it in just day-to-day life. For example, doubling a recipe. If it calls for two-thirds cup of flour, you have to—"

"Put in two-thirds cup twice," Jana replied flatly.

"Okay, yes, you can get around it in that case. But what if you need to calculate how much flooring to purchase?"

She rolled her eyes. "I'll call Handyman Connection and they'll calculate how much I need, and install it too."

"Okay. But what if you want to put in a round pond in your backyard someday? You'll need geometry . . ."

Jana shook her head, making her blonde braid whip out like a striking snake. "I will never do anything so foolish. Or I'll make my husband do it."

I laughed. "Okay, I get it. You hate math. And you can find a way to go through life avoiding it. But do you want to have to rely on your husband or other people for everything? Don't you want to be able to stand on your own two feet and do things yourself?"

"No," Jana replied. "I want to have *somebody* to rely on. Turn here. That's my school."

I pulled to the side of the road and she hopped out.

"Thanks so much!" she called, hoisting her backpack on her shoulder. "I'll come by after school and get my bike."

When Jana arrived that afternoon, Finn was helping me load a rented dumpster with rubbish. I had almost forgotten she was coming, and for a while I didn't notice her standing and watching us. Then she moved forward and caught hold of a roll of old carpet I was hefting and helped me toss it in the bin.

"Hey, thanks!" I said, smacking my filthy hands together to dust them off. "Perfect timing."

"Hi, Jana," Finn greeted her.

"Hi, Finn."

"You two know each other?"

They both sent me a "duh" sort of look.

"Oh yeah. Small town. I forgot. I'm from Toronto, okay?"

"Want a root beer?" Finn offered, the perfect host in someone else's house.

"Sure," Jana said, so he jogged into the house to get her one.

"I hope you weren't too late getting to class," I told her, reaching for some broken pieces of drywall and sending them after the carpet.

"Nah. My exam was second period anyway, so I was on time for the important stuff."

"How did it go?"

She shrugged. "It's over. That's all that matters."

I chuckled. "How's your mom?"

"Oh. I don't know. I haven't been home yet," Jana replied. "I came here straight from the bus. But I'm sure she's all right by now."

This rather confirmed my suspicion of a hangover. I wondered how often it happened.

Finn emerged from the house with three cans of pop, graciously offering me one as well. We all sat on the porch steps together to take our break. The root beer had just been purchased that afternoon and hadn't been in the fridge long enough to get really cold, but it was still refreshing.

"Hump day," Finn said gleefully. "Can I sleep in the fort Friday night?"

"If it's okay with your dad," I told him.

"What fort?" Jana asked.

"It's really cool. *She* made it for me." Finn jerked a thumb at me, and I couldn't help smiling.

"Lemme see," Jana said, forgetting she was supposed to be too old and sophisticated for such things. She and Finn deserted me to go inspect the fort, and with a sigh I went back to work. I liked building things, but I hated the clean-up it involved. I was nearly finished clearing the driveway when they came back, whispering together in a way that made me wonder what they were up to.

"Kerris," Finn said, coming to stand before me seriously with hands behind his back. "Can we ask you for a favor?"

Why stop now? "Sure," I said aloud.

"Could you fix us a picnic to eat in the fort?"

I glanced at my watch. "I guess so. But both of you need to phone home and make sure it's okay with your folks if you stay for supper."

"It is," Finn assured me.

"Phone anyway."

He looked a little mutinous, but Jana tugged on his elbow. "Come on, make the call."

Finn led the way into the house, and out of curiosity, I followed. He went to the wall phone in the kitchen, dialed a number, and paused.

"Dad? It's me. Is it okay if I eat at a friend's house?" He slid his eyes sideways at me. "Okay, thanks." He hung up abruptly.

"Didn't he want to know what friend?" I asked.

Finn shook his head. "He doesn't care."

I handed the receiver to Jana. "Your turn."

Jana dialed a number, and when it was answered, she said brightly, "Hi Mom, it's Jana. Is it okay if I have dinner at a friend's house?" There was a pause, and Jana looked at me. "Kerris . . ." she told the phone.

"Wells," I supplied.

"Kerris Wells. She's a friend of Finn's. Finn is here too . . . okay . . . okay, thanks. I'll be home right after . . . No, I don't know where it is. Maybe Kevin took it . . . Well, he'll just have to figure it out . . . I know it's my night to do dishes. I'll do them when I come home, okay? Just leave them. I'll be home later. Thanks! Bye." She handed the phone back to me with a "Satisfied?" smirk on her face.

"All right, one picnic coming up," I said. They ran back out to the fort, and I began to dig through the fridge for something suitable to serve. My suspicions had been confirmed, at any rate. I knew no numbers started with 555—that was why they used that sequence in books and movies—but I'd watched carefully when Finn had dialed, and it had been a 555 number. It was bogus. I was beginning to have my doubts that his father existed. But if not, where was he staying?

Jana Jameson obviously knew him. Maybe I could get her to spill the beans.

Chapter Ten

Thursday morning, I was just finishing breakfast and figuring out what to do that day when there was a knock on the door. Ian's car was at the end of the driveway, and Ian stood on the porch. It made me a bit breathless to realize how happy I was to see him. I kept my expression carefully neutral so that my feelings didn't show too obviously.

He greeted me cheerfully enough, but I thought there was a bit of a strain on his face, an anxiousness in his voice that I hadn't heard before, as he explained he was on the way to school and wanted to stop by to ask me something.

"Sure," I said. "What's up?"

"I wanted to ask if you're free on Mother's Day."

This took me by surprise. I had to think a moment. "When is that, a week from Sunday?"

"Yes."

"I'm free, yes. Why do you ask?"

"You're not spending the day with your mother or anything?"

"No. She died last year."

"Oh, I'm sorry. That's hard." Concern washed over his face.

"It's all right now," I said quickly. "But why are you asking?"

"Well, you see, Eamonn and his wife Shelley have invited us to lunch that day."

"They have?" Us? Had they been discussing Ian and me? The idea both startled me and filled me with happiness. Maybe Ian had been talking to them about me.

"I'd like to invite you, if you'll come," Ian unfolded his arms, pushed his hands in his pockets, and went on, sounding now as if he were rushing to get through the words before he could chicken out. "My father died last year too, and I think Mum will need jollying on her first Mother's Day without him. They're throwing a big lunch and the whole family will be there and, well, it would be great if you could join us. I know it's maybe a bit much to ask . . ."

"Sure. Of course. I'd be happy to come," I said, charmed by the earnest look on his face. "Thanks very much."

He relaxed into that great smile of his. "Good! I'm glad. We're a pretty big crowd," he added, "but don't let it overwhelm you. We're all pretty friendly."

"That's fine. It sounds fun." Even as I said it, my mind flashed to the fancy house in the forest with the monster willow tree, and I hesitated. I'd actually forgotten. I'd enjoyed his company kayaking and having fish and chips and . . . and I'd actually momentarily forgotten the differences between his world and mine. I told myself it didn't matter. It would just be a harmless family gathering, ordinary, like any family was going to have on Mother's Day. It might be ritzier than I was used to, but it was okay for me to go, even if—a recurring life theme—I had nothing to wear. Ian wouldn't invite me if he didn't think I could handle it. I knew him and Eamonn well enough to know they wouldn't judge me in any case. But I suddenly felt as if it was the prom all over again. I could envision myself standing awkwardly in his brother's posh living room in my best, inadequate dress with drywall dust in my hair, clearly out of my league. What would his family think of me? And why did it matter so much to me what they thought? Why did he want me to meet his family anyway? How was I supposed to read this?

In three seconds flat I had worked myself into a lather, spinning from charmed to panicked to horrified. Had I really said I'd go? I felt my heart rate speed up and my stomach tense. To Ian this might be a simple invitation, but to me it felt too intimidating. Too soon. I opened my mouth to say, "Sorry, no, I forgot I couldn't make it," but

Ian was already heading back down the driveway to his car, waving and calling over his shoulder, "We'll pick you up at noon Sunday. A week from Sunday, I mean."

A flash of his smile and he was gone. The sound of his car had faded before it dawned on me what he'd said. "*We'll* pick you up . . ." Who was *we*?

And where was my fairy godmother when I needed her?

After school, Jana and Finn arrived together, this time with another young blond-headed boy in tow. They barely took the time to introduce him as Jana's brother Peter, age eight, before they were heading for the fort. Judging from the exclamations in the backyard, the fort had won their approval. Musing, I arranged some cookies and mugs of milk on a tray and carried it out to them.

"This is the coolest! It's like your own little house!" Peter was saying when I knocked on the door. When Jana opened it and saw the tray, she beamed at me.

"Oh, that's so nice of you!" she said. She took the tray and the door snapped shut again. I went back to the house, laughing to myself. It seemed I'd created a hit.

It also seemed my place had moved from being my own personal oasis to something of a gathering place for local children. I would have to set down some rules with Finn about how many people he could invite over and when. I envisioned troops of children bounding through my yard, expecting picnics and treats on a daily basis. I didn't want to become a fast-food joint, nor could I afford to be one.

Then again, it was rather nice to have someone to prepare little treats for. I listened to the happy chatter coming from the fort, and for just a moment I pretended they were my children.

Miriam phoned as I was making myself an early supper (a can of chicken soup and a mini tower of garlic toast. I figured I would work off the carbs).

"Hi, kiddo! How are things in the back of beyond?"

"Same as ever," I said, holding the phone between my ear and my shoulder as I carried my food to the table. "The house is coming along. How about you? Anything new?"

"Nothing to report," she said. "Busy at work. Planning to go to Jamaica this summer, same place I stayed last time."

"In the summer? Won't it be too hot?" My own idea of a vacation leaned more toward Norwegian cruises or Alaskan adventures.

"There's no such thing," Miriam laughed. There was a pause, and I knew she was going to switch topics. I braced myself. And wondered how long it would be before I no longer felt the need to.

"And um . . . I just thought you might want to know, Maddie and Marcus's baby is out of the hospital and doing well. They've named her Crystal."

"That's good," I said. I waited for the pang of regret to hit me, the crush of disappointment and anger . . . but it didn't come. A twinge, that was all. I was genuinely glad the baby was okay. "That must be a relief for them."

"Yeah . . ." I could tell she was waiting for more from me. When she didn't get it, she moved on, with audible relief, to other subjects—mutual friends, a movie she'd seen, the traffic in Toronto. Fifteen minutes later, my soup was cold and she was wrapping up the conversation.

"Thanks for letting me know about the baby," I told her. I knew that had been her main reason for calling.

"Sure. Listen, does it bother you that I'm still in touch with Maddie? I mean, we were friends for a long time and—"

"Not at all," I said truthfully. "What happened with me and Marcus had nothing to do with you and shouldn't interfere with your and Maddie's friendship."

"I'm sure she feels really bad about the whole thing," Miriam added.

"I don't really want to discuss it," I said as politely as I could. "But really, it's okay you're still friends with her. I—I don't wish her ill or anything. I really do hope they'll be happy together." I was sort of surprised to hear myself say it.

"Is that really true, Kerris?"

I smiled at her skeptical tone. "Yes, at least I think it is."

"So you and I are okay?"

"Sure. You don't need to worry about that. And you don't need to worry about me. But you also don't need to keep me up to date on the baby's first steps or anything . . ."

"Gotcha. Okay."

"Maybe someday. Over time, I might feel differently about it."

"Okay. You take care, sweetie." She was the only person on the planet who called me that.

"You too. Thanks for calling."

I hung up and looked glumly at my stack of toast, now gone cold and crunchy. It did still hurt, and I wasn't thrilled my life had exploded. I still felt sorrow when I thought about the baby Marcus and I had never had. But I realized I wasn't raw with it anymore, and I no longer wished Maddie and Marcus had never been born, so I guessed that was a step in the right direction.

"I'm improving," I said aloud, and went to microwave my congealing soup. As I settled at last to eat, I pictured Finn's laughing face as he helped me with the dumpster. His sly grin. His open delight in the money he earned from me. His impish humor. The way he covered his need with spunkiness. Maybe, I thought, there's more than one way to be a parent.

On Friday, the second electrician scoffed at the first electrician's opinion.

"He's just trying to get money out of you," he declared, waving a hand. "You don't have to change all your wiring or receptacles. All you need to do is put a little of this special paste stuff on the joints between the copper and the aluminum in your outlets. I can show you how and you can do it yourself. No worries. I've been doing this for thirty years and I haven't burned down a house yet."

Somehow, I didn't find this comforting. I thanked him, told him I'd have to get back to him, and showed him to the door. As he got in his truck and drove away, I saw Finn coming down the road, lugging something heavy. I walked down the driveway to meet him. He carried a red plastic cooler. When he saw me, he grinned.

"Just some snacks for tonight," he announced. His expression was gleeful that it was Friday at last.

"It looks like you've packed enough to stay for a week," I laughed, taking one side to help carry it around to the backyard.

"I figured we'd eat a lot."

"We?" I shook my head. "Finn, I hope you're not . . . I mean, I'm not sleeping out in the fort with you, right?"

"Nah, of course not," he said complacently. "I mean Kevin and Seth and Peter and me."

"Wait. Who are—Are those the Jamesons, you mean?"

"Yeah. Just the boys, though. Not the girls. I mean, I don't mind the girls coming to the fort sometimes, after school, but not at night."

"You've invited three other boys to spend tonight?"

"Yeah." He finally caught the disapproval in my voice, set down the cooler, and turned to face me. "Isn't that okay?"

"I wish you had asked me first. I need to make sure it's all right with their parents."

"Oh, their mom doesn't mind. I asked Peter and Seth and—and it's all cool. They asked their mom and she said it's okay."

I studied his wide-eyed face and didn't trust him.

I sighed. "All right. But next time please ask me. And I'll have to talk to their mom myself so I know she's all right with this. I mean, she doesn't even know me."

"But—"

"What's their number?"

"I don't know."

"You're friends with them but you don't know their number?"

"Not off the top of my head. I usually just walk over."

"Oh. Are they close by?"

Finn shifted on his feet. "Yeah. They're going to meet me here."

"Well, when they come, please tell them I need their phone number so I can talk to their mother."

"Alright."

"And I don't want you four boys carrying on all night. You do have to sleep at some point, okay?"

"We will. My dad said lights out at eleven o'clock," he said, nodding. He spread his arms wide. "Besides, you don't have any close neighbors to wake up."

"*I* don't want to be woken up. Okay?"

"Okay. You won't even know we're here."

"Are they bringing their own sleeping bags? I only have the one."

"Yeah. It's all cool. Don't worry."

I went back into the house, shaking my head. They'd probably stay up all night telling ghost stories and frightening themselves, or drinking pop all night and making themselves sick. I could picture four little boys knocking on my back door at two in the morning, afraid or puking or needing the bathroom. Then again, maybe Finn had been a bit nervous about staying by himself all night. He seemed pretty tough and self-sufficient, but when it came down to it, I forgot sometimes that he was only ten years old, after all.

"They're here." Finn poked his head in the kitchen door. "What smells so good?"

"I'm making you burritos for a bedtime snack," I told him.

"Yum!"

I wiped my hands on my jeans and followed him out to the porch to meet my—his—guests. Peter and Seth I had met, but I was surprised when I saw Kevin Jameson. He had the same bright blond hair as his siblings, but he was as tall as I was and had two days' growth of beard. His t-shirt revealed a decent set of muscles. He shook my hand like an adult and said formally, "Pleased to meet you. Thank you for having us over."

I was caught off guard, and without thinking, I blurted, "How old are you?"

He chuckled, and his voice was deep. "Sixteen. Seventeen next month." He gave me a wry smile. "I know, I'm too old to be sleeping in forts. But I thought Petey might be a bit young to come, and he really wanted to." He ruffled his younger brother's hair with affection.

I felt better, knowing this hulking young man would be standing guard over the fort during the night. I didn't think he'd let Finn or his brothers get away with much.

"Thanks. Good. Um . . ." I had meant to ask for his phone number, but now it felt rather silly, checking up on him as if he were little. Finn jumped in.

"She wants to talk to your mom to make sure it's okay you stay over," he said.

Kevin looked at him, then at me, and I shrugged, feeling stupid. But Kevin just nodded.

"Sure. I'll call and let you talk to her."

"I hope she's feeling better now," I said, letting them all into the house and leading them to the phone.

"Better?"

"Jana said the other day that your mom was under the weather."

"Oh. Yeah. She's fine. In fact, I think tonight she's at some meeting at Kat's school, but I'll check." Kevin dialed—not a 555 number that I could tell—and had a brief conversation with whoever answered. He held the receiver out to me. "She's not home yet, but Jana's home."

"Jana? It's Kerris," I said.

"Oh hi, Kerris! Thanks for having the boys over. They're really looking forward to it."

"Sure. I—I just wanted to make sure your mother knew where they were and that it was okay with her."

"Oh, of course. She said the more they're out of her hair, the better," Jana laughed. "But she wants them home tomorrow by ten to do their chores."

"Okay. Thanks. Have a good night."

"You too."

I hung up and nodded at Finn. "Okay, they can stay."

The Jameson boys cheered and headed outside. In spite of Kevin's protest that he was only there to watch over his brothers, he looked as eager as the rest. But I caught Finn by the shoulder and stopped him from following them.

"Your turn. What's your phone number?"

He blinked at me. "Why?"

"So I can talk to your dad."

"It's okay with him. I asked—"

"I'm sure you did, but I think it's best if I speak with him directly," I said.

"I don't think he's home," Finn mumbled.

I bent over, hands on my knees, to look him in the eye. "What's your number?"

He studied me a moment, then apparently decided he couldn't distract me this time. He sighed and gave it to me with the aggrieved air of one who has unjustly been denied trust. I dialed the number and listened to it ring several times. No voice message service kicked in. Reluctantly, I hung up and looked at Finn, wondering what to do.

He raised his chin and met my eyes. "He's gone a lot," he told me.

"In the evening?"

"Yeah. He's with his friends. But he knew *I* would be with *my* friends, so it's okay."

"Does he leave you alone a lot, Finn?"

He shrugged and looked away. I hesitated, then gave up. I was no social worker, but from what I could tell, Finn was probably safer here with me tonight than he was at home with or without his deadbeat father, if such a person even existed. I'd figure out what to do in the morning, but I suspected a call to Children's Services might be in order. For now . . .

"Okay, out you go. I'll bring you your burritos later on."

Finn's face lit up. "Thanks!" He scampered out of the kitchen.

I had to hand it to them, they were well behaved. When I carried the burritos out to them at eight o'clock, they were all sprawled in the light of the lantern, reading comic books. They were surrounded by discarded pop cans and candy wrappers and chip bags. Peter looked ready to drop asleep at any moment. I didn't hear a peep out of them all night, and when I went to wake them in the morning, I found them already up, their sleeping bags rolled tidily, and the garbage collected.

"How was your first night in the fort?" I asked, bending down to Peter's level. He had salsa in his hair and a mosquito bite over one eye, but he looked very pleased with himself.

"Good!" he replied.

"Who wants breakfast?"

They cheered and flowed past me into the house, Kevin bringing up the rear. I put a hand on his arm.

"Thanks," I told him when he paused to look back at me. "I doubt they would have been so good if you hadn't been here."

He shrugged and smiled. "Seth and Peter are always good," he said offhandedly. "Finn, I couldn't vouch for!"

"I wanted to ask you about him," I confided. I checked to make sure the door had closed behind the others and they couldn't hear us. "I worry about him. He doesn't seem to have anyone to care for him. I told him to call home the other day to make sure his dad knew where he was, and he called a bogus number. But he acted as if he was talking to his dad. And then last night he gave me what may or may not have been the right number, and no one answered."

"Oh. Well, Finn just has a little thing about authority figures right now," Kevin said, sounding sixty instead of sixteen. "He's been running wild and getting into some trouble lately, and maybe he was afraid his dad wouldn't agree to let him come, so that's probably why he faked the call."

"Thanks. That's reassuring. I think." I ran my fingers through my bangs and laughed awkwardly. "I was starting to wonder if his dad even existed," I confessed.

Kevin frowned at me. "What do you mean?"

"Well, I get the impression Finn is on his own a lot. Does his dad care what Finn does and where he goes, do you know? I mean, is he a responsible sort of father?"

Kevin frowned at me. "Well, sure. I think Ian's a really cool dad. Finn's just a handful."

"I'm glad to hear it. I was starting to wonder if I should call Children's Aid." I had turned toward the house to go inside, but stopped cold, realizing what he'd said. "Wait. Ian? Ian who?"

"*You* know. Finn's dad. Ian McGrath. Jana said you're a friend of his." Kevin spread his hands, looking puzzled.

All I could do was stare at him. "Oh. I didn't realize . . ."

His mouth dropped open. "Don't you know Ian is Finn's dad?"

"No! I had no idea."

He frowned and rubbed his stubbly jaw. "I thought you knew him."

"I thought I did too," I murmured.

I went through the motions of making pancakes for the boys, but my mind was in a whirl. Finn *McGrath*? Ian's son? I kept glancing at the boy, but I couldn't see anything of Ian in his face or mannerisms. Maybe there was a small resemblance in the humor around the boy's flexible mouth. I hadn't known. I had assumed Finn lived in poor circumstances. I certainly didn't think he lived in that big fancy house with the trees. I thought about the little trail I'd followed, that I'd assumed had been made by animals. Now I realized it had more likely been made by Finn, coming back and forth to my house. Finn had said his mother died. Eamonn had mentioned Julia, presumably Ian's deceased wife. Why hadn't I put two and two together?

Because I would have expected more of Ian, quite frankly. How could he let his son run wild like this? How could he let him look like an orphan? Why was Ian out caring for neighbor families while his son obviously ached for adult attention? Above all, why hadn't Ian told me he had a son?

Chapter Eleven

After breakfast, I offered to give the boys a lift home in the truck so they didn't have to haul the sleeping bags and cooler on foot.

"We're fine. It isn't far," Kevin said, but I insisted. I rather hoped I'd get a chance to confront Ian. I loaded the boys and their stuff in the truck and, without asking directions, I turned left and went up the street. Around the corner, some way down, there was the driveway to the fancy house—the castle, I called it in my mind—and I turned in grimly, probably driving too fast. The boys, crammed in the back seat, didn't correct me. Sure enough, then. This was where he lived. I felt my temper start to rise.

I pulled up in front of the massive house and cut the engine. But to my surprise, it was the three Jameson boys who climbed out of the truck and collected their stuff from the bed. Finn just sat there.

I climbed out of the cab and watched, astonished, as the Jamesons went up the steps into the house, calling their thanks. The door closed behind them, and then I saw little Anne-Marie in one window, waving a hello. I waved back numbly and walked back to the truck.

"Where do you live?" I asked, in a sharper tone than I'd intended.

Finn clamped his mouth shut and frowned.

"I'm taking you home, so tell me, or we're going to sit here all afternoon. Enough monkeying around."

Finn sighed and jerked his head back toward the road. "Go out and turn left. Turn right on River Road, and it's the fourth house on the left."

I climbed back in the truck and turned it cautiously. As I drove at a slower pace down the driveway, I couldn't sort out my thoughts. I could have sworn it was Ian's car I'd seen pull into the garage of this house. But he didn't live here—the Jamesons did. What would he have been doing parking his car in their garage?

And then the idea occurred to me that Ian might have been coming to see Mrs. Jameson. The more I thought about it, the more I was sure of it. There was no other likely explanation. Why else would he go there in the middle of the day and hide his car in the garage? (Not that there were any neighbors close enough to see.) But then why, if he had a relationship with her, had he asked me out? Why had he kissed me on the cheek? Why had he gone so far as to invite me to meet his family? Was I being played for a fool? Was I being the "cover" to distract Eamonn and Shelley so that they didn't learn about Ian and whatever-her-name-was Jameson? I tried to remember what the children had said, if anything, about their father. Maybe he was out of the picture.

The fourth house on River Road was a tidy white bungalow with navy blue shutters. The driveway was empty and there was no garage; straggly yellow flowers bloomed along the sidewalk like an afterthought. It looked much more like the humble house of a biology teacher. Not the Lord of the Castle, then. But maybe the lover of the Lady of the Castle. At least, someone who knew her well enough to take command of her trees and summon an arborist for them. I felt sick.

I parked in the driveway and helped Finn lift the cooler down from the truck bed. We walked up to the front door, but it was locked. Finn began to fish in his pocket for a key. Just then, Ian's little white car zoomed down the road and parked with a screech behind my truck, blocking the driveway. I turned to face him, but whatever I had been planning to say flew out of my head when I saw his face. He leaped out of the car, leaving the door open, and was up on the steps beside us in three long strides. He dropped to his knees and pulled a startled-looking Finn into his arms.

Surely this was overdoing the loving dad bit, I thought. A little late for that.

But the strain on his face seemed genuine enough. Ian held Finn away from him and barked hoarsely, "Where on earth have you been?"

Finn didn't answer, just looked guiltily down at his tennis shoes. Nice shoes, really. Too good for a street kid. Why hadn't I noticed? I'd been a fool.

"You found him. Thank you for bringing him home," Ian said to me, climbing to his feet but keeping one hand on Finn's shoulder. "I've been frantic. I called the police. I drove around half the night looking for him. I didn't know where else to try."

I noticed for the first time Ian's unshaved face, the way his hair stuck out, the redness of his eyes. He wasn't faking.

"He was at my place," I said. Finn cringed at the tone of my voice.

"Your place?"

"He spent the night in the fort in my backyard."

"He . . . wait. You two know each other?" Ian looked confused, and maybe a little wary.

"You know my dad?" Finn frowned at me. I turned to Ian.

"I didn't know. I mean, I didn't know it was you. He told me his dad knew where he was and that it was okay for him to stay. I tried to speak to you myself to make sure . . . except you didn't answer." I was sure I sounded incoherent, and I couldn't keep the accusatory tone out of my voice.

"It's all right, Dad. It isn't her fault. I lied to her." Finn's lower lip jutted out, but he met his father's gaze squarely. "I gave her the wrong number."

"Why didn't you tell me where you were going last night? I would have given my permission," Ian said, his voice calmer.

"I didn't know you knew her," Finn muttered. "I didn't think you'd say yes."

"You should have at least asked," I pointed out to Finn. "After all, the Jameson boys' mother didn't know me, but she said yes."

Ian gave me a startled look. I spread my hands.

"It won't happen again," I told him.

"The Jameson boys were there too? Last night?"

"Yes. Kevin, Peter, and Seth."

"But—" Ian raked his fingers through his hair, spiking it further. "I went to the Jamesons' last night to ask if they knew where Finn was. He hangs out with the boys, and I thought if anyone would know, they would. But Anne-Marie told me her brothers were away, spending the night at a friend's, and she had no idea where Finn was. She didn't tell me he was with them."

"Maybe she didn't know," I said. "I spoke to Jana because their mother wasn't home. Maybe Anne-Marie wasn't aware, and Jana didn't mention it—"

"So all last night you four boys were together." Ian sounded as if he was still trying to put all the pieces together and understand what had occurred. "And you were at Kerris's house."

"It's a really cool fort," Finn said. "It has my name painted on it and everything. You should see it."

Ian licked his lips and pressed them together briefly, then loosened his grip on Finn's shoulder and put his hand on the boy's head.

"I will. If Kerris built it, I'm sure it's terrific. But next time tell me where you're going. I can't keep you safe if I don't know where you are."

Finn nodded glumly.

"Go put your stuff away and wait for me in your room. We're going to talk more about this, okay? But first tell Kerris you're sorry you lied to her."

Finn shot me a grim look, and instantly I was a child again, sitting on Mom's couch with Gillian, forced to stay there until we apologized to each other for some forgotten infraction. It hadn't taught us to be sorry, it had taught us to lie about being sorry so we could escape that couch. To say what was expected. Suddenly I didn't want Finn to have to do that. I reached out and gave him an awkward pat on the shoulder.

"I understand," I said.

Finn glanced at Ian, then pulled out his key and went into the house. Ian ran both hands down his unshaven face, leaving a smudge of dirt. And then I could see the resemblance between father and son.

"I'm sorry," I said. "When I couldn't reach you, I shouldn't have let him stay. But to be honest, I wasn't sure he even had a dad."

"What do you mean?"

I shook my head. This wasn't the time to tell Ian my hasty assumptions about his neglect as a parent. "It doesn't matter. All I can say is it won't happen again."

The anger and worry were gone from his face now. "How did you two meet?" he asked quietly.

I bit my lower lip and wondered if I should tell about Finn camping in my basement before I moved in. It would probably only anger him again. I shrugged. "He wandered over a while ago and helped me carry some stuff into the house. He's been over a few times since. I was going to tear down an old shed and he asked me to build him a fort out of it instead."

Ian shook his head again. "I didn't know. I'm sorry if he's bothered you."

"Not at all," I said. "We've become friends."

He looked at me then, closely, as if trying to figure out if I was telling the truth.

"What, don't you think it's possible to be friends with a child?" I asked defensively.

"Of course. I'm just not sure if it's possible for Finn to be friends with an adult," Ian replied. "Maybe you've noticed he doesn't exactly . . . get along with adults."

I heard my voice rise a notch. "He gets along just fine with me. Maybe he just doesn't know enough adults he can trust."

Ian looked a little taken aback at that. I folded my arms across my chest.

"Why didn't you tell me you had a son, Ian? Did you think I don't like children or something?"

"No, not at all."

"Are you ashamed of him?"

"What? Of course not," he protested. "Finn's a great kid. You knew I had a son. I just hadn't had a chance to introduce you yet."

"I didn't know you had a kid. How would I have known?"

"Eamonn told you."

"No, he didn't."

"He said he'd told you all about me. Finn's the biggest part of my life. I assumed he'd at least *mentioned* him . . ."

I shook my head. "Well, he didn't. I had no idea. And I didn't know Finn's last name until this morning."

Ian stared at me a minute, absorbing this. "I'm sorry," he said. "I thought you knew I had a son."

"That whole time we spent together the other day, you didn't talk about him."

He flung his arms out. "I was half a river away from you most of the morning! It's not something I would just bellow out over the water—"

"You could have talked about him while we were getting ice cream, or at the diner."

"Yes, I guess I could have. In my defense, I don't think it's all that unusual not to talk about your kid on your first date," Ian said drily. He sighed. "Look, I was planning to introduce him to you at the family dinner next Sunday and kind of ease into it slowly. He's my favorite person on the planet, don't get me wrong, but I'm sure you've seen for yourself he's not an easy child. There's a reason for that, and I'll explain it to you another day. For now, let's just say he's very good at pushing other people away. And I didn't want him to push you away, Kerris."

He had taken a step closer to me, and now I stepped back, keeping the distance between us. "He wouldn't have done that. He's a sweet kid," I protested.

"Well, thank you for saying that. You don't know how astounding it is for me to hear you say that. He doesn't exactly have a good track record when it comes to interacting with others."

"You could have fooled me."

"He's been suspended from school four times in the last two years."

"He's always been great with me."

He scrubbed his hand through his hair again. "Look, I'm sorry you're upset. I'm sorry for this whole situation. I didn't mean to come across as dishonest or—or not forthcoming. I really thought you knew about him. Let's start again, fresh, on Sunday, okay?"

I remembered now how he had said "Eamonn has invited *us* . . ." I had assumed he'd meant me and him. Now I knew otherwise.

"I'm not sure dinner's such a good idea," I said.

He looked dismayed. "Why not? It was just a misunderstanding."

"No," I said, thinking of Mrs. Jameson and the sight of the garage door closing behind Ian's car. "It's more than that."

"But—"

"Can you move your car, please, so I can go?"

He studied me for what felt like an age, then wordlessly went to move his car. I got in my truck and left without looking back at him.

I told myself it didn't matter. It was not a great disappointment. I hardly knew the man, after all. I'd only met him a couple of weeks ago. A few chance encounters. One golden day spent together. It wasn't much, really. But as I drove slowly home, I felt I'd lost something important. A missed opportunity. A dream grounded before it had the chance to explore its wings.

The next week I spent working hard on the house, avoiding the town or any place I thought I might run into Ian. He didn't call, and I told myself I was glad even while I felt drained with disappointment. I overhauled the sump pump in the basement, caulked around windows, tiled the tub surround, leveled the stones in the front walkway, and generally worked myself into exhaustion—my old trick to keep from feeling too much.

Sunday morning, I was up early, before the sun. I thought briefly of jogging down to the river to watch the mist again, but somehow I wasn't in the mood. Instead, I worked in the backyard, hacking out weeds and trying to tame the jungle into some semblance of order. I had decided to build a deck out the back of the house, and maybe put in a koi pond or some sort of water feature to add a pleasant sound, and then turn the rest of the yard to meadow. At some point I knew I'd have to stop tinkering with my own home and start looking for real work on someone else's house, but it seemed too daunting to think about. Maybe this fall, when people started thinking of indoors instead of outdoors. Until then, there might still be a little room on my credit card.

The highlight of the morning was discovering a short but healthy crabapple tree in the far corner. There would be jelly come autumn.

The idea brightened my spirits. It also helped me forget it was Mother's Day.

At eleven-thirty I poured myself a bowl of granola and flopped on the floor on a cushion to eat it, hoping to find a decent movie on TV. I didn't watch often, but I thought it might distract me from my grumpy mood. I had the choice of *A Bug's Life*, baseball, baseball, or baseball. I chose *A Bug's Life*. It had barely started, though, when the doorbell rang.

It was the two neatly dressed young women with the name tags again. They gave me their mega-watt smiles and the one—now wearing a pink blazer—said, "Hi again. We're missionaries from the Church of Jesus Christ of—"

"Look, I'm sorry, but I'm really not interested," I said tiredly.

I thought they would turn and go after that second refusal, but instead, the girl's smile dimmed a little and her head tipped to one side as she openly studied me. "Are you okay?" she asked.

"What?"

"I mean, you look a little upset. Are you all right? Is there anything we can do?"

I didn't know what to say to that. When was the last time someone had asked me if they could do something for me? Had looked at me with perception and concern? Well, Ian *had* helped with my countertop, and he'd checked on me in the storm . . . but I didn't want to think about him. I realized my mouth was open and closed it again.

"Listen, it's fine if you don't want to hear our message," the other girl spoke up. She had a British accent of some sort and wore what looked like the same floral dress as before. "But we're not here just to preach. We're here to serve, however we can."

"What, like you're my fairy godmothers?" It came out with a sharp laugh I hadn't intended.

"No," the first girl said gently. "We're your sisters."

For one insane moment, I thought wildly that my father's other family had somehow found me. But no, my half-siblings were much younger than these two were. And then I realized she'd meant it in a religious or metaphorical sense and blushed.

"Thank you." I struggled to keep my voice courteous. "But I'm okay, and I don't need any help."

"All right. You just looked a bit tired and upset, that's all."

A flash of anger rolled over me, and before I could stop myself, I barked into her innocent face, "Yes, I'm upset! I don't want you coming around and bothering me. Didn't you get the message the first time? It's none of your business how I am, and I want to be left alone."

The first girl took a step backward, looking startled, her sunny smile wiped completely from her face. I instantly felt as if I'd slapped a puppy. She began to stammer. "Oh. All right. I'm sorry. We didn't mean to upset you, we'd just hoped to share our message—"

"No, I'm sorry," I interrupted wearily. "Look, I didn't mean to shout at you. I know you're just doing your job or whatever it is. But I've got a bad history with religion. It's been my experience that religious people are hypocrites, saying one thing and doing the opposite, and using the cloak of religion to hide their bad behavior. So pardon me if I'm not interested in your church. But I shouldn't have taken it out on you like that."

I really expected them to turn and run, and I wouldn't have blamed them a bit if they had. But instead, the British girl stepped forward, put a hand on my arm, and said softly, "Oh, I'm so sorry you've had that experience. That isn't what religion is meant to do at all. That's so sad."

Once again, I was caught off guard by her warm sincerity. I couldn't think of anything to say as I watched her reach into her pocket and pull out what looked like a business card, which she pressed into my hand.

"We'll respect your wishes and we won't bother you again, but if you ever decide it would be okay for us to come back and talk to you, please call us. And if you don't want to talk religion but you need help with something—anything at all—all you have to do is call."

"Do you know how to install countertops?" I asked dryly, pushing the card into my pocket without looking at it.

This caught her by surprise, but she smiled gamely and said, "I can learn. Seriously, I'd love to help if you need us to."

I took a deep breath, feeling my anger diffuse. "Thanks. But I'm okay."

She eyed me, not believing me. I felt myself start to smile.

"Really I am."

She nodded once. "You will be," she said confidently. And the two of them went down the steps and walked away.

My granola was soggy by now and I threw it away and turned off the TV. I stood with my hands on my hips in the middle of the kitchen, trying to regain my equilibrium. I was chilled by the realization of the depth of my anger. I'd tried to cover over it, ignore it, but now I could see it was still simmering under the surface after all these years, like a boiling stew with an ill-fitting lid on the pot. I'd thought I was over my father's betrayal and hypocrisy, but maybe this whole thing with Marcus had stirred it up again.

As I stood there, I tried consciously to tune in to the peace I'd first felt in this house. I reached out for it like a blanket around my shoulders, pulling it close to ease the chill. I felt the tension slide from me, and I tipped my head back, closed my eyes, and addressed my guardian angel.

"Show me the way forward. I'm in a slump. I don't know what to do with my life."

The doorbell rang.

I looked at the door, then cast an irritated scowl at the ceiling. "So help me, if it's those missionaries again and you're trying to tell me I'm supposed to get religion, you're fired as my guardian angel."

Even I could sense the irony in that statement, and my lips were quirking with humor as I flung open the door again.

It was Ian, standing on the step in a nice black suit and gray tie. Behind him, I could see Finn sitting in the car, his hair slicked wetly down, watching me anxiously.

"I came to see if you'd change your mind," Ian said quickly before I could speak. "About dinner at Eamonn's. Please come. Finn thinks you're mad at him because of the mix-up and him lying to you. He's worried he won't be welcome here anymore. If you come, he'll see it's all right." When I didn't reply, he licked his lips and asked, "It is all right, isn't it? If he still comes over sometimes? I think it's important to him. He doesn't connect with many people, but he seems to like you. Now that the cat's out of the bag, it seems you're all he talks about."

I looked down at my mud-stained jeans and thought a moment. And remembered the vow I had made that no child would ever feel unwelcome in my home.

"It'll take me a few minutes to get dressed," I said.

Ian smiled. "Thank you," he said quietly.

I left him standing in the hall and ran upstairs to take a three-minute shower, pushing my hair into a cap because there wasn't time to wash and dry it. I went to my room and opened my closet. The old dilemma again. Since the divorce, my wardrobe consisted primarily of work clothes and ratty jeans. I owned one plain black skirt and a pearl-gray blouse that would look okay with it, but I hadn't pressed either one, and besides, if I wore it now it would look as if I were trying to match Ian's suit. Instead, I pulled on a short-sleeved muted floral print blouse and clean black pants, brushed my hair, slapped on some mascara, and went back downstairs. Ian was standing where I'd left him on the front steps. I could see his face change when he saw me.

"You look beautiful," he said.

"Thanks." I'd been thrown together in a hurry, and I still wasn't sure about not showing up in a dress, but his compliment seemed sincere. And when I came out to the car, Finn gave me such a huge, relieved smile that suddenly I felt radiant. My appearance was forgotten. Was Finn really that happy I wasn't angry with him? Did I mean that much to him?

Did he mean that much to *me*?

As Ian pulled the car into the road, I examined my feelings and discovered I'd been sad about missing the dinner today as much because I'd miss Finn's company as because I'd miss Ian's. Or maybe it was the other way round—Ian had grown on me as much as his son had.

As we sped away from the house, I glanced back at it, sitting smugly behind its trimmed bushes. I had the feeling it was smirking.

Chapter Twelve

There wasn't time for a lot of conversation before we pulled up in front of Eamonn and Shelley's house. It was a big redbrick home surrounded by maple trees with a tire swing hanging from one of them. A pair of rollerblades lay on the front steps, and the grass had been worn down in patches. One of the rain gutters jutted at a crazy angle from the eaves, like a cowlick. It was a plucky house, like a frazzled housewife who nonetheless had a good-natured smile for every guest.

"Should I have brought something?" I asked worriedly. "I hate showing up with empty hands."

Ian reached into the back seat and pulled out a covered dish, which he handed to me.

"You can carry the potato salad if it makes you feel better," he said.

Finn scampered ahead of us to the door. He was dressed in nice pants and a dress shirt, but it was coming untucked already and his tie hung askew. Ian saw me watching him and gave a rueful laugh.

"It's like trying to tame a cyclone," he said. "Just when you think you have hold of him, he slips around you and gets away."

"I like that about him," I said. "He has spirit. It will serve him well in life."

"Yes, well, unfortunately it doesn't serve him well in school." Ian followed Finn into the house without knocking, holding the door for me. The snug entryway was already filled with cast-off shoes, and we were bombarded with noise. People were laughing, talking, shouting, and somewhere a baby was crying. Ian leaned down and whispered in my ear, his breath warm on my cheek.

"Brace yourself. The whole family's here."

The family turned out to consist of Ian's petite and beautiful, white-haired Irish mother Peggy, his sister Margaret and her husband and two sons, his sister Jenny and her husband and four sons (one of them the crying newborn), and Eamonn and Shelley (who was off somewhere attending to something) with their six-year-old daughter. Even with only seventeen people in the spacious house, they were a rambunctious group and it felt more like forty people. Peggy greeted Finn with a shout and a big hug, which were returned with equal enthusiasm. She stood on tiptoe to hug Ian, and then she turned with open arms and a broad smile to me. My family hadn't been the hugging type, and I was caught off guard for a second. I returned her embrace awkwardly, but Peggy's warmth soon put me at ease. I found myself drawn into the kitchen and put to work slicing a large ham with an electric knife. Ian was sent to the basement to bring up bags of ice from the freezer. Finn was swept away into a game by his noisy cousins.

Jenny, standing next to me at the counter, laughed at my befuddled expression. She was taller than I by a couple of inches and her hair was a gorgeous mix between copper red and autumn brown.

"Things will calm down once the food is on the table," she assured me, dumping frozen peas into a pot and filling it with water. "We feed the kids on a picnic table in the backyard so we can get some peace."

"I don't mind a little pandemonium," I confessed. "My home growing up was always too quiet. This feels more celebratory."

Jenny set the pot on the stove and added a dash of salt. Her smile slipped a little as she said, "It is celebratory. But it's Mom's first Mother's Day without Dad. I'm sure Ian told you. He died of cancer last fall."

"I'm sorry, I'd forgotten," I said quietly. "It must be a difficult day for you, then."

"Actually, it feels better than I thought it would. Dad always loved having the grandkids over. He would have wanted us to make sure Mom enjoyed her party." She flipped her hair back over one shoulder. "Anyway, he's not really gone, you know? It feels like he's here, and I think he'll enjoy this day as much as the rest of us." She moved away to take her squalling baby from Peggy, who was bouncing him in her arms and making squeaky sounds at him.

I finished slicing the ham and arranged it neatly on a platter. I was poking through the clutter on the counter looking for plastic wrap to put over it when Ian came into the kitchen.

"That looks good." He snitched a piece from the platter and ate it.

"I can't find the plastic wrap," I told him. "I don't want it to dry out."

"You won't find plastic wrap here. Shelley is a green-living eco-fiend. Here, use aluminum foil. Though I've heard it asserted that aluminum has been linked to Alzheimer's. There's no escape—something will always get you in the end." He fitted the sheet of foil over the platter and wiggled his eyebrows at me. "Though a little dementia might go unnoticed around here," he added cheerfully.

He carried the platter into the dining room, and I followed. The table had been set with blue-patterned Corelle, and a blue glass vase in the center held a spray of spring flowers. The table was already groaning with food, and Ian had trouble finding room for the ham. Margaret was directing her husband Eric in placing the chairs. Peggy was now hunting through the drawers of a sideboard.

"I thought Shelley had blue candles. I could have sworn she said she did. Ian, be a dear and check above the fridge in that basket, will you?"

I wasn't sure about the wisdom of having open flames with so many children running about and jostling each other, but Ian went back to the kitchen to look. Peggy came over and took my elbow.

"Come here, Kerris. Let me show you."

She drew me over to a far wall, where an arrangement of family photos hung in matching black frames. She kept hold of my arm as she pointed to the largest frame in the center of the cluster.

"That's Patrick, Ian's father."

I could hear the warmth and adoration in her voice. It was the same tone Grandma had used when speaking of her deeply loved husband, my Grandpa Jack, who had died twenty years before I was born. She'd often told me stories about him and how she'd been left as a young widow to raise my mother alone. I had heard the loneliness in her voice when she spoke of him, even all those years later. In spite of Peggy's smile, I heard the same thing in her voice now.

I moved to take a closer look. It was a black and white photo, probably taken some years ago. The man in the portrait looked about fifty, with thick dark hair and a strong jaw. His lips were turned up slightly in a crooked smile, as if he found this whole portrait-taking thing a joke, and his eyes were friendly. He had the same impish look as Finn when he was up to something. I felt a sudden sense of regret that I hadn't had the chance to meet him.

"He looks like he should be in a movie," I said.

"Patrick was very handsome," Peggy agreed. "We were married for forty-four years."

"That's a long time."

"Is your father still living, Kerris?"

"Yes. He lives in California."

"Oh. Your mother too?"

"She died last year."

"Oh, then today is difficult for you too, dear," Peggy said matter-of-factly, giving my elbow a squeeze. "I'm glad you could come be with us. It must be hard to be without her today."

How to explain that my mother and I had never shared the kind of closeness I could feel in this house? That she hadn't been there to comfort me during my divorce, but wouldn't have really been there to do that anyway, even if she had lived? My last memories of my mother were of her shrieking at me from her hospital bed, brutal and enraged, almost unrecognizable. Even though my rational mind had understood that it was her brain tumor that had transformed her so completely, in my heart I felt it was as if the resentment and anger she had built up all her life had risen to engulf her entire mind at the end. I swallowed hard.

"Thank you. It's kind of you to have me," I said. I turned to the other photos on the wall. "Are these the rest of the family?"

She pointed them out to me, and I could hear the pleasure in her voice. "That's Margaret when she graduated from high school. Those are her two boys, Todd and Will, on the first day of school one year. And this is Jenny and Greg on their wedding day. She had braces at the time; she's mortified by this picture and is always after Eamonn to take it down, but I love it. These are her two oldest—Eamonn needs to update this wall, doesn't he? Greg Junior and Nathan aren't even on it. Oh my. And this is Eamonn and Shelley with their daughter Bridie."

"That's an unusual name."

"It's short for Bridget."

Bridie was a white-blonde pixie with a gap-toothed grin. Shelley was a plump blonde woman with pointy-framed glasses. I realized I had not yet met her, despite the fact that this was her home.

"Is Shelley here somewhere?"

"Out in the backyard fighting the bees away from the kids' picnic table. She'll be in soon," Peggy said. "That's me and Patrick on our wedding day." She pointed to a faded photo showing two solemn-faced teenagers, he in a suit that looked too big for him, and she in a frothy short dress and holding a single rose. It was charming. I could see her beauty developing even then, though I thought Peggy was the type of woman who became more and more lovely with maturity. I glanced at her now, thinking that her pure-white hair and the spray of fine lines around her eyes suited her. I was glad she hadn't dyed her hair or tried to smooth those wrinkles out. They illuminated the happiness in her face.

"And of course, this is Ian."

Ian looked a bit thinner but otherwise the same in a t-shirt and jeans. He held a chubby toddler in one arm, who had to be Finn judging from the scowl on the kid's face and the hair sticking up like a rooster comb. Ian's other arm was around the shoulders of a pretty, dark-haired woman who was laughing into the camera. She was slim and wore a button-down blouse and capri pants, her feet bare.

"Julia," I murmured.

"Julia," Peggy agreed. "She died when Finn was seven. But I guess Ian has told you about that."

"No, actually. He hasn't said anything. He has Finn, of course, so I assumed he was married before, and Eamonn mentioned Julia had died. That's all I know, really."

"Oh." Peggy seemed surprised at this. "Well, I'm sure there just hasn't been time to tell you about it. You haven't known each other long, have you?"

"No. Only a few weeks." It sounded ridiculously short.

"She died three years ago in a car crash. She was picking Finn up from a friend's house not ten minutes from home." Peggy reached out and touched one finger lightly to the photo, caressing not Julia, but Finn.

"That's terrible. I'm so sorry."

"Finn was in the car," Peggy said softly. "He hasn't been the same little boy since. It's like he doesn't trust the world anymore. All the light went right out of him." She turned away from the photos and called brightly, "Time to eat! Everybody come!"

The message was relayed from person to person through the house. It took a while to sort everyone out, filtering the kids out to the picnic table, slotting the adults into the chairs in the dining room. Eamonn and Shelley finally made an appearance, Eamonn slicked up so nicely in a suit and tie that he hardly seemed the same person. Shelley, in an unfortunate purple caftan that clashed with her red hair, gushed over me, swatted Eamonn's hands away from the ham as he tried to sneak a piece, and generally bossed everyone, but she was so good-natured about it, no one minded. I imagined she was the stereotypical big sister of the family. Her visible happiness distracted you from the caftan's lurid color.

Peggy sat at the head of the table and clapped her hands together. "Grace! We forgot grace. Call the kids back in again."

So the kids were trooped back in, and Eamonn said a brief but heartfelt prayer over the food. Everyone fell silent as he spoke, eyes closed, some of them with hands folded.

I kept my eyes on the floor and tried not to squirm. Demonstrations of belief always made me feel awkward and slightly resentful. My father's faith certainly hadn't kept him from breaking the commandment against adultery many times. Who knew where he was now and with whom? I could still hear Mom's voice, bitterly scoffing at ministers preaching on TV when she stumbled across them. Dad's desertion had so biased her against religion that she would even turn away from the Salvation Army woman who stood ringing her bell in the mall, collecting for charity at Christmas. Mom may have given me and my sister a cynical life view, but it was realistic.

But today is hardly the time to be dredging up all of that, I scolded myself silently. These people believe in what they are doing, and they seem genuine and nice.

I was distracted from my dark thoughts by the sound of my own name as Eamonn went on with his prayer.

"Thank you that Kerris could join us today and that we could all gather to celebrate Mother's Day with our wonderful mother. We're also thankful we had such a great dad and know that he's with us today."

I looked up then and saw that, like me, Finn stood somewhat apart. He held still, his fists at his sides, but his lips were pressed tightly together and his eyes were narrowed to little slits as he studied Eamonn. I reviewed in my mind what Eamonn had said. Was Finn wondering why his own wonderful mother wasn't there too? My heart ached for him, and it was all I could do not to cross the room and put my arms around him.

As if he felt my gaze upon him, Finn turned his head and looked at me. I couldn't read his expression, but I thought I saw his shoulders rise in a deep breath then fall in a long exhalation.

There was a heartfelt Amen, and Finn kicked into action as the kids scampered back to the backyard. Margaret and Jenny went to help serve them their dinner. Eamonn poured out ice water and there was a toast to Patrick McGrath. Then Peggy set down her glass and reached for the covered dish Ian had brought.

"I hope this is your famous potato salad. I haven't had it for ages."

"Remember the time you thought the chili pepper was paprika and sprinkled it over the whole salad?" Eamonn teased. He arched an eyebrow in my direction. "Blistered the roof of my mouth."

I watched the dishes being passed round, listened to the happy chatter, and felt drawn into it like a log sailing down a river. I should have felt totally alien and apart, but instead I felt carried along and completely at home. It occurred to me that I hadn't heard so much laughter in a long time, and my heart soaked it in. The McGraths treated me like one of the family, nudging my chair over a few inches to make room as Jenny and Margaret returned from helping the kids. Jenny sat on my left, jiggling baby Nathan on her lap while eating with one hand. Ian sat on my right, having an animated political conversation with Eamonn across the table from him. I felt as if I'd wandered onto the movie set of My Big Fat Greek Wedding. Only this was My Big Fat Irish Mother's Day.

Chapter Thirteen

"So tell us about yourself," Shelley suddenly said, her voice rising above the others'. I looked up to see she was addressing me. The others quieted and all eyes turned expectantly to me.

"Um . . . what would you like to know?" I asked, lowering my fork. It suddenly felt like a job interview, but I wasn't sure what I was applying for.

"You've just moved here from Toronto, Ian was saying?"

"Yes, just a couple months ago."

"She's in that old empty house on Rannick," Eamonn chipped in.

"That old place?" Shelley marveled. "It looks like it's falling to pieces."

"Kerris is fixing it up," Ian informed her. "She renovates houses for a living."

"Does she! How clever!" Peggy clapped her hands together. "Do you have your own business?"

"Yes."

"What a refreshing thing, to meet a woman who does something besides type or teach or clean teeth for a career."

"Now Mom, women do lots of things these days," Margaret protested. "They can be stockbrokers or judges or politicians—"

Peggy pointed to Margaret. "Admin Assistant." She pointed to Jenny. "Teacher." She pointed to Shelley. "Dental hygienist."

"Yes, well, we don't represent all women everywhere," Jenny protested.

"Eamonn thought I might know who used to own your house," Peggy said, turning back to me. "But I'm afraid I don't. I do remember seeing an elderly woman in the front yard, watering the flowers or sitting on the porch reading. But I never spoke to her or knew her name."

"A woman?" I wasn't surprised. The house had, after all, that definite feminine feeling about it, gentle and quiet. "Do you remember what she looked like?"

"Not really. Maybe about eighty years old. Gray hair, tall, thin. I'm afraid that's all I know."

"Why?" Shelley asked, looking from me to Peggy. "Don't you know who used to live there?"

"I inherited the house," I told her. "But I don't know who from."

There was a puzzled silence, and then Margaret murmured, "How odd."

"Well, maybe I can find another neighbor who knew her," I said, suddenly shy with so many sets of speculative eyes turned on me. "I really haven't gotten to know many people yet. Just—well, mostly just your family, really, and one neighbor who recently moved here, like me, so she wasn't able to help me."

"Have you tried the land registry office?" Greg suggested.

I blinked at him. Of course! Why hadn't I thought of that? It seemed so obvious.

"I'll try that, thanks," I said.

"Do you come from a big family?" Shelley pressed on, regaining control of the hijacked conversation.

"No," I said. "I have one sister, that's all."

"Imagine!" "How lonely!" "Is that all?" came the chorus of comments.

"I think it's cool," husband Eric ventured. "You'd hardly have to share the TV or wait in line for the bathroom."

"If you'd ever finish building that bathroom in our basement, you wouldn't have to wait," Margaret pointed out. "Maybe we should have Kerris finish it for us, if you're never going to get to it."

"I'd be happy to," I said, "but I'm sure Eric will do a fine job."

"No, actually, I'll bungle it up completely," Eric said brightly. "It'll take me ages to figure it out, and I'll probably flood the basement while I do it. Why don't you come have a look at it one day?"

"All right, if you'd like." I laughed.

"Kerris will do a great job for you," Ian added. "You should see how she's fixing up her place. It's turning out beautiful."

I couldn't help smiling at his words. "Thanks. It still has a way to go."

"Where does your sister live?" Shelley persisted with the original topic.

"Toronto. She's a cosmetologist." How to say I only talked to her once in a blue moon, that she wasn't really on my radar?

"Oh, I've always been interested in the stars and constellations and all that," Shelley said. "I had a telescope once, when I was young. I wonder where it ended up?"

There was a moment of silence at the table while everyone blinked at her.

"Cosmetologist," Ian finally said. "Not cosmologist."

Shelley frowned at him, puzzling over this.

"So what else do you like to do?" Jenny asked quickly, smiling at me. "Besides renovating houses, I mean."

"I don't have a lot of other hobbies," I said. "I read a lot. I sew a little."

Shelley had gone a bit pink, but she rallied again with enthusiasm. "Do you like to cook?" she asked me.

"I like to, but I'm not very good at it. I'm better with a table saw than an oven."

"Well, I hope you'll like our little town," Jenny began, but Shelley spoke over the top of her. "I'll be happy to help you out there. I'm told I've some skill in the kitchen. I'd be glad to pass along some of my recipes."

"Thanks," I said.

"We could get together and cook, even, if you like."

"Thanks," I said again, not sure I relished this thought.

"Leave her alone," Margaret said. "Not everyone has to cook like Jamie Oliver, you know."

"I was just offering," Shelley said. "If we brush up her skills a little, maybe we can help rustle her up a husband." She shot a grin at Ian, who stiffened beside me. There was an uncomfortable silence for a moment around the table, and then Eric began to say something. But Shelley cut across him too.

"I'm surprised you haven't settled down sooner, Kerris. I was married at twenty-one."

"Oh?" I couldn't think what to say to this.

"But I guess not everyone is lucky enough to find their perfect match right off." She twinkled her eyes at Eamonn, who looked down at his plate and poked at his ham.

"Shelley—" Margaret began.

I had known it was bound to come up sooner or later, but I hadn't planned on quite this venue for it. Oh well, it wasn't as if Ian had never sprung something on *me*. I cleared my throat and said, "Actually, I was married. For six years."

"Oh." Shelley's eyes widened with interest and she leaned forward. I knew she was preparing some consoling words on my loss. I heard my voice say flatly, "We recently divorced."

"Oh Kerris, I'm sorry," Jenny, beside me, said swiftly, and she briefly touched my hand where it lay on the tablecloth. I gave her a grateful smile.

"That's dreadful," Shelley said in dismay. I half expected, judging from her expression, that she was going to remind me that this was a good Irish Catholic family that didn't believe in divorce, but Ian shifted in his chair and spoke first.

"I'm not sure Kerris wants to talk about it," he said firmly. "Is there anything for dessert?"

Even Shelley realized she'd pried too far. She retreated quickly. "There's cherry pie and vanilla ice cream. Eamonn, come help me get it."

She left the table. Eamonn sent me an apologetic grimace and followed her. There was a tangible sense of relief around the table as the kitchen door closed behind them.

Peggy picked up her water glass. "When you have a close-knit family, there are sometimes boundary issues," she murmured to no one in particular.

Jenny's husband Greg gave a snort of laughter, and beside me, Jenny chuckled.

"Remember, Greg? We'd just been married, Kerris, just got back from our honeymoon, in fact. The first time we came here for dinner, Shelley met me at the door with 'What, married three weeks and you're not pregnant yet? What's wrong?'"

"Well, you've certainly made up for lost time," Peggy said wryly, nodding at child number four in Jenny's arms. Jenny collapsed into giggles. I felt my own face split into a grin.

"No harm done," I murmured.

I felt Ian lean slightly to bump my shoulder gently with his.

The easy conversation returned to the table with the pie and ice cream. I listened to stories about Peggy McGrath and some of her more daring moments—shingling her own roof in a rainstorm, driving alone up to Lake of the Woods for a vacation, fighting away a black bear with a broom—and heard the admiration and love in her children's voices. Then memories of Mom turned into accounts of Dad—Patrick McGrath as his children remembered him, his humor, his charm, his sly Irish wit. He sounded as if he had been as feisty and mischievous as his wife. Again, I wished I could have met him. I suspected his grandson Finn would grow up to be like him. I thought Grandpa Jack might have been something like him, too. I suppose that was understandable; they'd grown up in the same era, after all. Though Patrick had grown up in Ireland and Jack had been raised in Canada, they both had lived in a time when you made your own entertainment, and from the stories it sounded as if they'd both been quick to find trouble. Perhaps being teenagers through World War II, old enough to know what was happening but too young to join in, would have given them much in common, too.

Finally, after one story about how Patrick and his two brothers tipped over an outhouse with their younger sister in it, Ian pushed back from the table and sighed.

"If I keep sitting here, I'll keep eating, and I'm ready to burst. Want to go for a walk, Kerris?"

"Sure." I hadn't realized how long we'd sat at the table. My legs felt asleep. "But shouldn't we help clear up?"

Shelley jumped to her feet. "I've got it. Don't worry about it. You two go have your walk."

The children were still in the backyard, having abandoned the littered table in favor of a rowdy game of tag. Finn was in the thick of it, using a garden hose to squirt the others to tag them out. His shirt was soaked and he had grass stains on the knees of his nice pants. His tie had disappeared. Ian and I skirted the group and headed along a pathway that led from the backyard to a nearby park.

"I think I ate more today than I have all week," I moaned. "I will say, Shelley does have a way with food. That was the best pie I've ever had. Maybe I *should* let her teach me to cook."

Ian pushed his hands into his pockets and kicked a pebble along with his shoe as we walked.

"I hope she didn't upset you too much," he said. "She means well, but she's nosy and she talks without thinking first."

"No, I don't mind answering her questions. I just . . . it's fairly recent. I haven't figured out yet how to phrase it."

"What do you mean?"

"Your mother told me how Julia died. We were looking at her picture in the dining room."

He nodded but said nothing.

"If people ask you what happened, you can tell them. It was a car accident. People can grasp that and know how to react to it. She didn't mean to leave you." I stopped in the middle of the path and turned to face him, unconsciously gripping my hands together in front of me. "But Ian, how do you tell people your husband just stopped loving you? That you weren't enough for him? That he told you he didn't want a family with you, and then he turned around and had a baby with someone who used to be your best friend?"

I heard the tremor in my voice and looked down at the ground. Ian said nothing, only stood there looking at me. Far away, I could hear the shouts of children's laughter. I swallowed hard. The shame of it was overwhelming sometimes, the bewilderment, the disbelief. After my parents' nasty marriage, I had vowed I would make mine work. I would be careful in my choice. I wouldn't end up with a man like my father . . . but then I had.

My eyes refocused, climbing back up from the darkness, and I realized Ian was still just standing there. I didn't look up, not sure what I'd see in his face. I didn't want pity, and yet I wanted *something*.

There was a pause, and then I saw Ian's feet step forward until they were toe to toe with mine. His arms went around me, and I let myself rest against him, his chest safe and solid beneath my cheek, his chin resting on the top of my head. I waited for him to say the same useless things people had said to me before: "Such a shame." "Not your fault." "Unbelievable." "What nerve!" But he said nothing, only held me, and I found it immensely comforting.

How long we stood there, I don't know, but I felt as if strength were flowing from him into me. It was gentle and perfect and just what I needed. When at last his arms loosened, I was able to step back and smile up at him dry eyed.

"Thanks," I said.

Ian gazed down at me and asked softly, "Better?"

"Yes, actually. That helped."

He stepped back, took my hand carefully in his, and we resumed our walk along the path. I could no longer hear the children behind us. Above us, an airplane hummed steadily along through a pearl-white sky. The sun was already dropping lower behind the trees.

"Is this how it was for you after Julia?" I asked hesitantly. "Some days I'm fine and some days it hits me like a brick to the head. Like I don't quite believe I ended up alone here, like this."

"Yes. It's been three years, but I still have occasional days like that," Ian replied. Then he added, "I think Finn has a lot of them."

I thought about what Kevin Jameson had said. What Ian himself had said about his son. "Is that why he—he's a handful?"

Ian made a little puffing sound through his nose. "A handful. Yeah, something like that. Finn was in the car when it happened. He had only minor injuries, but Julia was killed instantly. It was . . . not a clean death." He swallowed and was silent a moment, then went on. "Finn was seven. He remembers all of it. He doesn't have as many nightmares as he used to have, though. It might be beginning to fade. His therapist told me it should fade a lot sooner than this, but Finn is nothing if not tenacious." He shot me a crooked smile.

"There isn't a timeline on grief," I observed.

"No, there isn't," Ian agreed.

I tried not to smile. "Somehow I can't picture Finn sitting and talking to a therapist."

"He doesn't seem to mind so much anymore, actually. He goes to see a really great guy who plays ping pong and video games with him while they talk. Says it draws things out of Finn without him realizing it because he's focused on the game and not on keeping his walls up."

"Does it help?"

"I don't know. Sometimes I feel he's returning to himself, and sometimes it feels like there's been very little progress. Until recently." Ian slid his gaze to me. "Finn doesn't seem to be battling the world quite as fervently these days. I hear he's even made a friend." He nudged me with his shoulder again, and I felt ridiculously pleased.

We reached the end of the park and turned back, walking leisurely along in the lengthening shadows beneath the maple trees. A boy sped past on his bicycle, followed by a yellow Labrador running with its tongue lolling out. Other than that, we were alone in the park. "Thank you for inviting me today," I said. "And giving me a second chance to come."

He gave my hand a little squeeze. "Thank you for not letting my family send you screaming for the door."

"They're nice. I like them. Especially Jenny."

"She's the best of the lot," he agreed.

"Finn is welcome to come over anytime," I said. "Make sure he knows."

"I will. Thanks."

"You're welcome to come over, too," I added.

We were nearing where the path emptied into the backyard, and we could hear laughter and shouting again. Someone yelled out, "Oh Finn, not the windows! Aim away from the house."

"I hope it's the hose he's aiming and not a baseball," Ian sighed.

I started to laugh. Ian stopped, looking down at me, and then he reached out and took my face in both his hands. I grew still as he dropped his mouth onto mine in a firm, intense kiss that left me breathless.

"That one wasn't for Shelley's benefit," he said roughly.

"Oh!" I couldn't think what to say. How to explain that his kiss had felt completely natural to me? As if a little voice in my head had responded, *Of course.* Had he felt it too? I stood a moment, surprised that the numbness that had coated me for so long seemed to have dissolved without my realizing it. When had it started slipping away? And why hadn't it left me exposed and raw as I had expected?

It seemed too soon to go back into the house, then. I wanted to be alone with Ian a little longer, to absorb this turn of events, and to have him all to myself before his family descended on us again. Apparently, Ian felt the same way, because he took my hand again and veered left, skirting the end of the yard and continuing on through the trees. We walked in companionable silence a while, and I pushed away the niggling question of Mrs. Jameson. I wouldn't think about that. I didn't really want to think of anything beyond the warmth of his hand around mine.

When the path emerged from the trees into the fading sunlight, I looked up, expecting to be back in the park again, but instead I saw rows of tidy headstones and the color bursts of flowers and realized we had entered a cemetery. The path continued through the grounds, meandering beneath occasional pergolas and around fountains. The air was thick with the blossoms' perfume. It was a pleasant if somewhat contrived spot, and the setting sun turned the granite headstones a pretty pink and lavender.

"I've always liked it here," Ian told me. "It's peaceful. Sometimes I bring Finn here for a picnic with his mom. Red tartan blanket, baloney sandwiches, and all. I draw the line at letting Finn bring a Frisbee, but . . . I don't know. I think he finds comfort in it, sitting and eating and feeling as if she's with us. Does that sound weird?"

"Not at all," I said. "I think it's sweet. You're a good dad."

"She's over there," Ian said, nodding toward a shady corner of the grounds. But he didn't head in that direction, and we continued along the asphalt path, winding our way toward the main gate that led to the street.

"Some of these stones look really old," I observed. "Are there pioneer graves here too?"

"I think it's the only cemetery in Smoke River," Ian said. "So it stands to reason that the oldest graves would date back to about

1850, when the town was settled. That part over there by the fence is newer. Once it's filled, I suppose they'll be looking at buying more land somewhere else."

I glanced toward the newer section, following his gesture, and paused. And looked again.

"That's funny," I said. I walked closer, squinting in the dusk.

"What?"

"The name on this stone. It just jumped out at me." I stopped in front of a short, square block of light-colored granite with dark letters etched deeply into the smooth surface. "Abigail Scott Borden. Born February 1st, 1931." A funny chill went up my arms. I drew my hand from Ian's to wrap my arms around myself, shivering. I looked up at him in confusion.

"That's my grandmother's name and birthdate," I said.

Chapter Fourteen

After Ian took me home that evening (with Finn sitting on one of Peggy's towels to keep from getting the car seat muddy), I sat at the kitchen table with my jacket still on and the lights off. I thought about making myself some hot tea but remained sitting, unmoving. I wanted to think about Ian's hands cupping my face, of his kiss sweet on my lips, but that granite headstone kept crowding everything else out of my mind. There could be other Abigail Scott Bordens, couldn't there? But what were the odds of finding one with the same birthdate? I couldn't swear the year 1931 was accurate, but the date February 1st I was sure of. We had moved from Ottawa to live with my grandmother soon after Christmas, when I was eleven, and we had celebrated my grandmother's birthday right after, on February 1st. I was positive about it. The day was etched in my memory because my mother had been so sour and angry since the move, but she made extra effort to be cheerful that day. We'd taken Grandma to brunch and Mom had smiled and laughed and given her yellow roses. I remembered.

But Grandma had died a year later, when I was twelve, much too suddenly and too soon, and I had mourned her—still mourned her—even more than I missed the father who had walked out of my life.

"So it can't be Grandma in the Smoke River Cemetery," I argued aloud with my reflection in the darkened window. My own face looked pale and elongated with strain. "Because she died in 1997, and the stone in the cemetery said that *that* Abigail Borden died March 11, 2012. And what would she be doing in Smoke River anyway? Grandma died in Toronto."

I rose stiffly from the table and realized I'd been sitting for over an hour, unmoving. I pulled the drapes closed over my pale reflection and plugged in the electric tea kettle. I took off my jacket and stood hugging it to me.

The thing was, I couldn't remember Grandma's funeral. I remembered everything else—the shock of Mom's sudden announcement, the gut-wrenching despair at the realization that my grandmother's comforting presence was no longer there, even the giant pink sympathy card that my friends at school all signed for me. I remembered Grandma's closet standing empty, her clothes and bedspread and things so swiftly packed up and swept away, as if Mom had been in a hurry to remove her memory from the house. That was all there, every detail etched into my mind. But I didn't remember going to the funeral home or the cemetery or seeing my grandmother's casket. It was a blank.

I waited until a decent hour the next morning before I phoned my sister Gillian in Toronto, knowing she wasn't an early riser by any means. She answered on the second ring, and when she heard my voice, she sounded genuinely happy to hear from me.

When I had first told her about the house-from-nowhere, when I'd arrived home shell-shocked from the lawyer's office, she had been as bewildered as I. "I wish I'd been left a house," she had responded, and then she'd laughed. "No, I don't. I can't imagine living out in the boondocks on my own. I could never leave the city. And Jeremy wouldn't be caught dead out of Toronto. He doesn't even go to the west end."

"Jeremy?"

"Latest boyfriend," my sister had said cheerily. "This one might be a keeper. He's a photographer. Gorgeous. Plays the piano like a dream."

I had suppressed the sigh before it could escape my lips. Gillian was always hopeful that *this* one would be a keeper. And without fail, the relationship never worked out. I sent a little silent wish across the phone line that this time would be different, and I tried not to sound hesitant as I asked her now, "How's Jeremy?" And crossed my fingers.

"He's great! He's out on a job today, in fact—some hot-shot wedding in Thornhill."

"That's good news," I said with relief. So he was still in the picture. (No pun intended.)

We chatted a moment longer, and then I worked myself around to the reason I had phoned.

"I need to ask you something, Gill. How old were you when Grandma died, seven? Do you remember going to her funeral?"

"What a morbid question, Kerris!"

"Do you? Do you remember Mom taking us?"

"No."'

"Neither do I."

"So maybe Mom left us home," she said. "We were pretty young. Maybe she didn't want us to attend."

"I guess," I said slowly, unconvinced. "I know I took her death pretty hard. Wouldn't Mom have let us go say our goodbyes, at least?"

"Maybe she died in some—disfiguring way," Gillian suggested. "And Mom didn't want to traumatize us."

"She didn't," I snapped without meaning to. "Mom said she died of a stroke. And when we were older, Mom never took us to visit the grave. I don't even know where Grandma was buried, do you? Don't you think that's weird, Gillian?"

"Well, I don't know. Maybe she was trying to spare us. Though frankly, that doesn't sound like Mom." She gave a sharp laugh. "I don't think Mom was overly concerned about protecting us from anything. I mean, look how she went on and on about Dad, every time he misbehaved or—or gave us another half-sibling we'd never meet. She didn't try to protect us from *that*."

I pondered this, hearing the bitterness in my sister's voice. We had never really talked about our father or our mother's bitter reaction to his betrayal. But from the tone of Gillian's voice, I thought she felt pretty much the same way I did about it all.

"Not necessarily," I said, wondering why I was defending Mom. "I mean, she found out about those half-siblings somehow. He obviously kept in touch with her to some degree. We never had contact with him after he left, but maybe that was because she was trying to run interference for us, to protect us."

"We don't know if Dad ever *tried* to contact us. What if he did? What if he wanted us, but she was so mad she just kept him from us?"

I had wondered this myself, as a kid, but the hope had died long ago. I didn't want to encourage it in my sister. "He could have pushed for access if he'd wanted it. And he hasn't reached out since Mom died," I pointed out.

"Maybe he doesn't know. I mean, who would have told him she died?"

"How could we have told him? We don't even know where he is, other than California."

"We could look him up on the internet. I bet we could find him," Gillian suggested, sounding wistful.

I shook my head, even though she couldn't see it. "I wouldn't want to, to be honest. And I doubt you should either. He has another life now. If he wanted contact, he could look *us* up."

There was a glum pause.

"We had a pretty messed-up childhood," Gillian said.

"Yes, we did."

"We're not the first kids whose father walked away."

"No, we're not."

"How many half siblings do you figure we have by now?"

"I lost count at six," I said.

And then suddenly both of us were laughing, howling into the phone, the laughter building to near hysterics before we managed to bring it under control. I wiped my eyes with the back of my hand and smiled into the phone.

"Thanks, sis. I needed that."

"Me too. So when do I get to come see your magic castle?"

"My what?"

"The house your fairy godmother left you. Are you settled in?"

I felt a funny shiver. "It's funny you say it that way. Did you ever feel like you had a fairy godmother growing up?"

"Gosh, no. If I had, I would have held her at knife point until she granted me three wishes. I would have wished for hair like Shauna Martinson's. I would have wished for a horse."

I chuckled. "And your third wish?"

"I would have wished for Grandma back," Gillian said softly.

There was a strained silence, and then I said quietly, "Me too."

"Though, you know, now that you mention it, I guess there have been a couple of things over the years that I couldn't explain."

"Like what?"

"Well, once I had bail posted for me and when I asked who had done it, I was just told 'a friend.' There's no way you and Mom would have even known I'd been arrested. And anyway, Mom wouldn't have done it even if she had known. But I don't know who else might have. I've always wondered."

"Oh," I said, feeling my heart clinch. "What was it for? The arrest, I mean." I was afraid to hear.

"Can't even recall now. Oh, no, that time it was possession. Oh, and once I did a stint at a private rehab camp, and at the end I was told the bill had been settled. I didn't have to pay a thing. I never did find out who paid for it. I guess having a fairy godmother is as good an explanation as any."

Her casual mention of jail and rehab gripped my heart and made it difficult to breathe. I hadn't known a thing about either.

"I haven't been a great big sister to you, have I?" I said regretfully.

I could almost hear her shrug. "I survived, didn't I? We both did."

"Yeah," I said, but I wasn't too sure it was the truth.

The land registry office would have to wait for a trip to Toronto, as I learned their records weren't online. But Monday morning, after a sudden idea, I went to the library and inquired about back issues of old local newspapers from 2012. The helpful librarian showed me how to use the microfilm reader, apologizing every other sentence for not having the entire collection scanned in electronically yet. Budget constraints. Dwindling staff resources. The project should be completed by Christmas, though.

After she returned to her circulation desk, it took me about ten minutes of scrolling through the film through ads and headlines, curling club announcements, and letters to the editor to find the obituary I sought.

Abigail Scott Borden, born February 1, 1931 passed away of heart failure on March 11, 2012 at the age of 81. Originally from Toronto, Abigail resided in Smoke River for the past fifteen years. A former nurse, she was extensively involved in charity work. She was predeceased by her beloved husband Jack Borden in 1965. Abigail will be sorely missed by her church family. Services to be held at DeGroot Funeral Home, 83 Anson Street, Smoke River on Wednesday at 2 p.m. Interment will be in the Smoke River City Cemetery. In lieu of flowers, donations to the Smoke River Friends of the Hospital are encouraged.

I sat staring at the screen for a long time, trying to puzzle this out until my head began to spin. It had to be my grandmother. The name was right, the birthdate, the fact that she was a nurse from Toronto—even my grandfather's name. There were simply too many coincidences. But how to explain it? What was she doing here? And how was it that she had died, not in 1997 as I had been told, but in 2012?

Quickly I did the math. She had been living in Smoke River for the past fifteen years. If she died in 2012, that meant she had moved to Smoke River in 1997.

A chill ran over my scalp and I shivered, hugging my arms around myself. Grandma had been living here all along and I hadn't known. Why had she left and why hadn't she gotten in touch with me since? Why had Mom said Grandma had died when obviously she had been very much alive right up until three years ago? I thought about her empty closet, seeing it now in a new light. She hadn't died. She had packed up and gone.

I *knew* Grandma had loved Gillian and me. When Dad had left, I knew he hadn't cared about us girls, not deep down. I had felt it. But Grandma had been different. Her love had been genuine, I knew it. Then what had happened? Why the lies about it? I was swept with a wave of fury, followed by devastating sorrow. All those years Gillian and I could have had her in our lives, but they had been stolen from us. How could she have done it?

She had left me the house.

The thought hit me clear as a bell, and I knew deep down I was right. I rewound the film with numb hands, pushed away from the table, returned the microfilm to its metal drawer, and left the library in a fog. Slowly I walked back toward home, hands pushed into my jeans pockets. There was so much to take in and there were so many questions cramming my mind, but the main point that kept asserting itself was that Grandma had died in 2012, but I hadn't inherited her house until 2015. Why now?

Because now my mother was dead.

The startling thought came out of nowhere, almost like words breathed into my ear, but I immediately recognized them as true. My inheritance hadn't come to me until after my mother's death.

When I got home—*her* home, I reminded myself—I hesitated in the entryway. Peggy's description of the thin, elderly woman who had lived here fit Grandma's description, and I found myself pausing to listen, to feel . . . I wasn't sure what. A presence? Her essence? Her spirit? She had been here all along, all that time when Gillian and I had *needed* her. I reached out with my thoughts, my very skin, trying to sense her there still.

But all I felt was chilly, and the only thing I heard was the old fridge muttering away. Surely if this had been my grandmother's home, I would have felt it, wouldn't I?

Then again, I *had* felt it, or at least I had felt *something* that first day when I had come to check out the house. I had felt a warmth, a welcoming, a feminine touch. It had felt like home. That flowery scent . . . was that what her home had smelled like when we'd lived with her? I had undeniably experienced that instant familiarity. And I'd felt that hug the other day . . . as if the house *wanted* me here.

I was being ridiculous, I told myself abruptly. I felt ferociously angry. Throwing down my purse and keys, I looked up the number for Grenville and Green and dialed it. Usually getting hold of Mr. Stephenson was difficult, but the administrative assistant must have heard the strain in my voice, because she put the call straight through to the lawyer.

"I know my grandmother is the one who left me this house," I said abruptly.

"Ah. Ms. Wells."

"She did, didn't she?"

"Yes," he acknowledged slowly. "She wanted to remain anonymous, but I told her you would figure it out eventually. Now that you have, yes, I'll confirm it was Abigail Borden who left you the house in Smoke River."

"Why?"

"She cared about you a great deal. She thought you would benefit from having it. And it's all she had to give."

"No, I mean why did she leave us in 1997? She disappeared and we went on living in her house in Toronto. We thought she was *dead*! Why didn't she get in touch with us all those years?"

"I can't really speak to that."

"My mother said she'd died."

"I'm afraid I can't speak to that," he repeated, more gently.

"Can you tell me why I didn't inherit the house until three years after her death?"

"Yes. I was left strict instructions not to contact you until after your mother was deceased. Camille Wells," he added helpfully, as if I didn't know my own mother's name. Then again, I wasn't sure what I knew anymore, or what was true. Mom must have known Grandma was alive. She'd lied about her death. Had Mom lied about Dad too? Was he really in California with girlfriend-number-whatever and a pile of new children? I shook my head to clear it and realized he had continued to talk.

"As soon as I learned of your mother's passing last year, I started the ball rolling."

"Why not until Mom died?"

"I couldn't say. It wasn't my place to ask, really. I just follow my clients' wishes."

"Who arranged for Grandma to be buried here in Smoke River? Was that you?"

"She left me instructions as to her funeral, obituary, and burial, yes, and she left money for the headstone too. The house had to be cleaned out and her personal things disposed of. I organized all of that on her instructions."

"So she knew she was dying?"

I could almost hear him squirming. "Well, no, I wouldn't say she had any intimation of it. But she was eighty-one, after all. She was prepared."

"But why would my mother tell me Grandma died in 1997 if she was still alive? If Grandma cared about me and my sister as you say, why did she just leave?" I heard the plaintiveness in my tone and blushed, but I had to know.

Mr. Stephenson coughed and cleared his throat. "She didn't tell me details, and even if she had, I don't think I'd be at liberty to say. She wanted to remain anonymous, that was all she told me. For what it's worth, I don't think she was happy about it. She disliked your separation. But she kept tabs on you and your sister over the years."

"She did?"

"Yes. She had me hire a private investigation firm to keep an eye on you from afar, so to speak, so that she would know where you were and—and how you were doing."

Someone had been *spying* on me for half of my life? I opened my mouth to exclaim over this, then stopped short. A new thought occurred to me, and the suspicion was hard in my voice as I demanded, "Did she arrange to pay off my student loan for me?"

"Er . . . she really wanted everything to stay anony—"

"You have to tell me. I mean, I think I know already. You just confirm it for me, yes or no. Please, Mr. Stephenson."

He sighed. "Yes, that was your grandmother. I was her intermediary."

"And what about the flowers I got when I graduated? And my prom dress in high school?"

"She had me arrange all that too, yes. You have to understand, I was her friend and assistant as much as I was her lawyer. I knew her—and admired her—for a great number of years."

That had been her hand, guiding me gently all my growing up.

But why wouldn't she let me know she was still alive?

"Was she Gillian's fairy godmother too?" I asked.

There was a pause and then a low chuckle. "Fairy godmother? Is that what you thought?"

"Some anonymous person did nice things for me," I said. "I guess that's how I viewed it. And for Gillian . . ." And now I realized why the kindnesses had come to a halt the last few years. Grandma hadn't been here to instruct him since 2012. I felt a sudden sting behind my eyes and blinked.

"She had me do some things for your sister too, yes. Maintaining confidentiality, as with you."

"She paid for Gillian's rehab. Settled the bill without her knowing anything except that it had been paid."

"Ah. You know about that," he said reluctantly.

"That was you?"

"Yes."

"How did you know Gillian had been arrested?"

There was another hesitation and I prepared to argue, but finally he sighed and said, "The private investigator informed me of it."

"So you paid her bail."

"Your grandmother—um, yes."

"I have a hard time believing a private eye has been spying on me and my sister for years and we never knew."

"Please don't think of it as spying, Ms. Wells. She wanted to be able to be there for you. I know she loved you, and this was the only way she could . . . well, *act* on it. She stepped in where she could to help you."

But why? I leaned against the kitchen counter and scrubbed my free hand down my face, feeling suddenly exhausted. I couldn't reconcile the loving compassion of her acts with her silence for fifteen years. What had made her leave us and only be in our lives thereafter through a private eye and a lawyer?

"Is there anything else, Ms. Wells?"

"Yes. Did my mother know? I mean, she must have known. I mean, in 1997 there wasn't a body to bury—" I couldn't finish the thought. Grandma must have signed the house over to Mom and walked away. They were in cahoots.

There was another pause, and then Mr. Stephenson said gently, "I can tell you that your mother never communicated with your grandmother, to my knowledge. Certainly not through me. I understand they were estranged."

"They were? But we were living with Grandma in her house!" I thought about this, and then had one last query. "Did you get rid of all of Grandma's belongings? Are there any things left?"

"Most of it went in the estate sale. Everything that didn't sell was donated to charity or disposed of, depending . . . I left some of the basic furniture that still looked useful, and some food cans I couldn't donate anywhere and hated to throw out. They still looked okay to use, so I left them in the house."

"Oh." I felt a sharp stab of disappointment. "So everything's gone?"

"Except for the photos. I couldn't bring myself to throw those away, so I tucked them away in a box here in my office. I didn't know what to do with them, considering. But now that you know it was your grandmother's house, I don't think there would be an issue if you wanted them."

I strangled the phone with shaking hands.

"Yes," I said. "I want them."

Chapter Fifteen

Insomnia kept me in its clutches that night, refusing to release me. I paced the house and alternately fumed and wept, missing Grandma one minute so intensely I couldn't breathe, and then so angry with her the next that I wanted to slam out of her house and never return. My anger was equally aimed at my mother. She had deliberately lied to us. Had broken our hearts telling us Grandma had died, and then had stood back and watched us sink into the despair caused by her lie. Knowing all along that she could have told us the truth, so we could have been reunited with our beloved grandmother. And yet Grandma herself had been in on the whole lie. My father's betrayal seemed like nothing compared to this.

How on earth was I to tell Gillian?

Finally, at about four o'clock in the morning, I dropped into a chair at the kitchen table and rested my forehead on my folded arms. I was drained and exhausted, with no shred of energy left. I closed my eyes and whispered into the table. "Why, Grandma? What made you leave us and fake your own death?"

Surely it had to have been something huge. Some grand design. Some devastating thing. Maybe she'd been put into the Witness Protection Program! But no, she'd kept her own name. She'd become demented . . . no, the lawyer would have said something to me. He'd known her for years. And all her careful preparations before her death seemed to indicate a sound mind. But then what? I could think of no good reason for it.

"Please help me understand," I pleaded. "Please help me to understand it so I can let go of this anger. I don't want to be angry with you. I loved you."

I waited for the scent of flowers, for the soft brush of air against my face. But there was nothing, only the house silent around me, and after a while I fell asleep with my head on the table.

The padded envelope arrived in the mail on Friday. It was small, not as big as a standard envelope, so I braced myself to find little in it. I was right. When I ripped the brown wrapping away, I found only five photographs in it.

I carried them to the kitchen table and spread them out, then sat down and stared at them, drinking them in, trying to understand them.

A photo of me and Gillian, when we were about nine and four.

An old black-and-white photo of a handsome man with wickedly laughing eyes, whom I knew instantly to be my grandfather, Jack. I remembered seeing this same photo on the sideboard in Grandma's dining room. He was posed formally, head and shoulders, in suit and tie. The photo had been removed from its frame at some point, and now there were multiple tiny pinpricks in the top edge of it, showing it had been pinned up and taken down several times over the years. I could picture Grandma holding it and tracing his image gently with her fingers. Did I remember her doing that? Or was it just something I could imagine, knowing her love for him?

The next was a group of seven women, all appearing to be in their fifties to seventies, and all wearing dresses or blouses with skirts. They stood in front of a brick wall with arms linked or thrown around each other's shoulders, most of them laughing or mugging for the camera like children. I knew none of their faces.

A snapshot of my mother, taken without her being aware of it, half turned away from the camera as she smiled at someone I couldn't see. It was an older photo, probably taken just before or after her marriage to my father, because her red-brown hair was still in the ponytail she'd worn until I was born. After my arrival, she'd chopped it off—as she'd said—for convenience. As if the burden of long hair was too much to be borne on top of the burden of a child.

The last photo was of my grandmother, looking as I had always remembered her, staring directly into the camera with a smile that looked more pensive than happy. She stood against what appeared to be the same brown brick wall as the women had posed in front of, but Grandma stood between two tall young men I didn't recognize. Their smiles were broad and genuine, and they were looking at my grandmother rather than the camera. All three of them were dressed completely head to toe in white clothing, the two men in dress shirts and white ties and my grandmother in what looked like a white prison coverall. On the back of the photo was written, in pencil, *April 15, 1997.*

I frowned over this last picture for a while, trying to decipher it. What was she wearing? Who were these young men? Where had it been taken? I ran my finger over her familiar face and swallowed back tears. Had Grandma gone to jail, maybe? And Mom was so embarrassed about it that she told us Grandma was dead rather than face the shame? But I couldn't imagine prison guards posing for a photo, or having such obvious affection and laughter in their faces as they gazed at my grandmother. And it didn't explain the seven laughing, loving women who had stood before that same brick wall for their photo.

It was no good trying to understand it. Anyone who could have explained it to me was now dead. I put the photos back in the envelope and slid it carefully on top of the fridge.

The third electrician shook his head in disgust at the other electricians' diagnoses.

"The paste is no good," he said firmly. "You have to buy these special boxes that are meant to join aluminum to copper wiring. They cost about twenty dollars each. Every outlet and light switch in the house needs to be changed."

I was stumped. If the so-called experts couldn't agree what to do, how could I know which was right? One would cost me five thousand dollars, one would cost me thirty dollars. This guy's plan would cost me something in the middle. I supposed that was probably the most realistic and honest.

"All right," I said. "Let's do that."

We arranged for him to return the following week, and then I drove, as pre-arranged, to Margaret and Eric's house to discuss the bathroom they wanted in their basement. As I passed the elementary school, I caught a glimpse of Jeri Shaanssen walking down the street, carrying a huge potted plant in a pink plastic pot. I had no idea why. Just out walking her philodendron? I waved and drove on, but I didn't think she saw me.

Margaret and Eric lived in an older house across town, a redbrick, cheerful sort of place with a stack of bicycles and a cement goose wearing a sunbonnet on the sagging porch. Margaret met me at the door, looking sincerely happy to see me, but the expression on Eric's face was one of undisguised relief. They took me into their cement-floored basement and described to me what they envisioned. I could tell they had been discussing it for a long time, because they knew what they wanted right down to the type of faucet and the color of the shower curtain. They had even already selected the tile they wanted from Home Depot. Their expectations sounded reasonable and practical, and I knew I could deliver just what they were hoping for.

As I listened and wrote, measured and sketched, I felt a surprising little zing of excitement shoot through me. I realized I was actually looking forward to this project. It was just the right size, the clients were friendly and likable, and I knew that I had been away from work for long enough. It was definitely time to get back into the full swing of things, and between this project and the Sellers' front porch, it felt like the world was starting to open up to me again. I felt the anxiety beginning to release its grip on me. Perhaps I was through the worst of it. Perhaps I was returning to myself at last.

The best part was, they didn't flinch at my estimate of the costs.

"I'm sure it will be just perfect," Margaret said with a brilliant smile. "When do you think you could start?"

"I'll have to get the materials together," I told them, "but I could probably start next week. Does that work for you?"

"Yes!" they both chimed.

Laughing, we returned upstairs, and I was about to take my leave when Margaret put a hand on my arm.

"Wait a sec. I have something for you." She hurried out to the kitchen, and Eric, once she was out of ear shot, leaned close.

"I'm so glad you came along," he said in a stage whisper. "She was driving me nuts to get it done, and my value as a husband was starting to come into question."

"I'm so glad you asked me to do it," I replied in a whisper to echo his own. "I really am looking forward to it."

Margaret returned with a large glass vase full of beautiful white peonies, full and frothy like whipped cream. Their scent was heavenly.

"A housewarming gift, though it's a little late," she announced, handing me the armful of loveliness. "To welcome you to Smoke River."

I was touched by her thoughtfulness and told her so. "Are these from your garden?"

"They are. They're about the only thing I can grow with any degree of success."

"I'm surprised they're blooming already. It isn't even June yet."

"They're up against a stone wall where the heat pools, so they seem to bloom first before anyone else's. The red ones bloom first every year, but I find them just a bit too powerful, and then they die off and the white ones come on. They're my favorite."

At that instant I knew they were my favorite too, and just what I'd needed. Margaret seemed to read my emotion in my face, because she gave me a quick kiss on the cheek.

"See you soon," she said, and then murmured low so that Eric couldn't hear: "You're likely saving our marriage, you know. I was turning into an awful nag."

I was still chuckling by the time I got home.

I found Finn and assorted Jameson children just heading around the side of the house, making for the backyard fort, and was surprised that they were out of school already. Was it really that late? I was used to time dragging and plodding, but today had sped by.

I showed the kids my lovely flowers and then carried them inside, where they redeemed my half-finished kitchen. I hadn't gotten the new counters yet—I'd probably been a bit premature hauling out the old ones before I could afford new ones—and the linoleum was still scuffed and curling, but the peonies in the center of the table made the whole place look welcoming and beautiful. For a second, looking at them and inhaling their heavenly scent, I could forget that I was standing in my deceitful grandmother's kitchen.

But no, I wasn't going to go down that path. Not today, when I'd finally pulled myself back into the land of the living and working. I set about making a plate of cut fruit to take out to the kids.

I found Finn and five others sprawled on their stomachs in the cramped space and reading through a stack of battered old comic books. They cheered when I set the plate of fruit where they could all reach it, and Finn went so far as to sit up and give me a high five. I was amused to see Jana among them, just as absorbed in her old Archie comic as her younger siblings were in theirs. I went back inside and left them to it. On the way I detoured to check on the crabapple tree. The foam of pink blossoms had gone and tiny little fruit was beginning to form. I could taste the pink jelly already.

About half an hour later, Jana came to the back door.

"Washroom's down the hall," I called without looking up from what I was doing. Assuming.

"Oh, no thanks. I don't need it."

She didn't add anything further, so I finally set down the curtain rod I was threading hooks onto and turned to face her. She lounged casually in the kitchen doorway, studying her fingernails.

"Do you guys need a pitcher of water or anything?" I prompted.

"No, we brought a thermos of Kool-Aid."

"Okay." I waited, but she said nothing else, so I shrugged and went back to my task.

"What are you doing? Do you need some help?" she asked, coming over to the table.

She just wanted to hang out, I decided. Tired of younger kids, no doubt, and ready to schmooze with an adult.

"Pull out a chair," I said. "I'm threading these onto the rod."

She sat down, picked up a few hooks, and began to help. For a while we worked in silence, but from the thoughtful look on her face, I knew she was working her way around to something, and I decided to give her a few nudges.

"School going okay?" I asked.

"Sure, thanks."

"When are final exams?"

"Not until June."

"Oh. A while, then."

Another pause, and I floundered in my mind for a topic. But she drew a deep breath and said, 'There's this boy I like in my math class."

"Ah."

"Chris. He's brainy, but not geeky, you know? And he's really polite and nice."

"That's good. Sounds like a nice person."

"He asked if I'd like to hang out this summer."

"That's cool."

"I said no."

My hands stopped moving and I looked up. She continued to work steadily, her face unreadable.

"Why did you say no?"

"Because I'm only fourteen, and . . . it felt like too soon, you know? I mean, not hanging out. I wouldn't mind if it was just that. But he wanted to *go* out. Like, exclusively."

"Oh. Well, yes, I guess fourteen is a bit young to do that," I agreed. "Sounds like you've made a wise decision."

"But now he probably won't want to see me at all," she added, getting down to the crux of the matter. "It's like it's all or nothing with these guys. I mean, what's wrong with just being friends and getting together with a gang of kids to do something in the summer? Like going to the beach or something?"

"Sounds good to me," I said.

"Why does it have to be going steady?"

"Do they still call it that?" I mused.

"My friends think I'm dumb for saying no. But I didn't want the pressure, you know? And I'm going to be busy a lot this summer . . . Do you think I'm dumb for turning him down?"

"Not at all," I said firmly. "You do whatever you feel comfortable with. But maybe this is the sort of thing you should be talking to your mother about."

She shook her head and a shadow seemed to pass across her pretty features. "I can't. That's just it, you see. She's—well, I can't, that's all. So I wanted to see what you thought."

I decided not to press or ask questions. I'd already figured out her mother appeared to have some issues, and I didn't understand all the family dynamics. If Jana didn't feel she could talk to her mother, well, I was flattered she thought I came in a close second.

"Well, I think if Chris is half as nice as you say he is, he'll understand how you feel and respect it. And still want to be friends. If he doesn't, he's not that nice anyway. And pretty dumb himself. So no loss."

She grinned. "Yeah, that's what I think too," she said simply. She stood and dusted her hands on her jeans and nodded in satisfaction. "Thanks, Kerris." She went back outside to rejoin her siblings.

When Ian came by that evening to pick up Finn, he offered the other kids a ride home. As they gathered their things, I thought about telling Ian what I'd discovered about Grandma. I hadn't told Gillian yet, though, and it didn't seem right to tell him about it before I told my sister. I was still getting my head around it, anyway. There were still too many unanswered questions.

I also briefly considered asking him about the Jameson kids' mother. If he kept tabs on the family, he might know what the situation was. But I chickened out, still remembering the sight of his car disappearing behind the slowly closing garage door. I wasn't sure I wanted to know what his relationship with Mrs. Jameson was. Because that would make me stop to consider what *my* relationship with him was, and I wasn't sure I was ready to go there quite yet. I hadn't even been considering starting to date again, when my friendship with Ian had suddenly become rather more—I guess *intense* was the word—than I had expected so quickly. I didn't know if he spent as much time thinking about me as I did about him, but if so, it was a wonder either one of us was getting much done. Between him and Grandma, my head felt pretty full these days.

There wasn't much time to chat, in any case, with the kids there. A quick smile and greeting, and they had all gone.

Chapter Sixteen

The next morning, I walked down to the river to watch the mist again. The beautiful phenomenon thrilled me as it had before and left me feeling calmer and filled with amazement that I'd ended up in such a lovely place. It was difficult to comprehend that one minute I'd been stuck in Toronto, brokenhearted and futureless in a cramped apartment, and the next minute I'd been granted this reprieve (for that's what it felt like). Who could have imagined I'd end up here in this beautiful spot with a house of my own, kids to nurture, and the beginning, cautious tendrils of a future again? In spite of my turmoil over Grandma and my distraction over Ian, my most overwhelming feeling that morning was gratitude. I just didn't know who to thank. I wasn't sure if I believed in God, so I just sent the thankful feeling wafting out over the river with the curling, sliding mist. If God was out there somewhere, he could pick it up.

That night I made myself dial Gillian's number. I knew she'd be out partying somewhere, it being the weekend, but I thought I would call and leave a message for her, and she could call me back on Monday. Deep down, I knew it was just another delaying tactic, but at least I could say I had taken the initial step.

But to my surprise, Gillian answered the phone. Her voice was croaky, as if she hadn't spoken in days.

"It's Kerris. Are you all right?" I asked. "You sound terrible."

"Just getting a cold, I guess."

Something in her tone made my stomach sink. "What's really wrong, Gill? Is it . . . Jeremy?"

There was a pause, and then she began to cry. Not gentle little tears, but big wracking sobs that garbled her words and made it sound as if she were choking. I had never heard her get this upset over any of the other men she'd dated. I gave her a moment and made soothing sounds and mentally cursed all men everywhere. Finally, she pulled herself together enough to blurt it out.

"We broke up just this morning."

"I'm so sorry, Gilly. What happened?"

"He's decided to take a job in British Columbia. He starts in June."

"Oh. And . . . you don't want to go with him?" I asked.

"Of course, I do! But I—I'm not invited," she said miserably. "He applied for that job without even telling me what he was planning." She gave a hiccupping breath, trying to pull herself together. "You know what, I don't care!" she exclaimed. "He wasn't The One anyway."

"I'm so sorry to hear it, Gilly," I said again, feeling useless. How many times had I said those same words to comfort my heartbroken sister? I knew if she kept to pattern, she'd be dating someone else within a couple of weeks anyway.

"Yeah, well. That's just my life. I should be used to this by now." She gave a tremendous sniff, and I imagined her straightening her spine, flipping her hair back from her shoulder. "So why were you calling? What's up?"

I hesitated. I didn't know if it was a good idea to spring everything on her while she was already upset. Maybe there was a gentler way to tell her.

"Listen, Gill, do you want to come stay with me for a few days? You know, just to have a change of scene?"

"Oh, could I? I've been wondering how I'll manage this week until Jeremy leaves. I don't want to just sit here and mope and watch him go, you know?"

"Come stay with me, then," I said. "Do you still have that air mattress you use for camping?"

"Yes."

"You'll need to bring that, because I don't have an extra bed, but I have lots of empty spare rooms."

"Are you sure I won't be in the way? I mean, I don't want to be a bother."

"Of course not," I said. "I'm excited to have you come. You can see the house and—and there's something I need to talk to you about, but I'd rather do it in person."

"That sounds ominous."

"No, it's okay. I mean, it's just sort of . . . complicated. I'd rather tell you in person. So it'll be great having you here."

"You're not sick or anything, are you?"

"No, nothing like that."

"Okay. Thanks, Kerris. I'll drive up Wednesday. Text me the address again—I've lost it. I can't wait to see your mystery house."

"Yeah," I said, but suddenly my throat was too tight to say anything more.

The next morning, I swept out a spare bedroom, choosing the brightest one at the front of the house, and dug out spare bed linens that might fit Gillian's air mattress. I hauled in an extra nightstand from my own room. The peonies, being such temporary flowers, had fallen to shreds already, but I put a vase of purple irises from my garden on the stand, thinking they might help cheer Gillian up. I set out fresh towels, thanking my lucky stars that the bathroom, at least, was finished. Then I made a list and headed for the grocery store. If Gillian was coming to stay for a week, I knew I had to be able to offer her more than root beer and hot dogs.

I was poking through the meager selection of condiments when I straightened and saw Jeri further down the aisle. It seemed I was seeing her a lot lately, now that I'd become aware of her. It was like when you learned a new word, and suddenly everyone around you seemed to be saying it. Was it that the word had suddenly come into more frequent use, or that you never really noticed what was going on around you until someone pointed it out?

Jeri caught my eye at the same time, waved, and came over. A brightly colored cloth hobo bag hung from her elbow, and she hugged a large loaf of French bread to her chest like a baby. Her hair was zanier than ever today, springing out from an orange scrunchie like ramen noodles.

"Hi again," I said.

"Hi. I remember meeting you, but I'm afraid I can't remember your name," she replied cheerfully.

I told her and she nodded.

"Ah yes. A great name."

"Thanks. I saw you kayaking on the river one morning," I told her. "It inspired me to go try it myself, and it was really lovely. I've discovered I adore kayaking."

"Oh good! It's one of my favorite things to do," she replied. "I'm glad you tried it."

"So how is the writing going?" I dared to venture.

"Great! I knitted eighteen rows this morning."

"Oh. I meant, how is the book going?"

"Great! I knitted eighteen rows this morning," she repeated in the exact same tone.

"Ah. Sorry to hear it."

"Not a worry. Must run," Jeri said. "Grooming the dog and polishing the silver this afternoon." She zoomed off, clutching the bread, and I laughed. If it wasn't writer's block, it looked pretty similar to it to me.

I had filled my cart and was heading for the cashier when I heard my name being called. Turning, I saw Peggy McGrath with another older woman. She was—impossibly—even shorter than Peggy and walked with a cane.

"Hi, Kerris!" Peggy called again, and I waited until they pulled their cart into line behind me before returning the greeting.

"This is my friend Bess Ingram," Peggy introduced the other woman. "I bring her shopping sometimes because she has trouble pushing the cart and reaching things. Bess, this is Kerris, the one I told you about who's going to do Margaret's bathroom."

"Oh yes!" The woman turned bright blue, eager eyes on me. "I think it's so wonderful that you have your own renovation business. When I was growing up, women were only allowed to be teachers or nurses. My husband wouldn't even let me do that. A woman's place was in the home."

"Well, for Kerris, a woman's place is *building* the home!" Peggy crowed, and Bess laughed.

Before I could say anything, Peggy gave the handle of her grocery cart an emphatic thump. "Say, Bess, weren't you telling me the other day that your son wants to build a new deck on his house? Kerris could do that sort of thing, couldn't you, Kerris?" She gave me a disingenuous smile and raised one perfect eyebrow.

I laughed. "Yes," I said. "I can do that sort of thing."

"There you go, then," Peggy said, and before I knew it, we had exchanged information and Bess had promised to have her son phone me.

As I drove away from the store, I couldn't help suspecting that Peggy had somehow contrived the meeting with Bess, though I knew she couldn't have. And I suspected that wasn't the only work she was going to drum up for me. Another warm flood of gratitude came over me at the thought of her kindness.

As I neared home, I saw Donna Sellers out walking her baby in a stroller and was glad to see her out and about. I gave her a wave but didn't stop to talk, knowing if I did, I'd be derailed for at least an hour, and I had too much to do.

My emotions were a bit of a roller coaster, fluctuating between happiness at having work again, at Peggy's friendship, at seeing my sister again—and also dread because of the conversation I knew I had to have with Gillian.

"You've really put me in a pickle, Grandma," I said aloud as I turned into my driveway. *Her* driveway.

I wondered if the house would ever truly feel like my own again after this. I was seeing Grandma everywhere in it. The cheap furniture she'd lived with. The paint colors she had chosen. The flowerbeds she had tended. I was eating her canned goods, for heaven's sake.

Gillian arrived after lunch on Wednesday, squeezing her little blue Kia into the space beside my truck. As she unfolded herself from the driver's seat, I couldn't help marveling for the millionth time that Gillian and I were related. Where I was five-foot-nine and sturdily built, with dark hair, Gillian was petite, slender, and graceful as a reed, and her blonde hair shone like wheat in the sun. She looked like something from an advertisement for Goodlife Fitness or some sort of high-protein energy bar. Even though I knew she'd likely spent the past twenty-four hours crying, her face was made up and perfect and delicate. Her hair was pulled into a shiny French braid. If I'd been in her shoes, I'd have been a blotchy-faced, red-eyed mess. Then again, I drove nails and unclogged sinks for a living. Gillian made people beautiful.

Even looking at my sister as she climbed from her car, I was reminded of Grandma. That summer we had lived with her, I had confided to Grandma that I felt like a gangly klutz next to my graceful sister (even at seven, Gillian had shone, and I'd known she was made of finer stuff than I). Grandma didn't try to talk me out of my funk. Instead, she had taken me on an outing, just she and I together. We went to lunch at a popular hamburger place, and then on the way home Grandma had stopped at the local art shop and gallery. Leading me round the paintings, she had pointed out in her soft voice the differences between the various art styles, the meticulous beauty of Monet, the scrawling freedom of Jackson Pollock, the lifelike glowing Rembrandts, the jaggedy weirdness of the Picassos. They were just prints, done up in nice frames, but to me they were magical, a world of color I knew little about.

Grandma had shown me all this, and then she had turned to me, a hand on my cheek, and said, "Kerris, your sister is a Monet. You are a Jackson Pollock. But both are beautiful, both are incredibly valuable, and both can brighten any home."

I knew what she was saying, and I'd never forgotten it. And I'd never felt frumpy or out of place next to Gillian since then.

I smiled at my sister now as she gave a little screech and ran to hug me as if we hadn't seen each other in years, though I'd just seen her at Christmas. Still, it felt wonderful, and I hugged her hard in return. She pushed her hair behind her ear and gazed up at the house, taking in the solid reality of it.

"Sure enough, it's a house," she marveled. "It's pretty."

"It'll look better once it's finished," I said. "Grab your stuff and I'll show you around."

We deposited her suitcase and air mattress in the upstairs room, which she declared to be just perfect, and then I gave her a quick tour of the place, from top to bottom. Gillian voiced approval of my color choices, snickered at the power tools in the front room, made sympathetic noises about the aluminum wiring, cheered my decision to knock through the kitchen wall, and echoed my curiosity about the cans of powdered milk in the basement. Then we sat at the kitchen table—since I lacked a living room couch, or a living room for that matter—and drank coffee while she caught me up on the Jeremy saga.

"I've decided any man who would apply for a job across the country without even *telling* me isn't worth crying over," she declared, but without conviction. "He'd be too selfish to live with anyway. I've had a narrow escape."

I eyed her over my cup, and after a pause, Gillian smiled, a wobbly sort of smile.

"If I keep telling myself that, eventually I'll believe it," she added ruefully. She let out a long sigh. "So, what was it you wanted to talk to me about?"

"Do you want to do this right now?" I asked gently. "Maybe you want to rest a while first. You've had a long drive through post-holiday traffic."

"For pity's sake, Kerris, you're scaring me. Are you dying of an incurable disease or what?"

"No. Okay." I spread my hands on the table and looked at them, not at her. "It's about this house. And our fairy godmother." She waited, not saying anything, and finally I looked up at her. Her face held curiosity but no anticipation of what I was about to spring on her.

"I've found out who left me this house," I told her. I took a deep breath. "It was Grandma."

Chapter Seventeen

She thought a little, a small crease appearing between her eyebrows. "How does that work? You mean Grandma Abby?"

"Well, it sure wasn't Dad's mother." We had never met our other grandmother, she having died when Dad was a teenager.

"But Grandma died a long time ago. And what would she be doing with a house in Smoke River?"

"Gol, I don't know how to tell you this, Gill. There's no easy way to say it. Grandma didn't die in 1997 like we were told. She moved here to Smoke River and Mom told us she was dead. But she didn't die until 2012. And in her will, she left me this house with the stipulation that I wasn't to inherit it until Mom died."

Gillian sat motionless, absorbing this. I had expected cries of outrage, tears, questions, confusion. I hadn't expected silence. When nothing was forthcoming for a full minute, I reached across the table and put my hand on my sister's.

"I've spoken to the lawyer who arranged it. He told me Grandma and Mom were estranged, and that had something to do with why I wasn't to inherit until after Mom passed."

Still Gillian said nothing. I cleared my throat. "There's more. Grandma was the one who paid for your bail and rehab. She bought my prom dress and paid off my loan. I bet she even got me that job offer somehow. It was Grandma all along, doing those things for us.

She—she had her lawyer hire a private investigator to keep tabs on us and let her know if we ever needed help. She watched over us. She was our fairy godmother; we just didn't know it."

Gillian stood abruptly and went to the sink. Grabbing a glass from the cupboard, she filled it with water and drank the whole thing in one go. Then she stood there looking at it in her hand—there wasn't a counter to set it down on. I went to her and took the glass, set it in the sink, then put my arms around her.

"Why?" she breathed raggedly into my shoulder. "Why did they act like she was dead? What would make her move away like that?"

"I don't know. The lawyer didn't know either. He said that as far as he knew, Mom didn't communicate with her after she moved here to Smoke River. Maybe she told Grandma not to have any further contact with us, and Grandma honored that. They must have come to some arrangement because we stayed in her house when she left. She—Gilly, Grandma is buried here in Smoke River. I've seen the headstone."

Gillian pulled away from me and slumped back into her chair. She planted her elbows on the table and pushed her face into her palms. When she spoke, her voice was muffled.

"How could she leave us like that? Didn't she know what it would do to us?" She raised her face to look at me with horrified eyes, and I saw her skin had gone sheer white. "She was just like Dad."

I sat across from her and reached to take both her hands in mine. "No, Gillian, not just like Dad. Dad took off to California and didn't look back once. Grandma kept tabs on us and made sure we had what we needed—"

"We needed *her*!" Gillian wailed, and then the tears finally came.

She even cried prettily. I let her go for a while, until the storm had passed and she once again grew quiet. Then I fetched her a roll of toilet paper to mop up her damp face and poured her another coffee.

"I can't say I understand any of it better than you do," I said softly. "But . . . well, you know how I can 'read' houses, the way they feel?"

"The House Whisperer," Gillian snorted.

"Yeah. And all I can tell you is the way I felt when I first walked into this house, back in February. I didn't know it was Grandma's house, of course, at the time. But I do know I felt it reach out and welcome me. It was a loving home. You could feel it."

"*You* could feel it." Her tone was bitter.

"Yes," I said quietly. "I could feel it. She did love us. That's what makes this all so difficult to understand. I'm as confused by it as you are."

Gillian breathed deeply and looked around the half-finished kitchen. "It's hard to believe she was sitting here the whole time. That we could have hopped in the car and come to see her any time, right up until a few years ago."

"I know."

"And then Mom dying, and you inheriting this place just at the perfect time, right when you needed it."

"Yes. She was my fairy godmother even after she died. She wouldn't have known I'd be in a pickle and needing to escape Toronto just then, but it worked out that way just the same."

Gillian pinched her lips tightly together, and I heard myself speak without realizing what I was going to say. "It's your home, too, Gill. If you want to live here with me, you can."

The words surprised both of us.

Gillian snorted again, the color returning to her face, her devastation replaced by healthy anger. "I can't just ditch my whole life in Toronto, you know. And Grandma wanted you to have it. She left it to *you*."

"Maybe because I was the oldest, but she'd want us both to have it," I said. "It was the last thing she was able to give us."

"Yeah, well, I don't want it." Gillian hesitated, then sighed and shook her head. "But thanks for offering, anyway."

"I meant it. I want you to stay, if you want to."

She shook her head. "I know you meant it. Thank you. But I'm only here for the week." She stood and put her coffee cup in the sink. "I think maybe I will go have that rest, after all."

Ian called that night, asking if I'd like to go out to dinner, but I explained that my sister was visiting and I wanted to be home with her that evening. His tone seemed as friendly as ever, and I felt my self-doubt grow. Maybe I was completely wrong about him and Mrs. Jameson, I told myself. Maybe there was a perfectly simple explanation for him hiding his car in her garage.

I made beef stroganoff and broccoli for dinner, but Gillian didn't come downstairs to eat, and when I checked on her, she was sound asleep with her long hair unbraided and flung over the edge of the air mattress. She had set up the mattress and thrown the sheet I'd left her over it before lying down, but the blanket remained folded on a chair. I unfolded it and gently lay it over her without waking her. I ate alone at the table with the scent of flowers all around me, so thick and perfumy throughout the kitchen that finally I snapped in irritation at the ceiling, "Knock it off, Grandma. I'm not in the mood." And the flowery scent retreated slightly . . . not disappearing entirely, but backing off. Respectfully. Gently.

"That's so like you," I muttered.

Gillian didn't appear for breakfast on Thursday, either, and when I left to work on Margaret and Eric's bathroom, she was still curled in a ball under the covers. I figured sleep was the best thing for her and left her alone. I left her a note telling her where I was going and that there was food in the fridge.

It felt good to take my energy out in my work, and it kept my mind off of everything. It also felt good knowing I was about to contribute to my bank account instead of bleeding the last drops from it. Eric had cleared a place in the garage where I could set up my electric saw. As the blade screamed through the pine boards, I breathed in the comforting smell of fresh sawdust and thanked my lucky stars, for the hundredth time, that I had my hands and skill, and that my tools had survived the divorce. I had found the right profession for myself, where I fit in, and I knew how rare that could be. I may not be able to completely repair people's lives, including mine or Gillian's, but I could repair the homes we lived in, and that counted for something. In spite of everything, I felt drenched with contentment.

At lunchtime I phoned Gillian. She answered promptly.

"I'm okay," she said briefly when I inquired. "I must have been zonked. I didn't even hear you leave this morning."

"Did you find everything you needed? Did you get some lunch?" I asked.

She chuckled. "Yes, Mommy, I ate my vegetables. Good stroganoff, by the way. I had it for breakfast. Want me to whip something up for dinner?"

"I'm planning to pick up a pizza on the way home," I said. "I feel like celebrating you coming and me finally getting a job."

"I'm not sure I feel celebratory, all things considered," she said.

"I understand, what with Jeremy and everything."

"Oh, Jeremy. He's so last week's problem!" She tried to say it lightly, but I could hear the pain in her voice. "Anyway, this thing with Grandma has kind of sidelined all that."

"So, should I skip the pizza?"

"Are you kidding? I want double cheese on my half. I'll pay for it."

"Yes, you will," I said. "See you around five."

"Hey, wait a sec. There was a phone call." I heard her fumbling with paper in the background. "Someone named Finn asking if he can sleep over this Friday even though your sister is in town." I could hear the amusement in her voice. "Something you're not telling me, sis? Anything I should know? He sounded awfully young for you."

"He's a friend's ten-year-old son."

"A friend, huh?"

"Yes," I said, ignoring her curious tone. "And sometimes he likes to sleep in the fort I built him in the backyard. The kid, not the friend."

"You have a fort?"

"Yeah, go look."

"Cool! How come you didn't mention this sooner? Maybe we can sleep out there one night. Roast marshmallows and tell ghost stories."

I laughed. "See you at five."

By the end of the afternoon, I had the bathroom framed, the plumbing half roughed in, and an appointment made with the electrician. So pleased with myself, I knocked off at four and headed out to buy pizza. Gillian had sounded much better on the phone, and I looked forward to a quiet night together, maybe watching a movie while we ate.

I was lost in thought and not really paying much attention to anything but the road in front of me, when I realized I had missed the turn-off for the street I wanted. I was heading into the new subdivision on the edge of town, the houses in their tidy lawns looking bland and repetitive on each side of the wide road. Maybe I could get some work putting up fences here; no one seemed to have one yet. My spirits lifted even more.

I looked for somewhere to turn around, mentally chiding myself for not being more mindful behind the wheel. Granted, I had plenty on my mind lately to distract me. I saw a parking lot to the right and pulled into it, preparing to swing around and re-enter the road. But then the sign on the building beside the parking lot caught my eye.

Bishop's Storehouse.

I thought of the cans of food in my basement, prepared "for the Bishop's Storehouse," and realized this was where those cans must have come from. There were two minivans parked in front of the building. On an impulse, I parked the car in the parking lot and got out.

The glass door opened into a tiled entry with a front desk. A round-faced man in a dark suit and tie sat behind the desk, doing some paperwork. He was about fifty, with thinning hair and a scrubbed look to his polished face. He looked genuinely surprised to see me.

"Can I help you?" he asked, and I suddenly wondered if whatever this place was was open to the public.

"Sorry to bother you," I stammered, not sure what to say or even what had made me come in. "I recently moved into a house not far from here, and I found a bunch of cans of food in the basement that had labels from the 'Bishop's Storehouse.' I'm assuming that's this place."

"Oh, yes?" The man rose to his feet, looking eager to be helpful.

"Well . . . I mean . . . "

"Is there anything wrong with them?"

"Well, no," I said quickly. "They seemed quite old, but they had expiration dates on them quite far in the future, so I think they're still okay to eat . . .?"

"Yes, most of the goods we can here are good for fifteen to thirty years, depending on the product," he said. "They're dehydrated or dry-packed in such a way that they have a long shelf life. If their expiration dates haven't passed and the cans are intact, I'm sure they're safe to use."

"So this is a cannery? I thought maybe it was a store of some sort."

His eyebrows went up and he gave a little nod, as if figuring something out. "You haven't heard of us? I take it you're not a Latter-day Saint."

"Not what?"

"A member of the Church."

"Oh no," I said. "I'm not religious. Why?"

"This facility is run by the Church of Jesus Christ of Latter-day Saints. You might know us as the Mormons. It is a cannery, yes, and also the Bishop's Storehouse, which is a part of the welfare program of the church."

"Welfare!" I couldn't help being taken aback. Surely Grandma hadn't ended up on welfare, had she? She'd thrown a lot of money at me and Gillian, all told, over the years, but surely she wouldn't have given away more than she could afford to. Then again, we had kept her house, and she must have had a limited pension . . . Did those cans in her basement mean . . .?

"Yes, we have our own system, so that any of our members having financial challenges don't have to turn to government assistance for food. We look after our own."

"So . . . so you're saying that if I found cans from this place in my basement, that means the person who previously owned the house was on welfare?"

"Not necessarily," the man replied. "That's the Storehouse half of it. The cannery part offers bulk food at good prices to anyone wishing to purchase it. The food in your basement might have been purchased by the previous owner. You see, we teach our members to store a year's supply of food at all times in case of emergencies or difficulties, such as job loss or unexpected disability. Would you like a tour of the facility?"

I was still mulling over the phrase "our members" and how it might apply to my grandmother, so I didn't react right away. He apparently took this a sign of agreement, because he came out from behind the desk and trotted toward a door at the back of the room, motioning for me to follow. Befuddled, I did.

The door led to a huge, cold warehouse full of tall metal shelving. The shelves were filled with shrink-wrapped skids of cans, sacks, and boxes, all neatly labeled. The abundance was staggering in scale. The wide aisles accommodated a forklift, which an elderly man in a hard hat was driving carefully along. We waited for him to pass, and the two men gave each other friendly nods. My guide resumed the tour, talking rapidly as he explained the church's welfare system. The only fact that really stuck with me out of all he said was that recipients were expected to chip in and serve in some way, and not just receive handouts.

As we walked, he explained a bit more about the cannery side of things, and I couldn't help being impressed by the whole operation, not just the scale and efficiency of it, but the philosophy behind it. I was all for self-reliance, preparedness, and industry, and this place and program epitomized it.

"Thank you for the tour," I told him as we returned to the front desk twenty minutes later. "I sincerely enjoyed it. I had no idea this place was here. But I didn't mean to take up so much of your time."

"It's my pleasure. It's what I'm here for," he replied cheerily.

I turned to go, then hesitated and looked back at him. "I wondered . . . would other people, just general members of the public, come here to buy food and supplies too? Or just members of your church?"

"Anyone can purchase food here," he said. "All are welcome, and keeping food storage on hand is a good idea for anyone, not just church members. But to be honest," he added sadly, "most of the public don't know we're here."

"Thank you," I said numbly, and went out.

As I turned the car toward home, gripping the steering wheel tightly, I remembered Grandma's obituary had referred to her "church family." My stomach felt suddenly queasy. Grandma was religious. Grandma was a *Mormon*. That suddenly made everything clear. Mom had hated religion passionately after my hypocritical pastor father had betrayed her. Had Grandma decided in 1997 to join the Latter-day Saints and they'd had a falling out over it? I could easily see Mom telling her not to have any further contact with us if she went through with this choice. That she was dead to us. Had Grandma gone away and chosen the church over her own daughter and granddaughters, even knowing that Mom would cut off all communication? Apparently so. She hadn't had any contact with us after that. But she had kept tabs on us from afar.

As I grappled with this shocking idea, I realized it also certainly explained why Grandma hadn't wanted me to inherit the house until after Mom's death. Mom would have seen Grandma's choice as just as bad as my father's betrayal. She would have hit the roof if she'd known Grandma was leaving me her house.

I could almost hear the click as the pieces all fit together.

If those young women missionaries ever came back to the house, I'd have such a story to tell them!

Chapter Eighteen

I ran my hunch past Gillian as we ate the pizza that evening. She didn't seem as astounded as I was at the idea.

"Is there some way to confirm it? Look up the local Mormon church and ask them if Grandma was part of their congregation?"

"I would think so."

"Let's try it. It would certainly answer a lot of questions if that turned out to be the situation." She reached for her iPhone and tapped on the buttons a moment.

"No Mormon Church in Smoke River. Hang on, it looks like that's a nickname."

"Yes. It's the Latter-day Saints or something," I said, trying to remember the full name.

"Here it is. The Church of Jesus Christ of Latter-day Saints. There's a chapel here in Smoke River. Highpoint Road. Where's that?"

"Across town, I think."

"The hours aren't posted that I can see," Gillian said. "And there's no website." She gave me a grin and wiggled her eyebrows. "It looks like Sunday morning we're going on a stakeout."

By Friday, I had Margaret and Eric's bathroom plumbing finished, the wiring installed, and the tiles and fixtures ready and waiting in their boxes in a corner of the basement. I was pleased with how things were going. Eric had ventured downstairs once to say hello and express his satisfaction with my work, but other than that they basically left me to it, not hovering the way some clients did. I worked extra carefully, wanting this particular job to go perfectly, not just because this was Ian's family, but because how things went on this job would determine whether I got any more jobs in the future. Reputations were vital in a small town, especially in my kind of business.

As I left the house, I glanced over and discovered Jeri on her hands and knees, quietly weeding Margaret's front flower bed, the pile of weeds in a tidy pile beside her. She looked lost in thought, so I didn't interrupt her.

That night Finn came over with a hand-held electronic videogame of some sort (not having kids, I wasn't up on the latest technology in that department), a flashlight, and a bag of popcorn. He and Gillian eyed each other frankly and made instant friends, as I'd known they would.

"Are any of your friends joining you?" I asked.

"Nah. I'm on my own this time," Finn said nonchalantly. "But if you want to come share my popcorn, you're welcome to."

We ended up sitting on cushions on the floor in front of the TV until eleven o'clock, watching three Pirates of the Caribbean movies in a row, and Finn fell asleep during the last one.

"Should we carry him out to the fort?" Gillian asked doubtfully, looking down at him where he lay on a pillow in a scattering of popcorn crumbs.

"Let's leave him. I don't want him waking up in the middle of the night and not knowing where he is. I'll just put a blanket over him."

I fetched one to drape over him, and then Gillian and I tiptoed out to the kitchen to clean up. Gillian eyed me thoughtfully as she washed the popcorn bowl in a sink of suds.

"You've changed," she said finally.

"What? How?"

"I don't know. You're domestic. Hanging out with small children. Making a home here. I just think you seem calmer and happier than I've seen you in a long time."

"I'm feeling like I'm just getting back into the swing of things, you know? Getting back to work. Back to my life. Things are finally starting to come together for the first time since the divorce," I told her.

"I'm glad. And I think it's cool that Finn likes to hang out with you."

"Because I'm such a cool old lady, you mean?" I laughed.

"He likes you. And I think you like him too."

I nodded. "He's the best kid. He came along at just the right time, I think. We needed each other."

"And his father? I suspect you like him too, don't you?"

I glanced at her. "How did you come to that conclusion? I haven't even mentioned him."

"You don't need to. It was the way you said 'a friend's ten-year-old son' that made me think he's more than a friend."

"You got all that from one phrase?"

"Yep. Come on, tell Gilly all about it." She dried her hands on a towel and leaned against the sink, arms folded.

I smiled. "I don't know that there's much to tell. His name is Ian McGrath, and he's a high school biology teacher. He's nice. I mean *really* nice. He treats little kids to ice cream, and he rescued me when my truck died. He doesn't get upset when Finn does Finn things. And I ate supper at his brother's house on Mother's Day."

Gillian put a hand to her mouth in mock amazement. "Dude, that sounds serious!"

I shrugged noncommittally. "Maybe. Maybe not. I—I have reason to suspect he's seeing someone else."

"While he's asking you to his mother's house? The nerve! I'll go give him a piece of my mind if you want."

"You can't spare it," I teased. "I might be wrong. He might have a perfectly good reason for going to her house in the middle of the day and hiding his car in her garage." The words cast a shadow over my good mood as I said them. I'd tried to think of a plausible explanation in Ian's defense but had failed to come up with anything.

"Ah. Mmm." Gillian nodded knowingly. "Doesn't sound good, I have to admit."

"No."

She sighed. "Ah well. It's too bad. I don't think Finn would mind having you for a step-mom."

I forced a laugh, but it sounded hollow to my ears, and the traitorous voice in the back of my mind agreed with her. *Too bad, indeed.*

When I woke up Saturday morning, after finally getting a refreshing sleep, I went outside in my bathrobe to get the newspaper and found a tall ladder propped against my house. Jeri was washing my living room windows.

"Good morning!" I called. "You don't have to do that, you know."

"Oh good, you're up," she called back. "I didn't want to do the bedroom windows until I knew you were awake, so I wouldn't startle you. Wouldn't want to wake up to my mug peering through the glass, now would you?" Her laugh was more like a manic bark. "You're doing a nice job on this house, you know," she added. "It was a shame to see it sitting empty."

"Thanks! Want to come in for a coffee?"

"Oh no, thank you. I'm working hard on the book this morning," she answered solemnly.

"Ah. Well, if you change your mind, come on in." I turned to go, then thought of something and turned back.

"Jeri, did you know the woman who used to live here in this house?"

She shook her head and dipped her sponge into her sudsy bucket. "No, I don't know many people in town, really. I'm usually too busy writing to socialize much."

I went back inside and left her to it. And spent the next ten minutes trying to explain to Gillian why a total stranger was up a ladder washing our windows.

"I guess she's harmless," Gillian said finally, shrugging. "If you can get her to wash my car, that would be great."

"I'm not going to take advantage of her," I said, but even as I said it, I wasn't sure just who was helping out whom, when it came to Jeri.

Finn woke and came into the kitchen, rubbing his eyes and yawning loudly. "I didn't sleep in the fort," he reported glumly.

"We thought it better to leave you where you were," I told him. "Gillian's making French toast. Want some?"

He was instantly awake and bouncing. "Cool!" He plopped into a chair at the table.

I sat opposite him with my own plate and watched as he and Gillian laughed and chatted and goofed back and forth. My own words came back to me—he *had* come along at just the right time. I needed a child to love, and he needed to be loved. If I could have chosen a kid to be my own, it would have been him. I was struck by how he was able to smile and be openhearted, despite all he had gone through in his short life. I could see a change in him, just in the time I'd known him. Apparently, Gillian had seen that change in me too.

"What's the matter, Kerris?" Finn asked suddenly. "Are you *crying*?"

"Just something in my eye," I told him, and fled to the bathroom.

Sunday morning came, and Gillian insisted we were going on the stakeout. I wasn't sure I wanted to find out the truth, but I couldn't very well chicken out if she was going. I showered and then hesitated over what to wear, dresses being foreign to me, but the missionaries had been wearing skirts so I figured it was likely the standard. I dug out my black skirt (still unironed), added my pearl gray blouse and flats, and pulled my brown hair into a braid.

When I emerged from my bedroom, Gillian was sitting at the kitchen table, turning her phone over and over in her hands. She wore jeans and a shot-at-the-neck t-shirt with a Star Wars logo on it. Even in those clothes, she looked glamorous.

"You're wearing that to church?" I asked, and then stopped, seeing her face. "What is it?"

She waggled the phone at me and swiped at the tears on her cheeks. "Jeremy. He texted me a few minutes ago. He says he can't stand the thought of going to BC without me. He wants me to call him when I'm awake."

"You're awake," I said. "Call him!"

"But—"

"Gillian, every indication I've observed this week tells me you love him. Regardless of how it all turns out and what you decide to do, you at least owe him a phone call. If you don't call, you'll always wonder how it could have turned out."

She nodded and rose from the table but paused in the doorway. "Oh! The stakeout!"

I flapped my hand at her. "We'll go next week."

She shook her head. "No. You go ahead and go this morning. I—I won't be here next week. And I kind of want the house to myself for this phone call, anyway, in case I feel the need to yell or throw things." She gave me a strained smile, and I went to hug her.

"All right. Just don't throw anything expensive. I'll be back soon. And don't go dashing back to his arms while I'm gone. At least wait to say goodbye."

"I can't anyway," she said. "I promised Finn we'd watch *Star Wars* tonight."

I sat in my car in the church parking lot, twisting my hands together for half an hour before I saw other cars begin to arrive at the chapel.

That was another thing. The chapel wasn't like any church I'd seen before. It was a single-story brick block with glass doors and looked more like a dental office than a church. I could see no cross, no stained glass, nothing that would indicate it was a place of worship other than the name on the wall beside the front door, written in plain brown letters. I watched five or six cars arrive and unload people before I dared open my car door and go in. And yes, all the women I'd seen enter were wearing dresses. I'd chosen correctly.

I had just entered and had only had time to register blue industrial carpet and brick walls (were they the same as the wall in the photos?) when the two female missionaries descended on me. I hadn't seen them come in; perhaps there was a back door. Delight was apparent in their faces as they each grabbed one of my hands and shook it, holding with both their own hands.

"Hi! You came! Welcome!"

I pulled my hands away and took a step back, a bit overwhelmed. "I—I hope you don't mind I came to visit," I said. "I'm not interested in converting or anything, so don't get your hopes up. I just wanted to come see . . . "

"Certainly! You're welcome anytime. Let us show you where to go."

They led me into a large room filled with folding chairs, with a small cloth-covered table and a podium with microphone at the front. More industrial carpet and brick walls, no windows, no ornamentation of any kind except for a bowl of plastic flowers sitting on the upright piano. The chairs were beginning to fill up with people of all ages, the men in suits with white shirts and ties, the women in nice but not fancy dress. An elderly woman was playing what I assumed was a hymn on the piano, and every time she pushed a pedal, the plastic flowers in the bowl quivered.

The missionaries explained to me that the first meeting—sacrament meeting—was held in this room for the first hour, followed the next hour by something called Relief Society, and they'd show me where to go for that.

"Hold it," I said. "Two hours? You're telling me you go to church for two hours? Every Sunday?"

"Yep," one of the missionaries said brightly. "Hey, count yourself lucky—it used to be three hours. Anyway, you don't have to stay for all of it, but I would encourage you to. It's a great way to meet the other women."

"That's the thing," I said. "That's why I'm here. That is . . . it turns out my grandmother was a Mormon, I think, and she attended this church. Maybe you knew her . . . Abigail Borden. She died in 2012."

"Oh! Well, we wouldn't know her, because we've only been assigned here for a few months, but I bet there are women in the branch who knew her."

"Branch?" It sounded like a bank.

"Congregation. We can ask around," the other missionary said. "How cool, that your grandma was a Latter-day Saint!"

"I only just found out. And I'm not even positive, but I—"

"There's the Branch President. Let's ask him if he remembers her," the other suggested.

But just as she turned to approach the youngish man in the brown suit who had just entered, I spied two women coming in the door who looked familiar. I was sure they were in the photo I had, at this moment, in my purse. I forgot the missionaries and walked straight over to the two women.

Both looked to be in their late seventies or early eighties, both had short gray hair and modest print dresses, and one clutched a key ring with enough keys on it to service a penitentiary. Their faces were older than in the photo, of course, but still recognizable. Both looked a bit startled as I strode up to them, then put on polite smiles.

"Hi," I said. "You don't know me, but my name is Kerris Wells, and I think you might have known my grandmother, Abigail Borden."

"Abby!" both women exclaimed together, and then the one with the keys put out a hand to grasp my upper arm. "You're Abby's Kerris!"

Chapter Nineteen

I felt a strange mixture of elation and disappointment. Grandma had indeed been a Mormon, then. My surmise was true. I fished the two photos out of my bag, the one of the women at the wall and the one of Grandma and the two men in white, and silently handed them to them. The women bent over them, giggling at the changes in their own faces, staring out at them from the photo.

"Oh, I remember this. There's me," the key-ring woman said, pointing to the woman on the end who was striking a silly pose. "And there's you, Gertie. My goodness, that's Hannah, and there's Emmy and Lucille, back when her hair was still long. Oh, and look at this one! There's Abby on her baptismal day."

"Baptismal day?" I asked.

"Yes. That's why they're all in white," Gertie explained.

"I thought she looked like she was in prison garb," I confessed, and both women laughed.

"Well, just the opposite I would say," Gertie declared. "You grandmother was set free that day. But what brings you here? Forgive me, but what I meant was, your grandmother told us your family would have nothing to do with religion. So I'm surprised to see you here."

"Yes, well, she was right. My mother was anti religion, and she raised me and my sister to be the same," I said, hoping I wasn't offending her. "But you see, Grandma left me her house here in Smoke River, and I just moved up not long ago from Toronto."

"Oh, you're living here now! That's wonderful. We wondered what was going to happen to Abby's house. It was sad to see it stand empty for so long."

"Yes. I've been here for a few weeks now. I only just found out . . . well, I *suspected* she was a Mormon, and you've just now confirmed it. I wanted to come see if I could find the women in these photos, and maybe find out a bit more about Grandma. It's a bit complicated, but you see, when Grandma left in 1997, my mother told me she had died. I've thought she was dead all these years. I didn't know she'd joined your church and moved here."

The women exchanged looks, and then key-ring lady put her arm around my shoulders and guided me toward the door. "Let's go find somewhere quiet where we can talk," she said.

"Thank you. But isn't your church service about to begin?" I asked.

They looked at each other again, and Gertie nodded.

"This is more important," she said. "Abby would have wanted us to explain it all to you."

As they gently led me from the room, I glanced back at the two missionaries and the man they'd called Branch President, who were watching with eyebrows raised. I let the two women—Grandma's friends—tow me down the hall to a quiet classroom. There was a semi-circle of folding chairs and a table and chalkboard, and that was all. Gertie settled herself to my one side and key-ring lady, who introduced herself as Catherine, sat on my other.

"Now, Kerris, the first thing you need to know more than anything else is that your grandmother loved you very much," Catherine said. "She told us all about you and your sister and took a great interest in your lives. But things weren't easy for her. She would want us to explain to you why she did what she did."

"Thank you. I would very much like to hear it," I said frankly. "Because from my view, it was pretty inexcusable."

Catherine coughed. "Well, let's explain, and then you can decide if you can forgive her or not. We first met Abby in . . . I guess it would be 1996, wouldn't it, Gertie?"

Gertie nodded again. "Yes, the year before she was baptized. She came to Smoke River for a quilt show at the museum, where Lucille was working, and they got to talking. I think it ended up they went to lunch together, I don't recall. Anyway, they became instant friends, just like that."

"Lucille died several years ago," Catherine added. "It's too bad you couldn't have met her. A wonderful lady. She would have liked to meet you." She pointed to the third woman from the left in the photo, who was grinning broadly at the camera. "That was Lucille."

"I remember Abby came back to Smoke River a couple of weeks later to visit Lucille and exchange some quilting fabric. She was here for the weekend, and Lucille invited her to attend church with her, and Abby accepted. And she was hooked."

"Hooked?" I felt a bit alarmed at the term, but Catherine shook her head at Gertie.

"I wouldn't put it that way," she said, a bit reproachfully. "It sounds too much like she fell for a scam. That wasn't what it was at all. She was genuinely interested in what she heard that day at church. She told me later that what we taught just drew her in and sounded right to her. She came back a few times after that. She said she felt at home here. We all got to know her and came to love her."

I rubbed a hand through my bangs. "She didn't say a word at home about it. At least, not to me or my sister. I guess she must have discussed it with my mother."

Catherine nodded. "Her daughter was anti religion, as you said, and told Abby if she joined the church, she wanted nothing more to do with her. She told her she couldn't have any contact with you girls if she were baptized. It was a terrible decision for Abby to have to make. She talked with both of us about it while she was trying to make up her mind, isn't that right, Gertie?"

Gertie nodded. "It was an awful thing to have to choose."

I felt tears prick at the back of my eyes and frowned them away. "How could she choose a church over her own grandkids?"

Catherine put her hand on mine, and to my surprise I didn't pull away. I could feel compassion radiating from her, and even while her words hurt me, the kindness in her tone and face comforted me.

"It was the hardest thing she ever had to do," Catherine said. "But you see, she felt she'd found the truth, and for Abby, it was impossible to act as if it hadn't happened."

I thought about this and knew my grandmother couldn't have ignored or turned against something she believed was good. It wasn't in her nature. But to embrace her new religion, she had turned away from *us*, and I wasn't sure I could forgive that. I fumbled in my pocket for a tissue and couldn't find one, but Gertie produced a travel packet of Kleenex from her bag and handed it to me.

"I know it must be hard for you to hear," she said. "Please believe she made the best decision she could at the time. She needed to be true to her own path, you see, and grasp happiness where she could find it. I know she held out hope that one day your mother would relent and accept her back. She told me she felt she was paving the path for you girls."

"Paving the path? Like, she expected us to follow in her footsteps and join the Mormons too?" My short laugh came out more like a bark. "Fat chance of that ever happening." I looked from one kindly old face to the other and said bluntly, "I have no intention of ever joining any church, including this one. Especially this one, if what you teach pulls families apart."

"It isn't meant to do that," Catherine said, her voice quiet. "It's meant to strengthen families and bind them together. But it can only do that if people's hearts are softened and teachable. Ultimately, it's up to each person to choose. Abby hoped your mother would come to understand one day."

"My mother told us she was dead. For years we believed it was true," I said, not bothering to hide the hurt in my voice. "I only found out recently that she didn't die until 2012."

Gertie nodded. "I understand your mother chose to keep you from her. I know it hurt Abby terribly, but she never gave up hope that one day your mother would relent."

"If she knew my mother at all, she'd have known it was hopeless. But she chose to be baptized anyway," I said.

"All of us have had to face the same dilemma to some extent or another," Gertie said, looking pensive. "My husband left me when I joined the church thirty years ago. And Catherine's got a sister who hasn't spoken to her in decades because of her decision to join the church."

"But if the cost is so high, why do you do it?" I cried. "What could be so important that you're willing to risk losing your family for it? What can your church possibly offer that's so valuable?"

Catherine grinned suddenly. "We could tell you," she said, "but then you'd go and join up too, and you've already made it clear you don't want to do that."

"I don't think there's any danger of that," I retorted. "But if I'm going to understand how Grandma could abandon us and my mother could fake her death to keep us girls from knowing about it, I think I need to understand what Grandma found so enticing about this church." I swallowed hard, fighting tears and also fighting my pride. "I'm filled with so much hurt and anger right now. I don't want to feel this way about my grandmother. Please, are you able to help me understand her decision?"

Catherine looked at me for a long moment, then exchanged glances with Gertie.

"If you genuinely want to know what Abby found here, we can teach you," she said at last. "But I should warn you—once you find truth, you only have two choices. Either you have to change your life, which can be painful, or you have to live a lie. And if you're anything like your grandmother—and I suspect you are—you need to be prepared for change. So don't ask unless you genuinely want to know."

This made me pause, and I gave it sincere thought for a moment. I didn't think I was in any danger of hearing anything that would lead to change, but then again, Grandma probably never thought she'd be in such a position either. Still, change was something I knew intimately. It was scary and hard, and I'd had far too much of it already, but I'd learned I could survive it.

The two women waited patiently, watching me, their hands in their laps and their eyes respectfully lowered, giving me space. Finally, I nodded.

"I think if I'm going to find any peace at all, I need to understand the choice Grandma made," I told them. And knew it was true.

"All right, then," Gertie said. "Why don't we arrange a time for us and the sister missionaries to come see you?"

"Do they have to come?"

She chuckled. "Don't you like them? They seem nice enough to me."

"Well, yes, sure, but can't you just tell me about it? I mean, I don't want to be too formal about it, or get their hopes up or anything."

Catherine laughed. "They won't pressure you—you'll see. But teaching is what they're trained to do. That's why they're here in Canada."

"What do you mean?" I asked.

"Sister Harper is from Arizona and Sister Davis is from England. They're here serving as missionaries for eighteen months, paying their way out of their own pockets, and their whole purpose is to help and teach people. They don't get the chance to do it often, so it would really brighten their day if you'd agree to let them come too," Catherine said. "There's a series of short lessons they go through, and they're really quite good at it, but of course we'll be there too to help answer any questions you might have."

Both women reached into their purses for their phones to check their calendars and find a date that worked for all of us. We settled on Thursday evening, and they took down my phone number.

"I'll make sure that's okay with the Sisters," Gertie said. "I'll let you know if there's any conflict."

And just like that, I'd agreed to let a bunch of Mormons into my house.

Mom would be rolling in her grave.

"Never mind Mom," I muttered as I drove home. "What am I going to tell *Gillian*?"

I hadn't stayed for the two hours of meetings. I was overwhelmed enough already, and I felt a strong need to get home to my sister, afraid of what I'd find.

What I found was Gillian, in the kitchen, making pancakes. Her hair was pulled back in a braid and she had changed into capris and a pink blouse that made her look rosy and fresh.

"Everything okay?" I asked, not sure which answer I wanted her to give.

"I told him I'm coming home tomorrow."

"Okay. That's good, isn't it?" If so, why did it sadden me so much to think of my sister leaving?

"I'm not going for long, though."

I blinked at her. "What do you mean? You're going to go to British Columbia with him, then?" It felt as if I was losing her just as I was really beginning to enjoy her.

"No. I'm cured," she announced. "All it took was ten minutes of talking to Jeremy on the phone, and I knew it wasn't worth the drama. He just called out of guilt, not because he loves me, and talking to him, I realized I didn't love him either. Not really. Not enough to uproot everything and leave Toronto. I just *wanted* to be in love with him, you know? You were right—the phone call made me see the truth of it."

I observed her carefully, but her eyes were clear and her skin radiant, and I knew she was speaking the truth. I went to hug her.

"So you're okay?"

"Yes. I really am. Or at least, I will be shortly," she said.

"And now you're making pancakes?"

"Yes. I felt a sudden craving for blueberries and maple syrup. And Finn will be here for supper, so we have to eat something boringly healthy then, so it's syrup and carbs for lunch. But tell me what you found out today."

"I will while we eat," I said. "First let me go change out of this skirt. I don't feel like myself in it." I paused in the door and looked back at her. "I'm glad you aren't moving to British Columbia, Gilly. I'd miss you. I feel like I just found you again."

"I'm glad you feel that way," she said, "because the other half of the story is that I've decided to take you up on your kind offer." She set down the spatula and looked at me, half smiling and half fearful. "I want to live here in Grandma's house with you."

I felt a surprising balloon of joy rise in my chest, and a goofy grin spread across my face.

"Really?"

"Yes. If the offer still stands."

"Of course, it does! But you just said you told Jeremy you didn't want to uproot everything and leave Toronto."

"Because," she pointed out patiently, "I don't love him. But I do love *you*. And I love Grandma, despite everything, and I want to live here in her house with you. I'll go back long enough to get the rest of my things and finish out my notice at work, and then I'll be back up in a couple of weeks. Deal?"

"It's a deal," I said.

"World's problems solved. So tell me about *your* day already!"

I grinned. "Let me change," I said, "and then I'll tell you what I've learned about Grandma."

As I bounded up the stairs, my own words whispered pointedly at me. *Let me change.* It was all I could do not to laugh aloud.

Gillian took it better than I'd expected. When I told her the missionaries and two of Grandma's Mormon friends were coming to teach me about the church on Thursday night, she simply said, "That sounds interesting. But I'd like to sit in on it, if that's okay. Can you wait until I'm back up here?"

"Sure, okay. But you aren't afraid Mom is going to rise from the grave and throw a hatchet at us?" I asked, only half joking.

Gillian shrugged. "It's just research, right? What's the worst that can happen? We have to have an exorcism in the kitchen to get the Mormons out of the house? That New Age friend of yours, Miriam—she could come do a sage smudging or something, couldn't she?"

"I just wanted to caution you, because Grandma listened to them and ended up joining them," I pointed out gravely.

"Which is precisely what we're trying to understand, isn't it?" she replied. "Oh! We can't very well have two old ladies sitting on cushions on the floor. You really ought to have a couch, Kerris."

"We'll have to sit around the kitchen table," I said. "I'll drum up some extra chairs."

I think I'd half hoped Gillian would talk me out of the mad scheme.

That night the insomnia hit me hard again, my brain refusing to turn off, and finally I got up to sit at the kitchen table in the light of a single lamp. I ran through the day again in my mind. I hadn't even gone to the church service itself, but the simplicity of the room and plain dress of the people had appealed to me. The kindness in Gertie and Catherine's voices still stuck with me. The caring in their elderly faces. The affectionate way they spoke of Grandma. The touch of Catherine's age-spotted hand on mine.

It couldn't hurt to listen to what they had to say, I told myself. It would help me understand Grandma better, and maybe—*maybe*—come to terms with her leaving. If anything could help me forgive her, I owed it to myself and to Grandma to give it a try.

Ian invited me to meet him for coffee at the café the next day during his free period. It was a gloriously warm day for May and the place was packed, so we carried our cups to the park to sit on a bench in the sunshine. I felt ridiculously happy to be sitting there with him and in such a pretty place, the sun soothing on my shoulders.

"How's Gillian enjoying her stay?" Ian asked. I'd told him about her but hadn't yet had a chance to introduce them.

"She's gone back to Toronto to get her stuff. She's going to move up here with me," I said.

"What, permanently? That's terrific!"

"It is?" I joked.

"I worry about you being here on your own," Ian confessed. "I'll feel better knowing you've got someone around."

"I grew up in Toronto," I reminded him. "I doubt Smoke River is a hotbed of criminal activity. You are the one who keeps insisting no one here locks their doors."

"I wasn't thinking of someone breaking in. I was thinking more along the line of you knocking a beam down on yourself, or falling off a ladder and breaking your back, with no one around to help," he replied peacefully.

"I've only fallen off a ladder once," I protested. "And it was my wrist that broke, not my back."

"Either way, I think it's good for you to have some family here."

"Actually, Gillian's not the only family I have in Smoke River. Or had."

"What do you mean?"

So I told him about Grandma leaving when I was young, not dying as I'd been told. About her joining the Latter-day Saint Church and coming to Smoke River. About it really being her headstone we'd found in the cemetery, and about her leaving me the house.

"That's astonishing!" he exclaimed when I'd finished. "Imagine your own grandmother living here all those years and you didn't know it! I'm surprised she let your mother tell you she was dead, though."

"My mother was a force of nature," I replied. "I'm not at all surprised she cut us off from Grandma. Religion was not a safe subject in our house."

I briefly told him why, and that led to other topics and an unburdening discussion of fathers in general, and by the time he said he needed to get back to the school and stood, the moment had moved on and I realized I hadn't told him that Gillian and I were going to meet with the missionaries to learn more about the church. I wasn't sure what held me back from telling him then. Fear? Embarrassment? My own self-doubt? Astonishment at myself that I was even doing such a thing? Probably a bit of all four. At any rate, I told myself I'd laid enough on him for one day and would save that particular nugget for another time.

We ditched our paper cups in the waste bin and he took my hand, entwining my fingers in his and pushing our joined hands into his pocket as we walked back. It was fantastically comfortable.

"Thanks for meeting me," he said. "I'm leaving tomorrow for a cousin's wedding in Sudbury this weekend, and then it's Victoria Day. How about if we meet for coffee again on the Tuesday after?"

"Sure thing."

He kissed me briefly as we parted, and I just let myself feel that slowly spreading happiness, like butter oozing off of pancakes, and didn't try to analyze it too closely.

It was a busy weekend, and before I knew it, it was the holiday and June was just around the corner. I had won the battle over the weeds in the backyard, and now I scattered wildflower seeds with Kat and Anne-Marie, who were delighted to help. They chattered so excitedly about the daisy chains they would make this summer that I fervently hoped the birds wouldn't eat all the seeds before they had a chance to germinate. We celebrated spring with root beer and some hot dogs toasted on forks over the stove burner, and then they headed home to get ready to go see the fireworks with their family.

"They aren't very good fireworks," Kat confided as they took their leave. "The fire department just shoots a few off over the river. But it's still fun."

"Do you want to come with us?" Anne-Marie asked.

"Thanks, but Ian is supposed to be home from Sudbury today. I thought I'd call and see if he and Finn want to go," I said.

"Oh, Ian's taking us," Anne-Marie said, then stopped abruptly. Kat had surreptitiously stepped on her sister's foot, but I noticed the movement. Anne-Marie clamped her mouth shut and shot me a worried look. I didn't know what it was about, but apparently Kat didn't want me tagging along. I felt foolishly disappointed, but I smiled and said, "Okay. Well, have a good time, then."

I watched them walk away, Kat's head tipped slightly as if she were hissing at her sister from the corner of her mouth, not wanting me to see. Puzzled, I went back into the house and cleared away the lunch fixings. So, Ian was taking Finn and the Jameson children to see the fireworks. Why didn't Kat want me to know that? And why didn't she want me to come along?

Unless it was because her mother was going along too.

I set the plates in the sink with a clatter and stood looking down at them, my heart sinking. I didn't know what to think about Ian, but if he really was seeing Mrs. Jameson, what did he think he was doing pursuing me? Because that was what he was doing, I felt sure. He had even phoned me once from Sudbury, after the wedding, his tone completely friendly, just to talk about nothing in particular. I definitely felt he was interested and sought out my company, and I enjoyed his. But was he being honest with me? I tried to give him the benefit of the doubt. Maybe he was just taking time to sort things out in his own head, to figure out where he and I stood. I hoped he'd eventually come to the same viewpoint I had, because no matter what doubt I had about where Ian wanted our relationship to go, I was pretty sure I knew where I did.

That night I could hear the pop and boom of the fireworks, but I didn't go out to look at them.

Gillian returned with a U-Haul full of her things Tuesday morning. I looked closely at her when she arrived, but she seemed dry-eyed and okay with her decision to let Jeremy go. As I helped her carry her boxes and clothes up to her room, I couldn't help feeling Grandma would have been pleased to know we girls were back under one roof again. It had been a long time.

"I'll build you some bookshelves," I told her. "And a table to use as a desk, if you want."

"Swell. This crate will do for now. I know you're busy."

"I am." Work had started picking up just by Peggy's contacts around Smoke River. I had lined up two more small jobs just that morning—laying flooring for one person and helping another put up a greenhouse from a kit. I was gaining confidence that once I really started working in earnest, everything was going to fall into place for me. After months of uncertainty and self-doubt, it was reassuring.

"Any more news on the McGrath front?" Gillian asked as we dished up store-bought lasagna for supper.

"Nothing more to report," I said, skipping over the whole fireworks thing. "He's back from his cousin's wedding, and we were supposed to meet for coffee this afternoon, but he called just a while ago to say he's busy getting school exams ready, so it's postponed. But I'm hoping to have him over soon to meet you." I felt that old twinge of doubt and quickly changed the subject. "Hey, I arranged the missionaries for Thursday night. Is that okay?"

"Fine with me."

"You haven't changed your mind about meeting with them?"

"No. Have you?"

"No."

On the other hand, I'd decided I didn't need to go through their whole series of lessons. I'd listen just long enough to get a grasp on what Grandma had found so important that she could choose it over her daughter and granddaughters, and then I'd tell them that was enough and ask them to leave. I'd never have to see them again if I didn't want to, after Thursday.

What I didn't expect was that Gillian would invite them to come again.

Chapter Twenty

"What they said made sense," she said after they'd left, shrugging as if a second appointment was no big deal. She went to forage in the fridge. "They've given us the basics, but I wouldn't mind learning more."

"This is just in the interest of research, right?" I said, eying her narrowly.

"Of course. What else would it be?" She took out an apple and bit into it. "If it helps us understand Grandma better, then there's no harm, right?"

"Hmm." I went upstairs and sat on my bed, needing a little quiet time to myself. What the missionaries and Grandma's friends had told us *was* interesting, all about prayer and personal revelation, but I wasn't sure there was anything so marvelous about it that it explained leaving your family to join up. I supposed it would be a good idea to learn more, to understand it better.

"But a second appointment is definitely the limit," I said aloud, reassuring myself.

I could have sworn I heard the house chuckle.

That Friday I went to watch a rugby game at the school . . . Well, I'll be honest. I went to watch Ian coach the rugby team. I didn't let him know I was there, not wanting to distract him while he was working. He wore jeans and a blue baseball cap that made him look much younger, like one of his own players, and his red sports jersey emphasized the breadth of his shoulders. I watched him call out instructions and clap at the various plays and could see he was in his element. When he spoke to the boys on the bench, he didn't speak down to them but crouched to their level, and what few callouts I heard him make were positive and encouraging ones, unlike the other team's coach, who seemed to be haranguing his crew.

I didn't know much about the game; it all seemed like a lot of running around and banging into each other without much regard for rules to me. But I enjoyed sitting in the hard metal bleachers and applauding and yelling along with the crowd, and when it apparently ended (I wasn't sure who had won), I worked my way down through the throng to where Ian stood debriefing his team. I watched him put his hand on their shoulders and coax a smile from each face (ah. They had lost, then.) and then he turned and saw me and I watched his beautiful eyes light up. (I *have* mentioned how beautiful his eyes are, haven't I? And I won't deny it made me proud that they were lighting up for *me*.) He jogged over.

"You came!" He sounded pleased.

"I did. It was very exciting," I said.

"You know much about rugby?"

"Not a clue. But it was fun to watch," I said.

"Fun to coach, too. We lost, though."

"I gathered that from the glum expressions."

Ian glanced back to where the team members were stripping off muddy shirts and digging in coolers for water bottles.

"Listen, I have to drive some of the kids home, but maybe I could come by and see you later."

"Actually, I was going to ask you to dinner tonight. You can meet Gillian. She's back now."

"Sure! Thanks. What shall I bring?"

"We've got it covered. Just bring Finn."

"Will do." He thanked me again and jogged back to his team.

They arrived at six o'clock, bearing a huge bowl of tossed salad. I had whipped up pasta and vegetables and Gillian had produced a pretty amazing strawberry shortcake. Finn took his plate out to the fort where he was setting up for another sleepover, this time with Peter and Seth. Once school was out for the summer, I suspected we'd be having sleepovers every night of the week. I might have to ask Ian to pitch in on the cost of all the snacks I knew I'd be doling out.

"So you are a cosmetician, I think Kerris said." Ian chatted with Gillian as we sat eating on the back porch. He shot me a twinkling glance, both of us thinking *cosmologist*.

Gillian slid her eyes at me. "I was, yes, until a few days ago. I've got to find another job pretty soon up here. My savings can only last so long. Any ideas?"

"I believe Shoppers Drug Mart is looking for a person for their cosmetics counter," he said brightly. "There's a sign in their window. It's sales, but it's in the same sort of field, at least. It would hold you over until you found something better."

"Thanks. I'll give them a try," Gillian said gratefully.

When there was a lull in the conversation, I took a deep breath. Feeling inexplicably nervous, I told him Gillian and I had decided to meet with the missionaries to learn more about the Church of Jesus Christ of Latter-day Saints in an effort to understand what had enticed Grandma away. I might have left out the fact that we'd actually already met with them.

He didn't freak out about it or try to dissuade us, only nodded and said it sounded like a reasonable thing to do, so I supposed it wasn't as big a deal, really, as it somehow felt.

"Imagine, this being your grandmother's house! And you and I stumbling over that headstone at the cemetery," he mused. "I've been thinking about it ever since you told me. If we hadn't gone for that walk, you might still be wondering who left this place to you."

I nodded and then felt my face grow warm, remembering the kiss he'd given me on that walk. He'd kissed me lightly a couple of times since then, but nothing like that one. I felt Gillian's curious eyes on my face and deftly switched topics, telling them about working on the Sellers' enclosed porch, and about Peggy drumming up more work for me.

"That sounds like Mom," Ian said ruefully. "The McGraths can be intrusive," he added apologetically. "Like the camel getting its nose into the tent. If they get too pushy, let me know."

"Not at all. I was flattered your mother would help me get work. It was very kind of her."

"Today a bathroom, tomorrow a greenhouse—who knows what will follow?" Gillian agreed, toasting me in my turn with her own pop can.

"Hopefully a big fat bank account will be what follows," I replied. "Grandma's bequest has soaked up every penny I had and then some."

"And then your little sister moved in to mooch off you on top of that," Gillian added. "Don't worry, sis. I'll call Shoppers Drug Mart tomorrow."

"What's left to do on this place?" Ian asked, looking around. "Besides the countertops, obviously."

"Just a few cosmetic things," I told him, feeling pleased with myself. I'd accomplished a lot, really, considering my budget. There were only a few things to wrap up, none of them urgent except the kitchen. "Some painting upstairs, installing the new bannister, putting up curtain rods. All easy stuff. I'm having a professional address the aluminum wiring." I gave a brief rundown of my encounter with the three electricians, playing up the humor of it, and Ian laughed.

"School is out the second week of June and then I'm free as a bird all summer," he said. "Let me know if I can be of help at all."

"Be careful—I might take you up on it," I warned him. "So don't say it unless you mean it." And then I stopped.

It sounded startlingly like what Catherine had said to me.

The evening passed pleasantly, and then Ian went out to kiss Finn goodnight before heading home. Or rather, to manfully shake Finn's hand, since Peter and Seth would be watching. As he picked his way across the yard in the near dark, Gillian and I stood watching from the back door.

"I approve," Gillian said, nodding. "He's a keeper."

"Except for that little Mrs. Jameson thing," I reminded her.

"Maybe you were wrong about that. He certainly seems to genuinely dote on you. He doesn't seem like the dishonest type."

"Every day after school, he goes straight to her house and hides his car in the garage. What other explanation can there be?"

"I don't know, but I think instead of skulking in the bushes every day watching her driveway, you should just ask him about it," Gillian said.

"I haven't been skulking," I protested. "I just—um—happen to go out for walks, and I happen to be observant."

Gillian sighed. "I haven't had much luck with men, I'm the first to admit, but I know a good one when I see one, and Ian McGrath doesn't seem like a two-timer to me."

He didn't to me either. But I could think of no other reason for his behavior, and I could more easily see myself flying to Mars than asking him about it. Because to do so, I'd have to reveal my own behavior, skulking in the bushes to spy on him. And how would I explain the reason I'd felt the need to do it? Well, no more. I didn't need to collect any more evidence—of his behavior, or of my own feelings about him. Both were pretty clear.

I finished the bathroom for Margaret and Eric, which they were more than pleased with, and it was with a feeling of accomplishment that I deposited their check in the bank. It had gone well. I hadn't lost my touch, the room had come together beautifully, and I knew they would spread the word and recommend me. I went to meet with Bess Ingram's son about his deck, and I got a call from another of Peggy's friends asking if I could repoint her brick chimney that was crumbling. The ball was beginning to roll, and I hadn't even had to do much advertising yet.

Early Wednesday morning there was a knock on the door, and I opened it to find Jana, red-faced and breathless, on the porch. She gripped little Anne-Marie, who looked no happier, by the hand. Anne-Marie's shoes were untied, her shirt was misbuttoned, and her hair was straggling from its hasty ponytail. Jana's bike lay on the sidewalk behind her.

"You're home! I'm so sorry to bother you, but I need help," Jana burst out the instant I opened the door. "Everybody else has already left for school and I can't reach Ian."

"Come in, come in." I pulled them both inside. "What's the matter?"

"I have a final exam today that I just *can't* miss," Jana said, looking near tears. "But Anne-Marie's got a temperature and threw up her breakfast, and I can't send her to school. I need someone to watch her just for a couple of hours, and then I'll come straight back after my exam. I didn't know who to call."

"Of course, I can watch her," I said, just as Gillian came down the hall from the kitchen.

"What's up?" she asked.

"Anne-Marie's going to stay with us this morning while Jana takes an exam," I explained. "She isn't feeling well. Stomach flu, maybe." I looked back at Jana. "Are you running late? Do you need a ride to school?"

"Oh, would you? That would be super!" Jana said, and did burst into tears this time.

I looked at Gillian. She looked from the embarrassedly mopping-up Jana to the pink-faced and pukey Anne-Marie and made her choice.

"I can run you to school in my car," she told Jana. "Just let me fetch my keys."

"Will my bike fit?" Jana asked. "I have to be able to get home again after. The bus doesn't run until three."

"Take my truck," I suggested.

As soon as they got on the road, I guided Anne-Marie up to my room, took off her shoes, and tucked her into bed with just a light sheet over her. I gave her half a Tylenol, put a glass of water and a strategically placed bowl near to hand, and then sat on the edge of the bed. I didn't know her as well as the other Jameson children, but she didn't object at all to being left in my care. I carefully brushed her blonde bangs out of her face.

"You'll feel better soon," I told her. "Just try to rest a little."

She nodded.

"Do you need anything else?"

She shook her head and swiped at the tears that rose in her big blue eyes.

"You know I'm glad to have you come here," I told her. "I'm just sorry you don't feel well."

"Yeah," she said miserably. "I threw up my breakfast. And it was waffles, too!"

I couldn't help smiling at the outrage and sense of injustice in her voice. "I'm sure you can have waffles again sometime when you're feeling better."

"Yeah. Jana makes good waffles."

"Is your mommy feeling sick too?" I asked gently.

Anne-Marie hesitated, then nodded again.

Maybe Mrs. Jameson was hung over again or something. I found it sad that Jana seemed to be carrying the lion's share of the mothering at home—cooking, childcare . . . How big of a problem did Mrs. Jameson have, when her fourteen-year-old daughter had to turn to neighbors for help? I struggled to understand Ian's attraction to a woman who clearly wasn't functioning all that well at home. Was it bad enough that the authorities needed to get involved? Surely Ian would be aware, would say something . . . He might like the woman, but he was a father and a teacher foremost, and he would have the children's welfare at heart. Wouldn't he?

Anne-Marie tossed and turned for half the morning, uncomfortable and bored in equal measures. I found her some paper and colored pencils to draw with, but she didn't feel well enough to do anything, and she wasn't interested in watching TV. Finally, I soothed her into lying still with a cool cloth on her forehead by singing to her. I wasn't a great singer, and I didn't really know any children's tunes beyond the Alphabet and *Twinkle Twinkle, Little Star*, but my voice seemed to calm the little girl, and she snuggled down at last, her eyes steady on my face. So I gave her my best rendition of *Born Free* and *We Shall Overcome* and the theme song from *Ghostbusters*. And then the song from the Tide Pods commercial. And a muddled version of *Country Roads*, to which I'd forgotten the words. Mercifully, she kept the Tylenol down and fell asleep by the time I had to resort to *The Eye of the Tiger*.

I fell silent, looking down at her flushed, little face and hoping she was all right. I thought about the lesson Gillian and I had had with the missionaries when they'd taught us to pray. They kept encouraging us to try it, and I supposed I had conceded—hoped—there was a God, but so far I hadn't tried addressing him. But I thought maybe now was a good time to try offering just a small prayer on Anne-Marie's behalf. I mean, it couldn't hurt, could it?

Feeling slightly foolish and glad no one could see me, I closed my eyes and thought, as if addressing a letter, *Dear God . . .* That didn't sound right. Maybe *Dear Father . . .* Okay, that sounded better. More personal. But what next?

I heard the front door click and knew Gillian was home, and in a rush of self-consciousness I blurted aloud, "Please let Anne-Marie get better and not be contagious! I so don't need the flu right now. Thank you. Amen." And then remembered the way the missionaries had taught me to close a prayer, in the name of Jesus Christ, but it was too late, and I jumped up and went downstairs to wash my hands. I figured God knew how it was supposed to go, and he could fill in the blanks if he was that strict about it.

"She okay?" Gillian asked, dumping her keys on the table. She'd gotten into the same habit I had of leaving everything in that spot.

"I think so," I said, feeling my cheeks still glowing warm with embarrassment. I wasn't sure why I felt so silly trying to pray, but I really didn't want Gillian to know about my feeble effort. "She's sleeping now. It's probably the best thing for her. Thanks for taking Jana to school."

"No problem. She seems like a great kid."

"She's amazing. I get the feeling she's filling in as mom a lot at their house." I briefly told her about the other time I had taken Jana to school, and about my suspicions that Mrs. Jameson had a drinking problem or depression or something along those lines that required Jana to step in more than most teens had to at home.

"That's awful," Gillian said, making a face. "I won't say we had a great mother, by a long shot, but at least she was functional. She fed us and dressed us and got us where we needed to be."

"I know. I have a hard time seeing why Ian is involved with her."

"If he is. Who knows? Is she drop-dead gorgeous or something?"

"I don't know. I've never met her," I confessed. "Judging from her kids, I'd say she's likely beautiful. But Ian wouldn't be swayed by that alone."

Gillian shrugged, clearly refraining from giving her opinion of the male half of the species. I shook my head.

"Maybe instead of judging her I should be a better neighbor and go see her," I said. "Maybe she'd be open to some help. Or maybe I'm completely wrong about the situation. Either way, it can't hurt for me to keep an eye on the kids and make sure they're all right. They're terrific kids. Very loving toward each other."

"Then maybe she's been a good mom to them after all, if that's how they've turned out."

I thought about this. "Is the kind of person you are entirely dependent on what kind of mother you had?"

"Wow, I hope not," Gillian said sincerely. "Otherwise, there's no hope for either of us."

Chapter Twenty-One

Jana arrived home before lunch, full of thanks and apologies. I waved them off and sat her at the table to share our lunch of tuna sandwiches and carrot salad. (I had upped my game since Gillian's arrival.)

"Anne-Marie's been fine," I told her. "She slept for a while and now she's listening to my iPod and eating a Popsicle. She'll be okay."

"I can't thank you enough. I didn't know who else to call."

"I like to think you can call on me any time," I assured her. "How did your exam go?"

"I think pretty well. I only have two more exams and then I've got the whole summer off." She looked very pleased with the prospect.

"What will you do all summer?" Gillian asked. "Will you look for a job?"

Jana shook her head. She carefully swallowed her mouthful of salad before saying, "I'm only fourteen. I'll probably be watching the kids, helping out at home . . . You know."

I decided to veer the conversation away from that subject. "You know, my first summer job was working as a receptionist for a construction company. That's probably what first sparked my interest and led to the work I do now. I've never had to flip hamburgers or babysit—I always managed to find a job that had something to do with building or decorating."

Jana looked interested at this. "Kevin's got a summer job with a roofing company. Maybe he'll end up doing construction too. And I remember my dad once said his first job was sweeping floors at a bank, and he ended up in finance." She looked at Gillian. "And you're a cosmetician, right? What was your first summer job?"

Gillian grinned. "Tagging and vaccinating skunks for the conservation authority."

"Skunks! But—"

"We had plastic shower curtains we'd hold up like a shield, and then throw it over the skunk to, um, keep the spray from hitting us while we treated them."

Jana shook her head. "There goes the theory, then."

"Not at all," Gillian said. "It made me all the more interested in a career where I looked and smelled good . . . and besides, it taught me a valuable life skill. I've learned to shield myself from a lot of skunks in my life." She winked at me, and I knew she was well and truly recovering from Jeremy.

I thought about Marcus and wondered if I would ever be as good at shielding myself.

"Let's go collect Anne-Marie and I'll drive you home," I told Jana.

When I got to their house, I helped Jana walk her little sister to the front door and then hesitated.

"Do you think your mom would like a visit?" I offered. "I could just pop in for a minute . . . "

"Oh," Jana said, looking startled, and then waved her hand. "No, I don't think she'd be up to company right now," she said. "Not when she's . . . yeah. Maybe another time, though. I'll tell her you asked after her. Thanks again for your help!"

She whisked Anne-Marie into the house and closed the door, leaving me on the steps. Musing, I went back to my car and wondered if I'd ever meet their elusive mother.

Friday night, Ian invited me to dinner again. I knew my heart was reaching the point of no return, if it wasn't there already, and I needed to finally ask him about Mrs. Jameson. I wasn't looking forward to the conversation and felt jittery when I thought about it. I didn't want it to become a confrontation. But didn't he need to make a choice at some point? How long did he intend to carry this on? What did it say about me that I was putting up with this situation yet still hoping that our relationship was going somewhere? I guess my experience with Marcus hadn't completely crushed my optimism . . .

But what if he didn't choose me?

Better to know now, I decided. I didn't want to pressure the man, but this was becoming ridiculous.

He picked me up after school and we went to The Keg, an upscale restaurant in Port Daley.

Ian ordered a steak and I ordered some sort of pasta with garlic bread. It was one of those restaurants where they keep the lights so dim you can hardly see your plate and you feel you need to speak in whispers. I suppose it is meant to make the ambience more romantic or peaceful, but I found it more a nuisance than anything else. Were they trying to disguise the portion sizes? Hide dirty tablecloths? Save on energy? Did they think the fancy-dancy ambience justified the outrageous prices? Or were they hoping you wouldn't see the prices on the menus in the semi-darkness?

Maybe they were hoping the hushed atmosphere would keep patrons from confronting each other in loud tones about certain personal relationship issues . . .

As dinner progressed, I found myself growing more and more on edge and irritated. The whole situation wasn't Ian's fault, I reminded myself . . . except I felt it sort of was. He may not realize how much I'd fallen for him, and maybe he hadn't set out purposely to win me over, but surely he had to take some of the responsibility for it in the end. Yet how could he sit here, practically nose to nose with me, cutting up his steak and murmuring about mundane topics like final exams and whether to sign Finn up for swim lessons, and not address the elephant in the room? The elephant with the fancy-schmancy house and the willow tree, not to mention the six children. I told myself I should trust him, give him the benefit of the doubt. But he'd had every opportunity to tell me about Mrs. Jameson but hadn't. Where did he think our relationship was going? Was it even a relationship? Had I misread his attention? That unforgettable *kiss*?

By the time dessert came around, I was in a fine state. I knew I was working myself up to becoming unreasonable and argumentative once I did broach the subject, but I couldn't help it. I wanted to know where we stood. And part of me was disgusted with myself for being so optimistic and stupid as to have allowed myself to fall for another man, after what I'd been through with Marcus. Did I learn *nothing*? Was I about to be let down spectacularly once again?

I watched the wait staff put a plate on the table between us containing two small white circles and a finger bowl of water, then retreat. I composed my thoughts, deciding how I should word it . . . *I'd like to explore where you envision this is going . . . Is there something you wanted to tell me . . .* My heart began to pound and I cleared my throat nervously.

"You know, Ian . . . "

He looked up at me, smiling, his fork of French apple pie halfway to his mouth. And my carefully composed sentences suddenly sounded dumb to me.

"Um . . . "

"Yes, Kerris?"

"I, um . . . " I reached for one of the breath mints and popped it in my mouth to give myself more time to think before I blurted the wrong thing and messed this all up beyond repair.

"Did you want to say something?"

"Yes. I wanted to . . . well, feel you out about . . . " There was something wrong in my mouth. Something terribly wrong.

"Yes?" He lowered his fork and leaned closer, his eyes lidded, his smile playing on his lips.

"I think we should talk about . . . "

Oh no . . .

I jumped up from the table.

"Excuse me," I mumbled and dashed for the washroom. Where I spent two minutes choking and spitting out the dehydrated (now rehydrated) hand towel I had mistaken in the dark for a breath mint.

Another woman came into the washroom and gave me a pitying glance where I stood bent over the sink.

"Bad date?" she laughed.

"The worst," I agreed and spit again.

Needless to say, the conversation never happened. By the time he'd stopped laughing, he was dropping me off at home. I admitted temporary defeat and invited him to come to a barbecue Saturday evening. We'd talk then, I consoled myself.

When I mentioned to Gillian the next morning that Ian was coming over that night, she immediately turned the private barbecue into a spontaneous hello-to-summer backyard party. Before ten o'clock she had invited the Jamesons and the Sellers family to join us. So much for private conversations. Ah well. We'd celebrate the end of school, I agreed. And what the heck, maybe I could put off the Mrs. Jameson discussion forever. I called to invite Catherine and Gertie too, and I would have invited Jeri, but I didn't know how to reach her, and I hadn't seen her about as much lately. Maybe the writing was going better.

The Jameson kids showed up while I was still trying to get the old barbecue started. Kat Jameson informed us that her mother was at a doctor's appointment and couldn't come, but that she'd said to thank us for the invitation and she looked forward to meeting us another time. And she'd sent a watermelon for the party. Kevin carried it, already nicely pre-cut, in a large Tupperware container.

"Isn't that thoughtful!" Gillian took the heavy container and set it on the board-and-sawhorse table I'd erected by the back steps. "I love watermelon. Once for my birthday I had watermelon with a candle stuck in it, instead of birthday cake."

I remembered that occasion, I thought with a stab of sudden sadness. It had been Grandma's idea, knowing Gillian preferred melon over cake. Mom had thought it was silly but went along with it because it meant less hassle than making a cake.

Donna and Craig Sellers appeared next, bearing a bowl of Caesar salad and with Blaine stuffed into a bright purple baby backpack. Craig, whom I'd met only briefly while doing their closet and porch, was well over six feet tall, no older than twenty-five, and as outgoing and chatty as his wife. He soon struck up a conversation with Kevin Jameson about basketball, which he'd apparently played in high school, while the younger kids gravitated toward Donna. I'd been wondering how to keep them all entertained, but when I went inside to bring out the fixings for the burgers, Donna was already sitting on the grass beside the fort, deep into telling a story, surrounded by rapt little faces, and Kat Jameson was bouncing Blaine in her lap.

"Even Finn's captivated," Ian remarked, coming to help me carry the plastic container of condiment bottles. "And it takes a lot to hold his attention."

"She ought to run her own day care or something," I said. "She seems to have the knack."

Ian looked thoughtful. "There's a poster up at the library saying they're looking for volunteers to help with their after-school reading program for kids. I bet she'd be good at something like that."

I nodded happily. "She'd be perfect for that, and I bet she'd love to do it. I get the feeling she gets lonely sometimes, and it would be a way for her to get to know some others in the neighborhood. And she obviously loves kids."

I set about dealing with the food, but the whole time I worked I was watching Donna Sellers from the corner of my eye. If ever there was a woman meant to mother lots of small children, she was one. Little Anne-Marie Jameson had crept forward, drawn in by whatever story Donna was telling, and now was leaning with her head against Donna's arm. Blaine had crawled away from Kat and taken up a comfy seat in his mother's lap, where he reclined happily. And Seth was paying such close attention to Donna's words that he'd forgotten the grape Popsicle in his hand, and it had melted and slipped unnoticed into the grass.

Some women had a talent for mothering, I decided, and some did not. Some were meant to have children and some just weren't. I pushed away the twinge of sorrow that followed that thought (and let's face it, a bit of envy too) and concentrated on slicing the hamburger buns. I became aware I was muttering under my breath (*What sort of bakery sells unsliced buns anyway? Anne-Marie Jameson never looked at* me *so adoringly, and I nursed her back to health, for pity's sake!* And other such unworthy things). I lost track of what was going on beside the fort, but when I turned back to the picnic table, I felt a small nudge against my leg. Looking down, I found Finn.

"Hey, Finn," I said, clawing my raw feelings back into my throat and swallowing them. "Are you hungry? This will be ready in a second."

"Nah, I had a bag of chips," he said.

I looked over at the knot of kids surrounding Donna. Like some Raphaelite painting. "Did she finish the story?"

"No, she's still going. I just wanted to come hang out with you," he replied offhandedly.

I looked at him a minute, blinking, fighting a sudden urge to grab him up in a big hug. The kid was a mind reader. Instead, I cracked open a root beer and handed it to him.

"You can hang out with me anytime, Stinky," I said. And he grinned.

The second appointment with Gertie, Catherine, and the missionaries was as interesting and low-pressure as the first. We sat in the kitchen eating oatmeal cookies and chatting as if it were the most ordinary conversation in the world, but I couldn't help wondering, as I watched Gillian's lively interest, what Mom would do if she knew. But really, I argued with myself, was it fair to condemn all religion and religious people just because of my father's one poor example?

Besides, Mom was dead and buried, I reminded myself. She couldn't hurt us anymore.

"So why did you decide to go on a mission?" Gillian asked. "Is it required or . . .?"

"No, but it's encouraged, and, well, I've just known all my life that I was meant to go," said Sister Davis. "Growing up, it was just something I knew would happen one day."

"Like being a government sleeper agent," Gillian said, nodding in perfect understanding. The missionaries burst out laughing.

"Something along those lines," Sister Davis agreed.

That night they told us more about Joseph Smith, who, at no older than Jana Jameson, had received revelation that had turned his world upside down and led him to go on eventually to found the Church of Jesus Christ of Latter-day Saints. (Personally I thought the name was quite a mouthful and he could have gone with something a bit more pithy. But apparently it wasn't up to him.) As I listened, my first thought was that Joseph's parents and siblings had been awfully nonjudgmental and supportive. If Jana came home one day and announced she'd been visited by heavenly beings in the forest, would her family believe her, or would they call for a psychiatrist? But Joseph's family apparently had believed him. There was *one* family, at least, that religion had drawn together, not pulled apart.

My second thought was that the story seemed somehow familiar. I was sure I hadn't heard it before, though. I knew Grandma had certainly never told it to me. So why did it seem I was hearing something I already knew? And why was I smelling that blasted flowery perfume again?

When the talk and the cookies wound to an end, I stood to thank our guests for coming. It was on my lips to say what I had been rehearsing all week—that while we appreciated them generously giving us their time and we'd genuinely enjoyed meeting them, we probably knew enough now and did not feel there was a reason to continue the discussion.

But even as I began to say this, Gillian spoke up.

"Would you mind if I came to church with you this Sunday? I mean, is that allowed?"

I stared at her, but she avoided my eyes. Catherine and Gertie laughed.

"Yes, it's allowed," Catherine said. "I can come pick you up just before ten, if you'd like a ride. That way you're not walking into the meeting by yourself."

"Thanks! That would be great," Gillian said.

"Kerris, do you want to come too?" Gertie asked.

I didn't want to hurt their feelings, but I wasn't sure I wanted to go. "I'll think about it," I finally said.

Gillian showed them to the door, and I heard her making an appointment with the missionaries for a third lesson on Tuesday. The front door closed, and Gillian came back into the kitchen, a defiant look on her face as if she already anticipated my objections.

"What are you doing?" I asked, struggling to keep my voice even. "You're meeting with them again?"

"Yes. The things we've heard are interesting, yes, but—well, they don't bring me any closer to understanding Grandma's decision to leave us," Gillian said. "I think there must be more to it, something they haven't told us yet, and I really need to know what it is. I don't want to give up yet."

I was silent, unable to argue with this, and after a moment she came to kiss me on the cheek.

"Good night, Kerris. I hope you're not too mad at me. Maybe I should have consulted you first."

I shook my head. "You're twenty-five years old, Gillian. You can do what you want."

"But I don't want to upset you," she said.

"It's okay. And you're right. We started this," I said, "and we should finish it."

Chapter Twenty-Two

I ended up going to church with Gillian that Sunday, for the whole two hours. And meeting with the missionaries again on Tuesday. And again on Thursday. Every time I told myself that was the last appointment, and every time I found I still had questions that hadn't been answered yet. There were things I wanted to know, perhaps more than I could admit to myself, and despite my misgivings, the missionaries seemed to have ready answers to all of my questions. Where was the harm in asking?

Lying in bed—my usual thinking time—I stared up at the dark ceiling and tried to imagine what Grandma's thought processes must have been. I tried to comprehend the sacrifice she had made for what she felt was important. It made me wonder what I had sacrificed for, if anything. What was important to me? What would I be willing to give for it?

I thought about my work, my tools, my skills and independence. My confidence, which I hadn't realized was so important until Marcus's betrayal had shaken it. My house, which was finally coming together into a home, a safe place where I could collect myself. But really, wasn't there something deeper that I wanted and would be willing to fight for? To sacrifice for?

Peace, I thought. I wanted peace in my mind and in my heart, like I'd fleetingly experienced on the river. I wanted that all the time.

And I wanted to be able to forgive—Mom for separating us from Grandma. Dad for disappearing.

Marcus for leaving me.

I rolled over and mashed my face into my pillow. Was that really it? Did I really want to forgive Marcus? I suspected I needed to in order to fully move on with my life. But, how could I? What would I give up to do it? The answer slid smoothly into my mind.

My injured pride. My resentment. My hurt. My envy of his new life with Maddie and their baby.

I would have to give up all those things in order to truly forgive Marcus and Maddie and find peace of mind. Could I do it? I wasn't sure, but I knew I needed to. I *wanted* to. Perhaps that was enough to start with. But how to do it? How to let go of all that pain and move toward forgiveness?

By the time the sun began to filter through the windows, I was no closer to the answer. I dressed silently and jogged down to the river to watch the mist, but I was too late, and the sun had already burned it away.

I was in a better mood by the next Friday evening. The day had been productive, Gillian had gotten the Drug Mart job, I had money in the bank—well, it was on its way to the credit card company, but all the better—and as an extra blessing, the weather had turned balmy. Jeri had dropped by with a platter of homemade spring rolls and stayed for a friendly if brief chat. She informed me she had planted her entire front lawn in potatoes.

To top the day off, I had discovered a family of rabbits in my backyard meadow, and it pleased me to think that wild animals would feel at home in my home. I set out a bird feeder and scattered some more wildflower seeds to thicken up the blooms that were starting to appear. I couldn't wait to show the kids the rabbits.

Ian brought Finn over for another sleepover in the fort with the Jameson boys (all three of them this time) and lingered to talk. We sat on the back steps and listened to the birds in the grass and the boys laughing in the fort. They'd been as excited over the bunnies as I was.

Ian, beside me, wore a chambray shirt and pants the color of the late-afternoon sky. He smelled faintly citrusy, embodying summer.

Ian had brought a bag of red licorice with him, but to my surprise he didn't send it out to the fort with the boys. He and I split it while we sat side by side, and it was the perfect ending to a perfect day.

I told him about Jeri's potatoes and we both got a chuckle out of it.

"I can't believe she actually ever wrote a book," I confessed. "She's never at her desk, anyway, as far as I can tell."

"She's written about eight of them, in fact," Ian told me. "You'll find them in the library."

"Really! I can't imagine it. Are they any good?"

"Exquisite," he said seriously.

"I'll have to read them."

"You won't be disappointed. However nutty she appears, she has a beautiful talent." He paused and cleared his throat. "So, the McGrath telegraph line tells me you've got work pouring in right and left these days," he said.

"Thanks to Margaret and your mother," I told him. "Another call came today about finishing someone's basement. I've got enough work to last all summer and into autumn. I have to say, I'd put off going back to work, but now that I'm back into it, I'm loving it. It feels good to do it again."

"I'm glad. And if your business takes off, you're more likely to stick around," he said.

I glanced at him and away. "I'm not going anywhere," I said. "This is home now." And I realized it was true. Somehow the shift had happened in my head without my being aware of it, and the house no longer felt as if it were just Grandma's. It had become an oasis of love for me and my sister, just as Grandma had provided us when we were young. I was still aware of her in the house, her scent, the feeling of her, but it was mine and Gillian's home now.

Ian smiled. "That's good."

"So . . . Gillian and I are still meeting with the missionaries to learn about Grandma's church," I said as nonchalantly as possible.

"That's good too. It might bring you some comfort and closure over everything, if you understand it better. Do you find you're feeling a bit less angry with your grandmother now?"

I looked out over the yard, admiring the wildflowers, the shape of the crabapple tree in the dusk. "Yes. I still don't entirely understand her decision, but I'm trying to. I'm getting to know her better, I think." I hesitated, then added, "The thing is, I started out wanting to learn about it for that reason. But now, I think maybe the—the reason has changed. I think now I'm learning about it for *me.* I—I like what I'm learning." It was the first time I'd admitted it, even to myself, and the words felt odd in my mouth.

Ian thought about this and nodded. "That's okay. More than okay, I think."

"Do you think so?"

"Sure. Why not? It can only help you, Kerris."

"I hope you don't mind my telling you all this. I was always told people aren't supposed to talk about religion or politics."

"I don't mind at all."

"It's not stretching any boundaries?"

"No. If it's important to you, it's important to me."

His response made a warm little wave wash over me. I smiled into the growing dark.

"Sometime can I tell you some of what we're learning? You might find it interesting too."

"Sure, if you'd like to. It might help me get to know *you* a little better." There was a pause, and then he said quietly, "I'd like to. Get to know you better, I mean."

I looked up at him, and without hesitation he leaned over and pressed his lips to mine. Then he moved back a couple of inches and looked into my eyes, waiting, silently asking me something I wasn't sure how to answer.

I drew a deep breath, knowing the moment had finally come. He began to speak too, but I held up my hand and shook my head. "Ian, I'm confused. You act as if you like me . . . "

"Of course I do. Isn't that what I'm leading up to here?" He set aside the almost-empty licorice bag and took my hands in both of his. "Kerris, I think I'm fa—"

"What about Mrs. Jameson?" I blurted. There. I'd said it.

He blinked. "Who?"

"Mrs. Jameson."

"The boys' mother? That Mrs. Jameson?"

"Who else? Ian, when were you going to tell me about her? I've been waiting for you to bring it up."

I saw a shutter close over his face like a light going out. He let go of my hands, his eyelids dropped half closed, and his lips pressed together a moment. I hoped he would deny it. But instead he said, "I don't know how you found out about it, but I don't see how it's any of your business."

I was stunned. "None of my—*Excuse me*?"

"Well, that was a rude way of saying it, I guess. I'm sorry. But Kerris, I don't want to involve you in it."

"But I *am* involved. I mean, you act like you want a relationship with me, but you don't deny . . . And you think I don't have the right to know?"

He spread his hands. "It has nothing to do with this. With us."

"Yes, it does. It has everything to do with us. Does *Mr.* Jameson know?"

"What? He died, three or four years ago. That's really what started all this, when he died."

"Oh, well, then I guess at least that makes it less messy for you." I felt as if, suddenly, I was looking at a stranger. I moved stiffly away from him and started to stand up to go back inside, but he put a hand on my shoulder, stopping me.

"Look, I don't know how you found out about it, because we've tried to be very careful. The less you know about it, the better. It—it isn't quite legal, you see."

"Not legal? I suppose it isn't very moral, but I wouldn't say it's exactly illegal," I said, feeling sorrow like a weight on my chest. *Stupid me. Betrayed again.* "I suppose it happens all the time."

He frowned. "I don't know of any other cases like this."

"No? My ex-husband for one," I spat, suddenly furious. "I guess by now I should be used to men lying to me and going behind my back! I thought you were different, Ian. I didn't think you were like that."

Ian raked his fingers through his hair and shook his head. "I wish I could have been honest with you, Kerris, but you have to understand it's a delicate situation. I have to put the children's needs first."

"The children's—! How on earth is this putting the children's needs first?"

Ian glanced anxiously at the fort and lowered his voice. "Of course it is!" he hissed. "This is all about trying to do what they feel is best for them. They're not alone. I provide the adult supervision. They're doing just fine. Please don't call Children's Aid."

I stopped, scowling in confusion. "Why would I call Children's Aid?"

"They're doing remarkably well when all is said and done. Jana is a big help. And Kevin's got a summer job now."

"What?" My mind was whirling. Nothing made sense.

"If we can just hold things together until he's eighteen, he can apply to be their legal guardian. Just one more year."

"Guardian! What are you talking about?"

"Unless she comes back, of course. I don't think it's likely, but the children still believe she will."

"Unless who comes back?" Had I wandered down a rabbit hole somewhere?

"Their mother. They think she just needed a break. It was so hard for her after her husband died. They're convinced she's just gone off to rest and recover a bit and then she'll come back."

"She's gone?" I asked stupidly.

"Well, yes . . . isn't that what we're talking about?" He stopped, confused.

"*I* was talking about your love affair," I said flatly. "What are *you* talking about?"

He gaped at me. "*What?*"

Relief flooded over me. "I apologize. I see I was mistaken. You're saying Mrs. Jameson left?"

"I—You thought—My word, is that what you thought? Carol Jameson and I?" He looked horrified.

"Obviously our lines have gotten crossed somewhere. You're saying Mrs. Jameson left the kids alone?"

"You didn't know." His face went from pink to white. He looked ill. "My word, you have to promise not to tell. She left them four months ago."

"Four *months*!"

"Kevin and Jana have been taking care of the children, and doing a very good job of it, too. They knew if Children's Aid took them into care, they'd be split up. No single foster home could take in so many children. But they wanted to stay together. They love each other, Kerris. They *need* to stay together. And Kevin is too old for foster care. He'd be left on his own."

"But they can't stay alone."

"They're not alone. I told you. I found out by accident, about two weeks after Carol left. The children had been holding things together on their own all that time. I've been checking in on them every day after school, ever since I found out, and so far they're managing just fine." He threw his arms wide in distress. "You have to understand, I can't let them be split up. If you tell anyone and they're split up, it will be my fault."

I put my hands on my cheeks, trying to collect my wits. "Do we even know if she's alive?"

"No, there's been no word. But no news is good news, if you think about it. If she were found dead, someone would have said something."

"Does Finn know?"

"Yes. He's over there every day after school, after all. Though he hasn't played over there as much since you moved in. He's been coming here instead."

"Maybe he needed some one-on-one attention." It came out more sharply than I'd intended.

Ian looked away. "I have been a bit preoccupied, you can imagine, taking on six extra children. He's suddenly had to share me more than he probably should. I'm doing the best I know how, Kerris. What else could I have done? I didn't plan it to be like this, you know."

I thought a moment, taking it all in, then asked, "How do they survive financially?"

"The family was well off, and Mr. Jameson was insured when he died. Mrs. Jameson left her bank card and PIN number when she left. And Kevin has his job with the roofing company. If they're careful, they can survive for quite a while on what they have."

"How come no one else has noticed this? Hasn't anyone noticed she's gone?"

"I only know because I was Jana's biology teacher, and one day I found her crying in the janitor's closet. She spilled the beans without meaning to."

"So you've known for months. And no one else knows?"

"Carol Jameson didn't have many friends. The ones she did have, the kids emailed now and then, pretending to be her, but gradually tapered it off. I guess the friends figured Carol didn't want to keep up the contact, and let it go. No one pursued it. It's sad, really. And as for everyone around town, well, a mother of six is spread thin. It was easy to spread her so thin no one ever saw her. 'She's not at parent-teacher conferences because she's at Peter's ball game,' and 'She's not at Peter's ball game because she's at Anne-Marie's dance recital,' and 'She's not at Anne-Marie's dance recital because she's at parent-teacher conferences . . . ' You get the idea."

"Yes. Pretty clever of them, really. I never could get her on the phone but there always seemed to be a good explanation for it . . . " I thought about Jana, leading me to think her mother was ill. Sitting at my kitchen table to talk about a boy she liked and saying she couldn't talk to her mother about it. The whole conversation now took on a different color for me. She really *couldn't* talk to her mom. And that day Anne-Marie had been ill . . . Jana had had no one else to turn to, quite literally.

"There are no other relatives?" I asked.

"No." He slid his eyes sideways at me. "Tell me why you thought I was . . . involved with Carol Jameson."

I felt a horrible embarrassment turn my face a sweeping red. "It was a misunderstanding. I've seen you go over there more than once. You parked your car in the garage, during the day, like you were hiding it." I hoped he wouldn't jump to the obvious conclusion that I'd been purposely watching.

"Well of course. I didn't want it to look obvious that I was checking up on them all the time. It would have raised suspicions."

"Well, yes, it did," I said miserably. "But the wrong sort. Forgive me for the wrong assumption. I didn't know."

He sighed, shaking his head. "Gee whiz," he said softly.

"You can see how I might have made the mistake," I pointed out, feeling defensive in my embarrassment.

"You think I'd do that, and all while I was seeing you?"

"I didn't think you would, but I couldn't explain it any other way. The evidence seemed to point to it," I said. "That's why I brought it up. I wanted an explanation."

"And I said it wasn't any of your business . . . " He began to smile.

"I was confused when you said it wasn't legal and then . . . well, there's no need to go over it again. We both know what I thought. I'm sorry."

There was a pause. "It occurs to me to wonder how you know I park my car in their garage every day."

Rats. There it was. I put my hands to my flaming cheeks again. "I thought it was a park across the street. I didn't know it was their yard. I was out walking, and I stumbled across the house. Then when you mentioned the arborist and the trees . . . well, I wondered if it was *your* house, and then I watched you pull into the garage. But then I found out the Jamesons lived there and . . . Oh, it's complicated. I'm not proud of myself."

He shook his head and reached for another piece of licorice. "I couldn't afford that house on my salary," he said ruefully.

"That's what confused me at first."

"Well, this has been quite the conversation this evening."

"Yup." I paused. "Ian, have you considered adopting the children yourself and making this formal and legal?"

"It's complicated when their mother is still alive, only missing. It would take a while to untangle and do all the paperwork involved, and as soon as I started the ball rolling, the authorities would know about it. They'd know they were on their own, and they'd take the kids into care. They'd be separated." His chin lifted slightly. "Their mother may come back, you know. They may be right about her."

"I'd say the odds aren't high after all this time."

"No," he said sadly. "But they have to have hope."

Chapter Twenty-Three

When the four boys emerged from the fort the next morning, I found myself studying the Jameson boys closely. Their clothes were clean, their manners impeccable—better than Finn's, who helped himself to an extra heap of pancakes when I wasn't looking. Kevin's gaze was open and direct as he thanked me for having them. I offered to drive them home, but they declined, shouldering their belongings and shuffling off across the street and along the path through the trees. Finn went with them, and I phoned Ian to let him know his son's whereabouts.

"How'd the sleepover go?" he asked.

"Fine. Finn had a big breakfast. He may not need lunch." I hesitated. "Ian, about last night—"

"There's no need to—"

"No, there's two things I want to say. The first is, I want to help. With the Jamesons, I mean. If there's anything they need, or if you're away and need someone to just call in on them, please let me know. They're great kids, and I don't want to see them get split up any more than you do. I'm not going to say anything to anyone."

"Thank you," Ian said quietly.

"You can let them know I know, and that way they can come to me if they ever need something and you're not available."

"I will, though I know Jana, at least, already feels she can come to you. But I'll talk to them. I think the girls may find it comforting to know you're in on the secret. I do my best, but I'm not a mom, and sometimes they need one."

I'm not a mom either, I thought. But perhaps it didn't matter. What made a person a mother, anyway? Was it the actual act of giving birth? I was inclined to think it was love, and in that case, I qualified.

"I think you're doing a nice thing, watching out for them," I said now.

"Someone has to," he said.

"The second thing I wanted to say is that we got sidetracked by the conversation last night and I never answered your question. I mean, you never really got to ask your question . . . I think I know what you were trying to say, but maybe you should try it again."

"What, now? Over the phone?"

"Yes."

He hesitated and I held my breath.

"Well, all right, I'll lay it out for you. I've been on my own for three years, and I've always resisted finding someone else because I couldn't see myself being happy with anyone else. But now . . . I think I've found someone who makes me happy. And just to be clear, it's you, not Carol Jameson."

We both laughed and he went on.

"I'm officially informing you that you intrigue me. I'd like to pursue this and see where it goes," he declared cheerfully, and then sobered. "I care deeply about you, Kerris," he said quietly, and I could practically feel the warmth of his voice on my ear. "More and more each time I see you. But what about you? I've reached the point where I want another relationship, but is it too soon for you? You haven't been divorced all that long, I know."

"No, it's not too soon for me," I said. "And I'd love to be in one with you. There. I've said it."

He began to laugh, and I joined in. It was that simple, after all.

"I'm glad we've got that settled," Ian said.

"But maybe it's better not to tell Finn we're officially seeing each other," I said, the thought occurring to me.

"What, *more* secrets?"

"Well, I don't want him to be upset if it . . . if it doesn't work out in the end." It sounded bleak, but I didn't know how better to put it.

"Finn," Ian said firmly, "knew I liked you before I did."

"Oh."

"How about meeting up and walking over for ice cream?" he asked, then paused. "Oh. It's only nine o'clock in the morning."

"It's never too early for ice cream," I said.

We wandered back by way of the park, the morning sun already hot enough to melt the ice cream and keep us busy licking for a while to keep it from dripping, so there wasn't time for conversation. When we got down to the cone part and the pressure was off, I grinned up at Ian.

"I think I'm making mint chocolate chip my new breakfast tradition."

"Well, you know, it has all four basic food groups in it," Ian observed.

"How do you figure?"

"Well, the dairy group is obvious. Mint is green and leafy, like lettuce is green and leafy, so it counts as a vegetable. Trust me on this, I'm a biologist."

"Go on."

"Cocoa beans, kidney beans, what's the difference? So the chocolate counts as a protein."

"I'll buy that."

"And the cone is the grains group. There you have it. All four food groups."

"I always knew you were smart," I replied and downed the last of my cone.

We walked for a while in companionable silence, just enjoying Saturday morning, the day stretching out free and cheerful in front of us. No matter how long it had been since I was in school, I still got that delicious shiver of happiness on Saturday mornings knowing I didn't have to get up and go.

"So . . . " I said after a while.

He angled a look down at me.

"We're officially going out."

"Yup." He looked a bit pleased with himself.

"I'm glad it's official," I chuckled, "but frankly, I'd kind of gotten the impression that we were already going out. I mean, I've seen you, what, four or five times a week since Mother's Day?"

"I think, judging from our track record, it's best we keep things completely transparent, so there are no misunderstandings." He shot me a grin.

"You're probably right."

"And to be even more clear, we're seeing each other exclusively."

"Got it," I said.

"So what would you like to do together next?" His grin grew wider as he looked at me and wiggled his eyebrows in that teasing way of his, and I felt my heart do a little backflip. But I think my response wasn't quite what he had in mind.

"Are you still open to the idea of meeting with the missionaries to learn about the church?"

"Oh! Um." He recovered himself. "I said I was open to discussing it. I don't remember saying I'd meet with the missionaries."

"But they're much better at explaining it all than I am," I said. "It's all still new to me."

"Okay," he said after a pause. "I'm willing to listen, but don't get your hopes up that they'll convert me. My blood is Irish, remember."

"I know. I totally get that. I don't know that I'm converting either, remember. But I'm glad you're willing to hear them out. I'd like you to hear what I'm learning."

"If it's important to you, then I will."

"It is."

"What's important to you is important to me," he said simply.

Ian came over the following Monday evening, and while Finn and Gillian made cookies and played board games in the kitchen, we perched on pillows on the living room floor among my power tools and the sister missionaries went over everything they had taught me, in one bold marathon session. I hadn't planned it quite that way, I'd thought we'd start with the basics and then schedule a follow-up appointment or two or three to go more into depth, depending on how it went. But Ian kept asking questions and drawing out the answers from the astonished but thrilled sisters, even going so far as to pull out a notebook and write down the things they were telling him, and it was nearly eleven o'clock by the time the discussion wound down.

"Wow, we've really got to get home," Sister Davis croaked, catching sight of the clock. "We're way past curfew. I didn't realize what time it was."

I thanked them for coming and walked them to their car, but I paused a moment before going back inside. The air was still warm from the day and a soft breeze shifted the trees across the street. I stood looking up at the jewel-splashed black sky (so many stars compared to Toronto's sky!) and sent up a prayer of thanksgiving that the evening had gone so well and Ian had seemed so receptive to the information. He had made no commitments and hadn't gone so far as to accept any of the challenges the missionaries had given him, but he'd listened, and that was enough for now.

I didn't pause to consider why it was so important to me that he was open to the things being taught. Or, for that matter, to wonder when it was I had begun to believe for certain there was a God. But it seemed natural now to direct my prayer of thanksgiving to him. It had also been good for me, I realized, to hear the information all over again for a second time. It seemed to have settled into my mind and heart more solidly this time.

I turned to go back into the house and saw Ian standing framed in the golden light of the doorway. He stepped outside, closed the door behind him, and came to join me on the sidewalk.

"Finn's asleep on the kitchen table," he reported with a chuckle. "Gillian's a real trooper."

"So are you. I didn't intend the discussion to go on so long," I told him. "I think it's kind of unusual, actually."

"Sorry I kept everyone up. I just found it . . . interesting. I wanted to keep going until I'd heard it all."

"You did?"

"Yes." He grinned suddenly, his teeth white in the dim light coming from the curtained windows. "And that's all I'm going to say about it until I've had a chance to think about what I've heard tonight."

"Fair enough," I said. "You're caught up now in the lessons to where I am."

He linked his arm through mine and without really noticing, we started meandering down the sidewalk. There was no one outside tonight, but I could hear the baby wailing at the Sellers house, and every light was on. A tiny part of me was briefly envious, and then instantly grateful I didn't have to deal with midnight feedings. All things considered, I didn't mind inheriting half-grown kids instead.

"I feel like there's a bale of hay stuffed inside my head," Ian said suddenly. "There's so much to sort out. I don't really know where to begin."

"I thought you weren't going to talk about it," I teased.

"I'm not," Ian said, and then proceeded to. "It's as if all the nice orderly wires in my brain that have never been questioned and have just always boringly gotten on with things have suddenly become tangled up. The connections are different. I think it's what's called cognitive dissonance. I can't stop poking at it and trying to straighten out the mess." He gave a low laugh. "I guess messes want to be straightened."

"Just like broken houses want to be fixed." I spoke without thought, not seeing anything overly profound in what I'd said, but Ian stopped and looked at me.

I couldn't tell what he saw in my face in the darkness, but he said softly, "I think you're right. Broken things need to be fixed. Seemingly meaningless and hurtful things in our lives want to be given meaning and purpose. A moral has to come from the story or else there's no point to it. If there's no meaning, then the things that happen just shatter us."

I knew then that he was thinking of the terrible accident that had taken his wife and traumatized Finn. I tugged lightly on his arm and we continued walking, our footsteps the only sound as we crossed the road and headed toward the river. When we reached the bridge, I released his arm and leaned on the railing, looking down at the black water slipping past below. The starlight glinted here and there on a ripple, a little swirl, and was swallowed into blackness again. It was a while before I could find my voice.

"I don't see you as shattered," I said quietly. "I see you as brave and kind."

"Thank you. But it's a front. Inside it's all just smashed glass. Chaos, really."

"I can relate to that." I thought a moment. "Maybe that's why we need God," I suggested. "We know deep down that we're not in control, and we can't make sense of the things that happen. But God can restore order out of the chaos and give meaning to the things that hurt us, so that instead of shattering us, they strengthen us."

"I suppose *somebody* has to be in control of the universe," Ian agreed, leaning beside me. "It's a comforting thought for us, but it puts a lot of pressure on God, don't you think? Does he ever goof? Or get tired? Does he ever throw his hands up and say, 'It's beyond me'?"

I smiled down at the river. "I hope not. I'm relying on him pretty heavily right now."

"Yes, well, he's made a fine mess of things so far," Ian said, a note of bitterness creeping in that I hadn't heard before.

I took a deep breath and tasted the dampness coming off the river. "I haven't told you a lot about the family Gillian and I came from, but I think you know enough to know it was pretty dysfunctional. Pretty broken. I think that's maybe why I ended up fixing houses for a living. I can't fix the families inside them, but I can at least repair the house." I put my hand on his arm. "Sometimes that's the best you can do, Ian. Shore up what you can. Slap on the best patch job you know how. And then step back and trust God to fix the rest. I'm learning that he can. But I don't think he'll shove you aside and say 'Here, let me do that.' I think you have to ask for his help."

"Ah. The Great Architect. I can see why that image appeals to you." He considered this for a little, then nodded and turned back the way we'd come. I fell into step beside him. "I don't know if I'm at that point yet, Kerris, but I'm glad you are. I can see a peace in you that wasn't there before. Maybe once I've sorted through everything I heard tonight, I'll be that much closer to it myself. I hope so. But it's going to take time."

He looked up at the sky, and I didn't know if his next words were for my ears or God's. "I'm still pretty angry, you know. I don't see any purpose to what happened to Julia."

"That's understandable," I said gently. "I went through the same thing when my world crumbled. And I'm not saying it's perfect now, but it's on the road to better."

"Be patient with me?"

"Of course. And I think God will be, too."

He reached to take my hand in his and we walked in silence back to the house.

I woke to the distinct smell of bacon frying. My heart instantly leaped with joy—and then it occurred to me that I was alone and no one was downstairs cooking breakfast. Gillian had gone to Toronto to see friends for the weekend. I sat up groggily, pushing away my covers and brushing the hair out of my eyes. Had Finn let himself in?

I pulled on sweatpants and a t-shirt and padded downstairs. Even as I descended, the smell of bacon faded, and when I reached the empty kitchen, the scent was completely gone. No one stood at the stove. But somehow I had the impression that if I had just hurried a little faster, I would have caught them. *Her.*

Grandma used to make breakfast for us—French toast and boiled eggs and oatmeal with dried blueberries . . . and bacon. It had been a delight and a surprise for me and Gillian, since our mother had never gone all out for breakfast. Growing up, it was usually just a bowl of cereal eaten, more often than not, on the couch or in our rooms instead of together at the table. But for that charmed year we'd lived with Grandma, there had been order and routine and hot breakfasts. Grandma was at the stove and all was right with the world.

Boy, how I still missed her! How the phantom smell of bacon evoked such memories! Why couldn't she have stayed with us just a little longer, until we were grown?

I went to the window and looked out at the sunrise coming pink and gold over Finn's fort. "I needed you, Grandma," I murmured. I lay my cheek against the cool surface of the window glass and closed my eyes. "I still do."

The house drew close and comforting around me, a gentle shifting of walls and light, the shadow of an embrace. That was the sensation I had craved. Filled with peace, I went back upstairs to bed and fell back to sleep.

I knew now why Grandma chose what she did.

I headed out of the house, just walking, not paying attention to where I was going or which direction I went, only needing to get out and walk in the fresh air. The thump of my shoes on the pavement, the brush of the fresh breeze in my face, the high clouds overhead—I was only vaguely aware of them. My mind was too churned up to take note of much else.

The missionaries had told me about it last night, as if they'd saved the best for last. If they'd led with that, I mused, we basically could have skipped the rest and saved ourselves a lot of time. I had no doubt at all that this was the exact morsel that led Grandma to choose the church despite Mom's ultimatum. All the other principles I'd learned were reasonable and comforting and solid and rang true, but this last idea was the one that figuratively broke the camel's long-suffering back.

I knew now it wasn't about choosing religion over family. It was about choosing religion *because of* family. Because of the simple but profound idea that stated that families could be together not just until death, but afterward, through the eternities.

Even as a child I'd recognized the deep passion Grandma had had for her husband Jack who had died so young, only ten years into their life together. She still missed him every day. Grandma's marriage to him in 1955 had been "'til death do you part." But the Mormons taught that, with an ordinance performed in the temple by the right authority, Grandma could have her beloved Jack back again as her husband in the next life. She loved her daughter and grand-daughters, I knew, but she had adored her husband. She had spent most of her adulthood separated from him. Who could blame her for jumping at the opportunity to have that ordinance done and be sealed to him for eternity while she could?

The only thing that could have convinced Grandma to leave us was the hope of rejoining him one day. If I had known about it and understood it as a twelve-year-old, I wouldn't have stood in her way. I would have encouraged her to follow her heart. To get her Jack back.

I slowed my steps and looked around, uncertain where I was. There were fields on either side of me, and a great maple tree at the side of the road with a hand-lettered sign nailed to it saying "Brown Eggs $3/doz" with an arrow pointing down a dirt road branching to my right. My legs felt wobbly, and I leaned against the thick tree trunk for support, catching my breath. My stomach churned, because now I knew Catherine's words had been true. I shouldn't ask the question if I didn't really want the answer.

Now that I had the answer, how could I choose any differently than Grandma had?

I straightened away from the tree and headed slowly back toward town. What would Gillian say if I told her I wanted to join the Latter-day Saint Church? This was just supposed to be research. I wasn't supposed to *convert*, for pity's sake! But she at least had seen me go through the learning process and knew at least some of what I'd studied. I didn't think she would object too much, but it made my stomach jumpy to think about telling her. Above everything, I didn't want her to feel I'd betrayed her or let her down—too many people in her life had already done that. Now here I was, thinking of following in Grandma's footsteps.

But it isn't the same, I thought fiercely. I'm not leaving Gillian. I'm not disappearing from her life.

I didn't either.

The words appeared sharply in my mind, and I paused, as stunned as if I'd heard an actual voice. Grandma *hadn't* disappeared from our lives. She had hovered, always, in the background, watching and caring and stepping in wherever she could without actually breaking her word to our mother. She hadn't disappeared.

I knew she still hadn't.

I continued walking, the sun warm on my head, my hands pushed into my pockets, nursing the fragile little feeling that had come to me, and trying to put a name to it. Love? Peace? Both of those, but something more. A connection, and a joy I hadn't felt in many years. I didn't want it to leave me, but after a while, my own tumbled thoughts intruded again and I could feel the peace slipping away again, like melted wax through my fingers.

In its place came worry. Gillian might reconcile herself to my decision, I knew, but what about Ian? What would he think? I hadn't seen him since our meeting with the missionaries two days ago, but I knew he now had a fairly good understanding of what they were teaching me. He said he was open to learning. He had asked so many questions and genuinely seemed to like their answers. But it was all still new to him. What if in the end he decided against what they taught? He came from a big Irish family, after all, where Catholicism wasn't just a religion, it was a culture, handed down for generations. It was practically engrained in his DNA. If I became a member of the church, would he pull away from me? I hoped fervently that he wouldn't . . . but was it a risk I was willing to take?

You can either change, or live a lie. Once I knew in my heart which path I needed to take, how could I turn away from it? Now that I knew what I wanted, what was I willing to sacrifice for it? Would I be willing to lose Ian if that's what resulted?

"You never know," I comforted myself aloud. "He might be cool with it. He might even decide to learn more and end up joining too." But I couldn't count on it, and the thought of discussing it with him filled me with anxiety. He had become extremely important to me. He and Finn both.

That thought started the tears down my cheeks. I wasn't sure I could live without Finn. Official or not, I was his mother at this point, in my heart if not on paper. Losing Ian would be awful, but losing Finn would devastate me.

I rolled my eyes at the hot August sky.

"Stay close, Grandma," I muttered. "I'm going to need you."

Chapter Twenty-Four

"I don't want to tell Gillian until after it's done."

"Why not?" Sister Davis asked, eyes wide.

"I've given it a lot of thought, and I think it would be best to tell her afterwards. Present her with a done deal. She deals a lot better with facts than with anticipation. She'll just get herself worked up about it, but if it's already done, she won't fight it as much. I know her, trust me."

Sister Harper looked at her companion and then shook her head at me. "Your sister will understand. Really. Just talk to her."

"No. Otherwise she'll argue with me and I'll chicken out and not go through with it."

"If you aren't sure about your decision—" Sister Davis began.

"I am," I said quickly. "I'm more sure of that than anything else in my life. But it's a scary thing, being baptized. My whole life is changing. I need to get comfortable with it first before I say anything. It's like—I don't know—buying a new hat you love, but wanting to wear it a while first to see how it fits before wearing it out into public. I'll tell her afterwards, I promise."

"All right," Sister Harper said. "But we've gotten to know your sister pretty well over the past while, and I really do think she won't judge you the way you think she will."

"I'm hoping you're right," I said. "I'm *trusting* that's true. But it's still how I feel."

The baptismal date was set for a week from Saturday. I found myself thinking a lot that week about sacrifice, in all its forms. Jana Jameson's giving up her teenage life to become a mini mom to her younger siblings. Ian giving so selflessly of his time to help the Jamesons, even at the cost of his time and some of his closeness with Finn. The sister missionaries left their families and countries and put school on hold for eighteen months to find people to teach. Compassion and strength were all around me, if I looked for it.

Then there was the sacrifice Grandma had made for her newfound beliefs. I liked to picture her reunited with Grandpa Jack. I looked forward to meeting my grandfather one day and getting the chance to tell Grandma I understood her decision. I *appreciated* her decision. I wouldn't have found the same path and embraced it if she hadn't led me to this point. I only hoped I would be as strong as she was if I were called upon to sacrifice as she had.

I had never seen my mother's sullen parenting as sacrifice before, but I suppose that was what it was. She had had to work so hard to raise us girls alone after Dad left. That took on a new appearance to me, or maybe it was that I was looking at it with new eyes. Dad's choice to leave meant he had given up his family, and I couldn't know what that had cost him, really. In the end, people just did the best they could with what they had. It wasn't my place to judge their choices, and I couldn't see into their hearts. My only job was to love them and sincerely wish them peace in my soul.

But was that also true when it came to Marcus and Maddie? Was I able to sacrifice my anger and hurt toward them so that I could move forward? I mulled over this, and it was with a mixture of surprise and joy, slowly dawning over me like morning sunshine, that I realized I was. I was still sad and there were things I regretted, but the anger was done and over with, and rather than being left empty or shaky with the letting go, I found I was filled with comfort. My pride had taken a kick, but it hadn't destroyed me. And that was how I really knew I was making the right decision. Anything that could lift from me all of that pain had to be powerful and right.

That night I did what the missionaries had been after me to do for weeks—I knelt beside my bed and said a prayer. It wasn't well thought out, perhaps, and was a fairly incoherent jumble of gratitude and anticipation and promises to try to live up to the commitment I was taking on, but it was heartfelt. As I finished, I asked for a blessing on all my loved ones, as I'd heard someone do at church. Then I sat back on my heels and pondered that phrase.

In my former life, I hadn't had many loved ones to speak of. I hadn't been close to Gillian, I'd lost Marcus and Mom and Grandma. But now, here in Smoke River, I could make a long list of my loved ones, from Gillian, Ian, Finn, and the Jameson kids to the whole big McGrath clan, Donna Sellers, Jeri, and my new church friends. I was no longer alone, nor did I want to be. And that was probably the biggest miracle of all.

I went over to Ian's house mid-week to talk to him, deciding this conversation was too important to have over the phone. He had just gotten home from grocery shopping and I interrupted him putting the bags of food away.

"Come on in. Do you mind if I keep working while we chat?" he asked. "I want to get the frozen stuff in the freezer."

"Sure." I sat and found myself drumming my fingers nervously on the kitchen table. I folded my hands in my lap. "Is Finn around?"

"He's over at Jenny's playing with his cousins."

"Oh, that's nice. Listen, I dropped by because I want to tell you something."

"Sounds serious," he joked, then sobered when I didn't smile back. "What is it?"

"Swear to me you won't tell Gillian what I'm about to tell you. I mean, I'll tell her myself, but not yet."

"Okay . . . " He lifted his eyebrows and waited.

"I've made a decision. I'm—I'm going to join the Latter-day Saint Church. I'm being baptized at nine o'clock this Saturday. And I'd like you to come."

He paused and just stood there looking at me, a forgotten bag of oatmeal in his hands.

"Say something," I said, desperately trying to quell the anxiety in my stomach.

He shrugged, and a small smile played on his lips. "What's to say? It sounds like you've made up your mind."

"I have. I finally understand my grandmother now and—and I'm making the same choice she did."

"I take it you discovered what made her do what she did," he said. "Did you find the same thing?"

"Yes," I said. "It's hope."

His frown turned quizzical, and I couldn't help smiling.

"And it's what you're going to learn about the next time you meet with the missionaries," I added.

"In that case," Ian said thoughtfully, his beautiful eyes on mine, "I'd better call and make an appointment. I could use some hope myself."

Saturday morning, I slipped out of the house while Gillian was still in her room and arrived at the church just before nine. I brought with me a towel and clean underwear in a bag, as instructed, and met the Sisters at the door. I felt like a little kid running away from home with a knapsack on her back . . . but no, that wasn't the right image. I wasn't leaving home, I was finally finding it.

"Come with us and we'll get you changed into your white jumpsuit," Sister Davis said. She laughed. I'd told her I'd mistaken Grandma's baptismal clothing for prison garb at first. I followed her to the bathroom, where there was a cubicle where I could change. The white suit zipped up the front and felt weird and cozily comfortable at the same time. It was a strange sensation to walk into the hall in my bare feet. Sister Davis was waiting for me when I came out.

"There will be a short meeting in the Relief Society room first," she explained. "The Branch President will say a few words, we'll sing a hymn, and Sister Harper will give a short talk on baptism. Then Elder Ellesmere will meet you in the font, where he'll baptize you, and then you'll get changed into dry clothes. Then we'll meet back in the Relief Society room and the Relief Society President will welcome you officially into the group. I'll give a talk about the Holy Ghost. Then there's punch and cookies in the gym. Tomorrow you get confirmed in sacrament meeting. Got all that?"

"Yes, I think so." I wiped my palms on the towel I clutched, nervous but excited.

As we entered the Relief Society room, I saw the rows of church people waiting, all come to celebrate my baptism with me, and I felt a bubble of joy rise in my chest. I thought about my reluctance to so much as meet the neighbors when I'd first come to Smoke River, not wanting the burden of friendship, and now here I was surrounded by all these new friends, who considered themselves my church family. Just as Grandma had had. Catherine and Gertie gave me big toothy grins, and Catherine winked.

Ian and Finn were in the back row, Ian's face carefully neutral, his tie looking tight enough to strangle him. I still worried about what he thought of all this, but he gave me a little thumbs up when I caught his eye.

Finn, of course, was beaming and waving and squirming around on his folding chair, his hair slicked wetly down but his tie already undone and mismatching light and dark blue socks poking out between his pant legs and his shoes. I gave him a grin.

"Here goes nothing, Grandma," I whispered.

Sister Davis led me to a seat in the front row and, as I sat down, I glanced at the person next to me. All dressed in white.

"*Gillian?*"

"*Kerris!*"

"What are you doing here?" I demanded, forgetting to keep my voice down. The woman at the piano faltered mid-hymn, and everyone craned to stare at us.

"The same thing you are, apparently," Gillian said drily, holding up her rolled towel.

I looked at the missionaries, and they were smirking.

"I told you she'd understand," Sister Harper said.

"Why didn't you tell me?" Gillian demanded.

"Why didn't you tell *me*?" I retorted, hugging her.

"I was afraid you'd try to talk me out of it, and I didn't want a big fight surrounding my baptism. I wanted it to be a peaceful thing. I was going to tell you afterward, honest."

"Me too," I told her, pulling back to look her in the eye. "That's just how I felt too. I didn't want you to feel I'd let you down or something."

Gillian squeezed my hand. "Never. I've never worried about that with you."

I craned to call to Ian in the back row. "Did you know about this?"

He just grinned and wiggled his eyebrows.

"I invited him. I thought maybe he could help me break the news to you afterward," Gillian confessed.

"I invited him too. He never let on at all!"

"Settle down, girls. We're about to get started," said Gertie in a stage whisper.

We both sat up straight, staring ahead, holding each other's hand tightly and trying not to giggle.

"Boy, Mom really is gonna throw the hatchet this time," Gillian murmured from the side of her mouth.

I couldn't help it, I started laughing. The piano stopped, the Branch President stood up to speak, and I still couldn't stop laughing. Great loud guffaws that brought tears to my eyes. But it was okay, because everyone else in the room was laughing too.

When we all traipsed at the end into the gym to where the punch and cookies were laid out on a long folding table, Finn was waiting for me. His shirt tail was untucked, he held a fistful of cookies in one hand and a glass of red punch in the other, and there was a ring of red around his broad smile.

"Hi!" he called with his mouth full.

"I should have known you'd sniff out the cookies," Gillian piped up behind me.

I looked around and saw Ian standing to one side, his hands in his pockets, his tie slightly looser looking now. He gave me a sheepish grin as I approached.

"You knew Gillian was being baptized too!" I said.

"Yes. She'd told me the day before you did. It was all I could do not to let anything slip to either of you."

"I'm glad you came."

He looked down at his feet as if double-checking that yes, he really had come. "I wouldn't have missed it." He reached out and tweaked a damp strand of hair hanging on my shoulder. "So you went through with it."

"Yes." I looked down at my feet and up again, as if confirming that yes, I really had gone through with it.

He gave a short laugh.

I looked around the milling crowd and saw Gillian and Finn talking with Catherine.

"They can keep an eye on Finn for a minute," I said. "Do you want to go for a walk or something?"

"Don't you want to be with your friends?"

"I want to be with you," I said simply.

So we went out the back door of the church and walked slowly down the street. Ian kept his hands in his pockets, and for a while we didn't speak. Finally, I gathered my courage and said, "Tell me honestly, are you okay with this?"

"A little late to be asking that, isn't it?" he said dryly.

"But I want to know."

"I'm here supporting you, aren't I?"

I drew a deep breath, anxiety fluttering in my chest. "And I'm so grateful you are, Ian. It means a lot to me. Being baptized was a choice I felt I had to make. But I need to know how you really feel about it and discuss it properly. I don't know if—or how—my decision is going to affect, well, *us*."

He stopped at this, turning to look at me.

I kept my eyes on his, and the chatter in my head slowly stilled and crystallized, and I knew at that moment the position both our hearts had taken.

He seemed to read this in my face and felt it too, because his expression gentled and he reached to touch my cheek lightly with the backs of his fingers.

"Not possible," he said. "It'll take more than that to get rid of me."

I could feel relief flooding through me.

"I'm glad," I said.

He took my hand and we continued walking in the quiet morning. My anxiety had been replaced with happiness, and I knew it was shining out ridiculously all over my face. It would be all right, I knew. Whatever he felt about my newfound beliefs, at least I knew he wasn't going to turn away from me.

"Besides," he said lightly. "In the eyes of my Irish family, you were going to hell anyway, because you're not Catholic, but at least believing in God is a step up from being atheist. It's moving in the right direction."

I grinned at him. "I'm happy to hear it. But really, it's your opinion that matters to me."

He stopped and drew me closer, putting his hands around my waist.

"I think you've taken a step that brings you happiness, Kerris. I can see it in you. And *that's* what matters to *me*."

Sunday morning, Gillian and I were confirmed members of the Church, and Ian and Finn were in the front row, grinning at us. It was somewhat of a miracle that Ian had gotten Finn into a suit and tie two days in a row. The missionaries had told me I'd probably feel a calm peace after the confirmation, but instead it was more like giddiness. Celebration. A feeling as if I'd finally come home after being years away. I could see clearly how all the time I'd spent in Toronto I'd felt disconnected somehow, but now that had changed. Here, I was part of a community. And Gillian was beaming beside me. And Ian was here. And the sun was shining. And Gertie and Catherine were dabbing at their eyes with the backs of their hands and laughing at each other for being emotional. And Finn was totally going to cause chaos in Primary. And I couldn't have been happier.

"Thanks, Grandma," I murmured, very softly so that no one could hear me. But I thought Grandma heard.

Chapter Twenty-Five

It was the crack of dawn, and Jeri stood on the front steps, a big red bucket at her feet. It was full of crabapples.

"These make good jelly," she told me. "I have way more than I need, if you want these."

"Thanks, that's great! I actually have a tree in my backyard," I told her, rubbing the sleep from my face. "But it's pretty small and I was worried there wouldn't be enough to make a batch. I wanted to make some for Finn McGrath. You've come to the rescue."

"Glad I could be of help. You'd be surprised how many people think they're just ornamental." She hefted the full bucket and handed it to me. I nearly dropped it, the weight catching me by surprise. "You probably have enough here for about two batches," Jeri added. "I have a steam juicer you can borrow if you don't have one."

"Thanks. I'll take you up on that."

Her eyes narrowed and she scanned the front of the house, pinching her lips together.

"You're doing great with this place," she said. "But you really should do something about this vinyl siding. It doesn't suit the age of the house."

"I know. It's next on my list of things to tackle." I cocked my head to one side, noticing her pause. "Would you like to come in and see what I've done inside?"

She smiled but shook her head. "Another time. I'm hard at work on the book this morning."

I set the bucket down, thinking how much time it must have taken her to fill it. She must have been up picking when it was still dark.

"How's the book going?" I asked.

"Terrific! I kayaked clear to Springwater yesterday. Thanks for asking."

"Jeri," I couldn't help saying gently, "I'm sure the book will happen in its own due time. Don't feel bad if it isn't flowing well right now."

"Oh, but it is," she replied happily. "And frankly, I think it's my best one yet."

"But you never work on it," I protested. "It seems I see you all over Smoke River, always busy doing things for other people. You're everywhere. We appreciate all you do, don't get me wrong, but how can you possibly find time to yourself to write?"

Jeri shook her head, her ramen hair springing out vigorously over her ears. "You don't understand. Very little of producing a book actually involves sitting in front of a keyboard," she asserted. "I'm writing and composing and editing all the time, up here." She tapped her temple.

"While you're planting potatoes and washing windows and weeding other people's gardens?"

"Of course. I get my best ideas from those things. Life is happening out here, not in my office with the door closed. It doesn't take any time at all to type it up of an evening. It's like having a baby, really. Nine months of gestation followed by a few hours of hard labor."

I laughed. "Well, then I won't stop you from washing my windows any time you want to."

"Thank you," Jeri said in all seriousness. "I'll bring over the steam juicer, then, shall I?" She gave me a brisk nod and strode off, and I hauled the crabapples into the kitchen.

When Finn came over that afternoon, the kitchen was filled with steam and the heavenly smell of cooking apples, and six pint jars of sunset-pink jelly already stood cooling on the table.

"Whatcha making?" Finn asked, peering at the jars. "It's pretty."

"Crabapple jelly. When it's set, I'll give you some on homemade bread. Best thing you ever tasted. Gillian used to call it candy jelly when she was little."

Finn reached over and picked up one of the tiny red apples from the half-empty bucket. Before I could stop him, he'd bitten it in half. Instantly he grimaced and spat it out into his hand.

"They taste terrible! No wonder you call them crabby!"

"You're not supposed to eat them raw like that," I told him. "They're only good cooked with sugar."

"I don't think I want any of that crabby berry jelly, no matter how pretty it is," he said doubtfully.

"Crabapple. And trust me, you'll love it."

And, of course, the next time he came over, when I gave him a thick slab of homemade bread with butter and jelly, he took a tentative bite and then inhaled the whole thing in an instant.

"That's the best thing I ever tasted," he agreed. "Can I have a jar of crabby berry jelly to take to my dad? He'd *love* this."

"Yes indeed," I said. I'd already selected who I was giving the jelly to—Gertie, Catherine, Sister Davis, Sister Harper, Margaret and Jenny and Peggy . . . and of course Ian and the Jamesons. Gillian was already whining that I was giving so much of it away, but it was the best possible thing to do with pure pink goodness. It was just a lucky thing Jeri had brought me extra crabby berries.

Distributing food gave me an idea, and I ran it past Ian the next morning.

"I'd like to start a little tradition," I told him. "If you think they wouldn't mind, I'd like to start cooking Sunday dinner for the Jamesons, and you and Finn of course."

Ian's expression grew soft, and he reached to take my hand. "They wouldn't mind at all. Thank you for thinking of it," he replied. "Jana's becoming a pretty good cook out of sheer necessity, but it's a big burden for her. And I'm sure they get tired of my limited repertoire."

That Saturday, Gillian and I loaded the car with a bag of soft buns, containers of cut vegetables, a crockpot of barbecue pulled pork, and a freshly baked cobbler, and made the short drive to the Jameson house. The happiness on all those young faces warmed me as they gathered around, and I was touched to see the kids had gone out of their way to set the table as nicely as possible. A jug of coneflowers sat center stage on the table, each place had a carefully folded napkin, and Anne-Marie had even hand drawn place cards with pink crayon.

"It's beautiful," I told them. "Like something out of Downton Abbey."

Jana snorted and poked Peter, who wore jeans worn out at the knees and a Dragonball-Z t-shirt. "Should have worn your dinner jacket," she laughed.

Gillian shooed everyone into their chairs before the food could get cold. The dining room was twice the size of my whole kitchen, but we were a big group. Ian had rigged up extra seating with a thick board laid across cinder blocks, and with a bit of jostling and good-natured nudging, we all fit around the table. Squeezed between Finn and Gillian, I looked across the table at Ian and caught his eye. He sent me a grin, and I suspected he had chosen his career wisely. He was happiest surrounded by hordes of children.

"Which one of you wants to say grace?" he asked, looking around the table.

The younger children squirmed, and Finn slid down in his chair until his nose was level with the table.

"Come on, you heathens. Show Kerris I haven't completely neglected your spiritual upbringing. Kevin, technically you're the head of this group."

"Okay." Kevin lowered his chin, and around the table his five siblings and Finn followed his example. "Lord, we are glad Kerris and Gillian and Ian and Finn could join us today," he intoned, taking on the solemn voice of a TV evangelist. "We're mindful of the kindness of our neighbors and are glad to have them in our lives, to help us and watch over us. We're thankful for what we're about to eat."

"A great big pot of barbecued meat," Finn murmured in the same tone, eyes closed. Anne-Marie giggled.

"We ask that you keep us in your care," Kevin went on, undeterred.

"Hey Finn, quit kicking my chair," Peter hissed.

"And help us be grateful for our blessings."

"Please pass the poppyseed dressing," murmured Seth, head bowed.

"We're thankful for the bounty provided at this table."

"We'll stuff our faces as long as we're able," sang Finn. I felt Gillian's shoulders begin to shake beside me.

"We thank you for our daily bread."

"We're starving and we're nearly dead," said Peter.

"We're thankful for the help you send."

"Will this prayer never end?" Kat sighed.

"And bless Mom to be safe wherever she is," Kevin ended.

There was a deep silence, and then Jana straightened and declared briskly, "Amen."

There was a clattering of dishes and lids as everyone helped themselves to pork sandwiches. I was busy helping Anne-Marie with the bottle of barbecue sauce and hardly heard the soft click of the front door. And then a woman appeared in the doorway and the room went abruptly still.

She was thin and tall, her blonde hair pulled into a ponytail, scraped back to frame her pale face. The blue of her blouse and jeans emphasized the blue of her eyes. But what transfixed me was the stunning mix of uncertainty and joy on her face. She looked around the room hungrily, fearfully, taking in each face and skipping over me, Finn, Gillian, and Ian entirely, seeking out only the Jameson children. There was the pause of an indrawn breath, and then the room exploded as all six children jumped from their chairs and flocked around her.

I didn't need to hear their shouts to know that Carol Jameson had come home.

Surrounded by her family, she dropped to her knees, trying to hug all of them at once, and she began to sob. After a moment, Ian stood, gently pulled the children's arms from around her neck, and helped her to stand. He led her to a chair, and the children grouped around her, standing and kneeling, as if they couldn't be near enough. Jana and Kat were crying. Peter, unable to reach closer, laid one finger on her shoe, as if reassuring himself she was real.

"Let her breathe, now, kids," Ian directed softly. "Let her sit a moment."

The children drew back slightly, but Jana kept her arm around her mother's shoulders. After a minute, Carol's sobs grew still, and she wiped her tears on her sleeve. She was one of those women who cry prettily, like Gillian. I could see Jana's beauty in her mother.

Carol looked round at all the faces hovering over her and reached a trembling hand to touch each child's cheek in turn.

"You're here! I can't believe it," she marveled.

"You're here too," Jana said shakily.

"I was so afraid I'd get here and . . . "

Jana knelt beside the chair and took her mother's hand in hers. "Mom, we didn't let anyone know you'd gone, so they wouldn't split us up and take us into care. We're all here."

"I've missed you so much," Carol whispered.

"We've missed you too," Kevin said, and the others chorused their agreement.

"You've grown," Carol said, sounding surprised. "You're taller. You too, Seth." She raised brimming eyes to Ian, then to me and Gillian, questioning.

"Well, we let Ian know you were gone," Jana corrected herself. "He's been looking out for us. And Kerris too. This is Ian's friend, Kerris. And her sister Gillian. But no one else knows."

"Are you hungry, Mom?" Kat asked, as if realizing supper was still on the table. "There's pulled pork sandwiches and salad and—and green beans."

Carol Jameson began to laugh, shaking her head, and then the laughter turned to tears again. Anne-Marie turned her face into Jana's shoulder and began to cry.

"Why don't we take this into the living room?" I suggested briskly. "Come on, everybody. Don't crowd around. It'll be more comfortable for your mom on the couch. Kat, can you get her a glass of water? And Seth, maybe you could fetch an afghan or a blanket." It wasn't cold, but it sounded comforting, and Seth jumped up to find one.

Having tasks to perform energized the kids, and they scampered ahead of us into the living room to straighten pillows and claim spots. Ian helped Carol to stand, and she gave him a grateful smile.

"How can I thank you enough?" she whispered.

"No need," Ian said. "I'm just glad you've come back. Are you all right?"

She nodded. "I am now."

Once she was comfortable on the couch and the kids had found places around her, Jana, leaning her head against her mother's upper arm, asked softly, "Where were you, Mom?"

Carol took a deep breath, but she looked stronger now and had recovered herself. "I was in the hospital," she said. "The psychiatric hospital in Ottawa."

"Ottawa!" Kevin exclaimed.

I tried not to smile. Apparently being in the capital city five hours away was more shocking than landing in a psychiatric hospital.

"That's where I ended up," she explained. "You know I wasn't too well after your dad died. I wasn't holding up, it all became just too much, and I was very sad." Peter, leaning against her knees, nodded, remembering, with his own tears drying on his cheeks. She put her hand gently on his head, smoothing his hair.

"When I left that day," she continued, "I thought I'd just go for a drive to, you know, clear my mind a little. I thought I'd be gone a day at the most. But I left the bank information, just in case . . . in case I was longer than that."

"Yes, we found it," Kevin said.

Carol reached to take Kevin's hand, as if seeking strength from him. Her face was full of apology. "But the longer I drove, the more terrible I felt, and . . . well, the more impossible it felt to come back. I knew I wasn't strong enough. When I got to Ottawa, I knew I shouldn't keep driving, because it wasn't safe."

Seth, Anne-Marie, and Peter looked puzzled, but the older children nodded as if her words confirmed something they'd already known. I felt my own throat grow tight with unshed tears. Carol looked down on her littlest children with her lips pressed tight a moment, and then she said simply, "I was afraid I might hurt myself. I didn't want to, because I knew I needed to take care of all of you, and I loved you so much. So I took myself to the hospital, and the doctors there took very good care of me."

"But you're okay now, aren't you, Mommy?" Anne-Marie asked anxiously.

Carol smiled. “Yes, sweetie. I’m okay. My depression is being treated, and I feel so much better. Ready to take on life again. And so the doctors let me come home.” She turned to the older children. “I—I’m sorry I didn’t phone you to tell you where I was. I didn’t know myself, for some of the time. I didn’t mean to worry you. But I wanted to wait and make sure I was going to be strong enough to come back.”

“We understand. I’m just glad you got help,” Kevin assured her.

“I didn’t tell the doctors about all of you here at home. I didn’t know what they’d do. I’m so sorry I left, but I’m so glad to be home, and that you’re all here. I didn’t know if you would be. I don’t know what I would have done if you weren’t . . . ”

“It’s okay, Mom,” Jana said quickly. “We’re alright. We were just fine.”

“Your children did very well,” Ian piped up. “Jana and the others have been doing the cooking and everything. They made themselves a job chart and all worked together.”

“And Ian’s been checking on us every day,” Kat added.

“Oh, you’re all so beautiful!” Carol smiled around at all their faces, drinking in the sight of them.

“We love you, Mom,” Jana said, putting her arms around her mother. “It doesn’t matter what happened or what could have happened. We’re just glad to have you back.”

It was the children’s turn, then, to catch their mother up on all of their activities and school adventures, each squirming impatiently until it was their turn. Ian, Finn, Gillian, and I withdrew to the kitchen to give them time together, and set about putting away the interrupted supper.

“I can’t believe she’s back,” Gillian said. “The children believed she’d come back, and she did, just like they said. It’s a miracle.”

“It’s a great relief, I have to say,” Ian confided. “I would have hated it to turn out differently.”

“I put the pork in a container so they can have it later,” Gillian said. “I don’t think anyone wants to eat now.” She put the plastic box in the fridge and then carried the emptied crockpot out to the car.

I glanced toward the living room, where I could hear laughter now. “Do you think she’s all right? I mean, just stepping back into her old life . . .?”

Ian nodded. "I'll have a long talk with her later, privately, to see what she needs and how I can help. She'll need some strong support for a while. I'm sure the hospital will have referred her to a local therapist or clinic when they discharged her. I'll make sure there are safeguards in place."

"Good. Do you think there will be any, well, legal repercussions for her leaving like she did?"

Ian pursed his lips, thinking this over. "I don't know. It *was* abandonment, I guess, but I could argue that she left them in my care. And really, no one knows she's been gone, so who would raise the argument? The kids certainly won't, and neither will I. The important thing is, she's back, she got the help she needed, and the kids are okay."

"They are, thanks to you."

He shrugged. "I'll still come in frequently to see how she's settled in and check on things. I mean, they're practically my family now."

There was an odd tone in his voice, and I looked up, noticing the strain drawing lines around his mouth. I put a hand on his arm. "They love you, Ian. You are their hero. You were there when they needed you, and they'll never forget that. Neither will I. And I'm sure they'll still need you sometimes. You're as close to a dad as they have."

He nodded. Finn, uncharacteristically quiet, came over to lean against his dad's leg. Ian put his hand on his son's head to rough up his shaggy hair.

"Just me and you again, huh, buddy? Will it be nice to have me back all to yourself again?" Ian said lightly.

Finn thought about this, then shook his head. Surprised, Ian looked down at him.

"It's not just you and me," Finn said earnestly. "There's Kerris too. That's even better."

Ian looked at me, and his smile slowly spread to light his whole face, warming my heart.

"Yes, there's Kerris too," I said and put my arms around them both.

"Even better," Ian agreed and kissed me. He pulled back and studied me thoughtfully.

"What? Have I got food in my teeth?" I asked.

"I was just thinking about our conversation that night by the river . . . "

"Oh?"

"I'm not saying there was a reason for—for what happened. The accident," he said, glancing down at Finn. "I still think God messed up on that one. But maybe he's trying to make up for it." He touched my cheek softly with his finger. "By giving me you."

I gazed into his sea-colored eyes and felt my heart swell. A blanket of warmth and joy settled over me, and I drew breath and my lips parted to give voice to all that I was feeling.

"Cut the mushy stuff," Finn said. "Can we have dessert now?"